Stefan wanted to touch her hair.

His fingers still remembered the feel of spun silk the color of sunshine.

At thirty-five, Lindsey was every bit as beautiful as she had been at twenty-one. More beautiful, perhaps. She had floated through the years, danced along their boundaries as if she wasn't a part of time. Green-eyed, ivory-skinned and so slender she seemed to live on air, she was fragile, ethereal, a fairy princess in a world that no longer believed in fairy tales.

Emilie Richards believes that opposites attract, and her marriage is vivid proof. "When we met," the author says, "the *only* thing my husband and I could agree on was that we were very much in love. Fortunately, we haven't changed our minds about that in all the years we've been together."

The couple live in Virginia with their four children. Emilie has put her master's degree in family development to good use—raising her brood, working for Head Start, counseling in a mental-health clinic and serving in VISTA.

Though her first book was written in snatches with an infant on her lap, Emilie now writes five hours a day and "rejoices in the opportunity to create, to grow and to have such a good time."

FROM A DISTANCE

EMILIE RICHARDS

Published by Silhouette Books
America's Publisher of Contemporary Romance

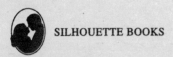

SILHOUETTE BOOKS

ISBN 0-373-51170-1

FROM A DISTANCE

Copyright © 1992 by Emilie Richards McGee.

This edition published by arrangement with Harlequin Books S.A.

® and TM are trademarks of Harlequin Books S.A., used under license.
Trademarks indicated with ® are registered in the United States Patent
and Trademark Office, the Canadian Trade Marks Office and in other
countries.

Visit Silhouette at www.eHarlequin.com

Printed in U.S.A.

Prologue

So far from home, problems were inevitable.

No one expected otherwise. No one was surprised or angry if problems occurred. Of course, for those on the ship's bridge who were busy scanning the small island for a place to land, there was little time for emotion, anyway.

"Shipwrecked," the captain said. "An honorable tradition here, I'm told."

The ship's first officer looked over the land mass just coming into view. "Not so honorable for us, if we're discovered."

"We won't be."

"You're certain? There are dwellings here."

"But no life forms."

"It's so close to civilization."

"That does seem odd, I'll admit. But either this portion of the island's been abandoned, or it's only inhabited for part of the year."

"Can we trust our biological tracking systems?"

"I'm afraid we have little choice. We have to land. We can't make repairs in motion."

"It's oddly beautiful, isn't it?"

"More beautiful in daylight, I suspect."

The first officer braced himself, as he had often done on other voyages. There was a dark mirror of water beneath them, then treetops. A field appeared. He felt the ship settle and descend. There was one gentle bump.

"A fair landing," the captain said. "That's a good sign. Maybe repairs won't need to be as extensive as we thought."

There were voices from the back of the ship. Fluid, musical voices. All was well. The landing had been a safe one.

And then a discordant note.

The first officer moved toward the voices, but the captain stopped him. "No."

"I'm afraid what they're saying is correct. Look."

The first officer glanced at the monitor the captain had indicated. Then he looked away. "One of those who breathe."

"At least we know a part of the ship that definitely needs repair."

"It's a female. A woman."

"And she's seen us," the captain confirmed.

"How could she not?"

"Well, we've contacted them before."

"Unsuccessfully."

"We have no choice but to try again."

"There might be others, too."

"I don't think so," the captain said. "Our tracking system might not be working, but the monitors would show us if anyone else was in the immediate vicinity.

"We have to be sure she'll be safe."

"That will be your job. Also to communicate with her."

"If she's not too terrified to listen."

"She doesn't look terrified."

The first officer examined the monitor again. The woman

was gazing at them as if in awe. She didn't look frightened at all. "Either she has rare courage or she doesn't yet believe what she sees."

"Or perhaps what she has is even rarer than courage. Perhaps she has the necessary intuition to know we won't harm her."

"I hope so. For her sake."

"Prepare to bring her on board."

The first officer turned to his instrument panel to begin the procedures that would make that possible. Halfway through, he paused. "We are not in harmony," he said. "I feel it strongly."

"Probably because we aren't supposed to be here. We must make harmony and leave harmony in our wake."

"That will be difficult. Perhaps impossible."

The captain didn't dispute his words. His crew was top quality but small, so small that each member of it served in many capacities. In his opinion the first officer was the finest member of the finest crew on the finest ship in the galaxy. He trusted him completely. "Can you feel what's wrong?" he asked. "Can you assess it?"

"No."

"Then proceed as before. We have no choice, and we have no time."

The first officer obeyed, but he gave a warning, gathered from his own intuition. "What we do here tonight will change the history of this planet."

"For the better?"

"I don't know."

Both stared into the monitor when the procedure had been completed. The woman was being slowly drawn toward the ship.

"She comes willingly," the captain said.

The first officer watched, but his spirit was troubled. "I hope she has no cause to regret this."

"But you think otherwise."

"And you?"

The captain turned toward the door to welcome their guest. "I think otherwise, too," he admitted. "And I think that already we are powerless to change what has been set in motion."

Chapter 1

Stefan Daniels had been only peripherally aware of the reverent hush in the operating room. The applause was harder to ignore.

He stepped back from the patient on the table—not a patient, really, a brain, a small circle of human knowledge and experience surrounded by sterile drapes—and looked up, acknowledging the applause with a lift of his eyebrows. Then he nodded to the resident waiting to finish the surgery. The young woman, one of the most talented of the senior residents at Cleveland Neurological Hospital, would now put back together what it had taken Stefan twelve hours to take apart.

Twelve grueling hours when, thankfully, everything that could have gone wrong had not.

"Brilliant." Stefan's friend and colleague George Le-Grande stepped forward to eagle-eye the resident as she began her tasks. "I didn't think it was possible, Stefan. I truly didn't."

"We'll see how brilliant it was when we wake the patient up. If we can."

"He'll wake up. And he'll have a long, useful life, thanks to you and your new procedure."

"Dr. Daniels?"

Stefan turned. Interested physicians had come and gone during the twelve-hour landmark surgery, but he had not expected the nurse-practitioner who worked with him in his private practice to observe. After one glance behind him to be sure the final moments of the operation were proceeding as they should, he crossed the room.

"This must be important," he said. *It had better be,* hung unspoken in the air between them.

"You know it is, or I wouldn't be here."

He nodded. Most of the hospital staff stood in awe of him, but Carol could be counted on to treat him with no more respect than was due any man. Age had taught her the relative value of fame. He had hired her because he was far too busy to spend his time building up or tearing down the presumptions of others.

"It's Mrs. Daniels," she said softly.

"My mother?"

"Lindsey." Carol was dressed in sterile garb. Above her mask, her eyes were troubled. "She was taken into emergency at University this morning. They sent her over here about noon when they realized who she was."

"And you waited until nine o'clock to let me know?" He paused, remembering exactly where he was. "Of course you did," he amended.

"No one could have taken your place here. I didn't want to upset you."

He was too logical to pretend that nothing would have changed had he known his ex-wife was lying in a hospital bed somewhere downstairs. Surgery demanded complete concentration, and Lindsey had always been able to disturb his. "What happened to her? What's wrong?"

"She's awake. She's alert. The preliminary examination doesn't show anything unusual."

Stefan knew that Carol, who always shot straight from the hip, was evading an answer. His hands, still encased in blood-stained surgical gloves, felt oddly restless, as if they needed something to do. "What exactly happened to her?"

She rarely called him by his first name, but she did now. "Stefan, I'm sorry. I guess there's no way to spare you this. She was found on the side of the road out on Kelleys Island just after dawn, unconscious. She claims she saw a UFO. Nothing anyone's said or done to her since she was found can get her to change her story."

Lindsey Daniels was not confused. Once, half a dozen years before, she'd fallen off a horse and hit her head hard enough to knock her out for a minute or two. There had been no real damage—Stefan had made certain of that—but for the rest of that weekend, stringing thoughts together had been more difficult than usual. Now thoughts flowed one into another, like the mesmerizing themes from a new age symphony. She was not confused.

But everyone else was.

She swung her legs over the side of the hospital bed, just in time to hear the door open behind her. She didn't attempt to see who it was. She didn't even care anymore. Instead, she bent and searched the floor for her shoes.

"I'm going home," she said. "There's no indication that anything is wrong with me. I've been scanned and radiated, pricked and questioned. I've touched my nose with my index finger so many times I've probably made a dent in it. I've walked a straight line to China and back. Now I'm going home."

"You're not going anywhere."

The man's voice was all too familiar, and, as always, something stirred inside her before she could repress it. "No?" Her blond hair sailed over her shoulders as she turned around. "Even when we were married, Stefan, you didn't give me orders."

"Those orders come from your physician."

"I have no physician. I didn't ask to be brought here."

"I'm your physician. As of twenty minutes ago."

"I didn't request you."

"Lindsey." He moved closer to her, stopping several yards from her bedside. "Are you saying you don't want me here?"

Even after a year of divorce, she couldn't say that. She let herself ponder him as she tried to rein in her emotions. He did not look like a neurosurgeon fresh from a precedent-setting operation. He did not look as if he had been on his feet since six o'clock that morning. He did not look like a beleaguered husband confronting his crazy ex-wife. He looked like Stefan, the man who had once been the center of her universe.

"I want to go home. That's what I'm saying."

His expression was reassuring and maddening. A doctor's expression. "The children are with my mother. You don't have to worry about them."

"I know where our children are. I've spoken to them twice." Lindsey stretched out her hand, then let it fall helplessly to her side before Stefan could reach for it. "What have you been told?"

"I spoke briefly to Carol. I've seen your chart."

"And the physicians at University?"

"I've spoken to two of them."

"Did they tell you they wanted to put me on a psych ward? That if I hadn't been married to you for twelve years, I'd be there now?"

"No one thinks you're crazy."

"No? What *are* they thinking, then? That I'm temporarily disturbed? Depressed? Delusional? Or do they think it's something tidier, like a brain tumor or a blood clot? Something Stefan Daniels can work his wizardry on?"

"You've overwrought."

"No. I'm naturally, sanely emotional." Lindsey leaned back against her pillow, drawing her legs beneath her like a little girl. With Stefan she often felt like a little girl, confused, raw, hurting, pleading. Almost worse, she also felt like a woman, too much like a woman, considering that she should no longer be feeling anything for him at all.

"I saw something incredible last night. I know how that sounds to anybody who wasn't there. I knew how it would sound before I told the people who found me and the doctors who've examined me."

"Suppose you tell me about it."

"You sound frighteningly like the shrink I saw at University."

He released a long breath. It was almost imperceptible, but in a dozen years of marriage Lindsey had learned to read the tiniest signs indicating what Stefan felt. No other evidence had ever existed. Something twisted inside her as she tried to piece together the sigh, the way his fingers seemed to dance against the legs of his slacks, the casual remark about their children. He had called Mandy and Geoff before coming to see her. That was a clue of sorts, too.

She patted the bed in front of her. "Sit. Please."

"Who, the man who used to be your husband, or the doctor?"

"Neither. Just be Stefan. I want to tell you what I saw."

He sat. Several feet of space separated them, but for the first time that day she didn't feel completely isolated from the rest of humanity.

She searched for words as she watched him for more clues. He was an easy man to look at. Never in all the years that she'd known him, even after their divorce, had she tired of looking.

His face was broad, his features strong and somehow intangibly European. On a woman, his nose would have been unfortunate. Balanced with his brown eyes, heavy brows and high forehead, it was exactly right. Accented by a wide mouth—some might say cruel, but they would be wrong—

the whole picture was arresting. There was nothing about Stefan that didn't speak of strength and intelligence. And nothing that spoke of the emotional, sensitive man trapped inside.

There were no other clues to his feelings except that his eyes were busy, too. He was searching, just as she was. She tucked her hospital gown over her knees, aware, for the first time since he had come into the room, that he was fully dressed and she was not.

"I was out on the island," she said.

"Why?"

She tried to smile and failed. "We'll never get through this story if you stop me after every sentence. The children were both spending the night with friends. I love the island this time of year when there aren't so many day-trippers. You can almost hear it thinking." She stopped. She could almost hear *him* thinking. "You know what I mean. I don't really believe the island thinks. It's just a…a…"

"Figure of speech?"

She shrugged.

"Go on."

"It was a beautiful night. Perfect. Did you go outside last night? Could you see the stars in the city?"

"I wasn't thinking about stars."

"I suppose not." She looked away, completely aware of how all this sounded. "I went for a walk."

"I've told you before, it's not safe to walk alone at night."

"There are lots of things you've told me." And lots more he had never told her, but she didn't remind him of that now. "There was no reason to worry. Kelleys Island is virtually crime free. And virtually deserted for a few more weeks. I went for a walk."

"And ended up unconscious by the side of the road."

"Can you listen? Not accuse? Not jump to conclusions?" She knew it was a weakness, but she needed to touch him, had needed to since she had seen him in the doorway. Now she let herself. Just a touch, a brush of her fingertips across the back of his hand. The slightest touch and suddenly the empty place inside her was a chasm.

She pulled her hand away, but he captured it in his own, gently imprisoning it. "What happened on the walk?"

She could no longer meet his eyes. She shut hers, and the symphony inside her crescendoed. "I saw lights in the sky," she said. Her voice was husky, a droning bagpipe woven in and out of her memories. "Colored lights, like none I've ever seen. Colors I can't even describe. There was a field in front of me, and the lights seemed to hover over it. Then they dropped to the ground. I walked closer. I was curious."

She opened her eyes, but she still couldn't look at him. And she knew she wouldn't see him if she did. She would see the lights again, *was* seeing the lights again, just as she had each time she repeated the story.

"I walked closer, and then I wasn't walking at all. I was drawn through the air toward a central beam. I wasn't frightened. Something beyond comprehension was pulling me. All I remember after that was a feeling—the most intense, overpowering sensation of love and goodwill you can imagine. It was so tangible, I could almost touch it."

"And then?"

"Nothing. I can't remember anything else until a man and a woman found me beside the road this morning."

"You were there all night?"

"I don't know. I've told you everything I remember." She looked at him. His eyes didn't waver. He had compassionate eyes, eyes the same warm brown as his hair.

His words were less compassionate. "I could give you a dozen possible explanations for what you might have seen."

She pulled her hand from his. "Might have seen?"

"I'm sorry. I don't dispute that you saw something. But either there's a perfectly logical explanation no one has thought of, or…"

"Or?"

"The brain is a complex organ, Lindsey."

"I see." She tucked her arms together so that he couldn't, wouldn't, reach for her hand again.

"You're angry at me."

"No." She was surprised at the sound of tears in her voice. She hadn't realized she was crying.

"Lindsey."

"Don't touch me, Stefan."

"No matter what happened to you, I know it must have been frightening. I understand why you're crying."

"You haven't a clue!" She reached for a tissue. "I saw what I saw. My neurons didn't misfire. The blood flow to my brain wasn't blocked. My blood sugar didn't plummet. I saw what I saw. I was part of something, something so extraordinary that even you can't comprehend it."

"Tell me what you think you saw."

"I know I had a close encounter. The lights were from a ship of some kind. I encountered beings from another planet. I'm as sure of it as I am of anything else about last night."

"But you say you can't remember what happened after you were pulled toward the lights."

"I can't remember every moment, any moment. I can remember feeling welcomed. I can remember feeling part of something so vast, so…" She threw her hands apart when words failed her. "I remember that. And I know I wasn't harmed, that I was cared for. Whatever I encountered, who-ever, were beings so intelligent, so far beyond us in every way, that I was never in even the slightest bit of danger."

"You can't remember anything specific, yet you can re-member that?"

"I can't explain." She met his eyes. "And what good would it do to try? You've already decided something's wrong with me. At the least I'm exhausted. At the worst I'm psychotic."

"Are you exhausted? Was that one of the reasons you went out to the island? To rest?"

"Of course! The island is a restful place. It's a wonderful place, and it rejuvenates me. But I'm not exhausted. I don't work twenty-hour days. I don't push myself until I fall asleep on my feet.''

"You're raising two children, running a successful business."

"I saw what I saw." She leaned forward. "And I'm going home."

He sat a little straighter. "Tomorrow. If all the results of your tests come back negative."

"Tonight. Without any results other than those you have in my chart already."

He stared at her, but his eyes gave nothing away. Hers didn't waver. "All right," he said at last. "I'll take you home myself."

"You don't have to. I can call a friend."

"I'll take you. And when I get there, I'm staying with you." He held up a hand to ward off her response. "I'm staying."

"It's no longer your house."

"And you're no longer my wife." He leaned forward, too. "Do you think a piece of paper, any kind of paper, matters right now? I'm staying, and I'm going to keep my eye on you to be sure you're all right. I won't argue about it!"

She was too tired, too emotionally drained, to argue anymore. She shut her eyes, and she saw colored lights. She wished she could feel the tranquility, the tremendous surge of hope and joy, she had also experienced. But it was gone, and in its place were the doubt and confusion she always felt when she was with the man she'd loved since the first day she met him.

"Let me dress."

"I'll square this with administration."

She felt lips against her forehead. For a moment she thought she had imagined them. Then she felt an emptiness so vast she knew she had not. She opened her eyes, and Stefan was gone.

* * *

Someone, a neighbor probably, had come over to turn on the porch light. Windows had been opened to catch the evening breeze, and neither mail nor newspaper cluttered the front porch. Stefan held out his hand for Lindsey's key. He had turned his over to her as part of their divorce settlement. Lindsey had asked only for child support and the deed to their summer cottage on Kelleys Island. He had insisted she take their House in Rocky River, too, as well as a sizable portion of their investments.

Tonight he wished he had refused her the cottage.

"How do you feel?" he asked.

"There's no way to answer that."

He turned the lock and pushed the door open. The smell of coffee welcomed them. "Someone's been inside."

"I called Mrs. Charles before I left the hospital."

"She's a good neighbor."

"You don't have to stay. She offered. She'll come back if I call her."

"She's not a doctor."

"And I'm not sick."

"Lindsey, please." Stefan ushered her inside. She kept her head turned from him, but he knew what he would have seen on her face. Despair, fear, confusion—and the strength to overcome all of them.

He touched her shoulder, and reluctantly she turned. "I want to stay," he said. "Not for you as much as for myself. Humor me."

"I wish the children were here."

He didn't tell her he was glad they weren't. The divorce had been difficult enough for Geoff and Mandy. Seeing their mother like this would only compound their insecurities. "My mother will take good care of them."

"They'll come home reciting Kant in German."

He smiled. "Child abuse, for certain."

"I don't want them told their mother is crazy."

"They won't be." He wanted to touch her hair. His fingers still remembered the feel of spun silk the color of sunshine. At thirty-five Lindsey was every bit as beautiful as she had been at twenty-one, more beautiful, perhaps. She had floated through the years, danced along their boundaries as if she weren't part of time. She was fragile, ethereal, a fairy princess in a world that no longer believed in fairy tales. Green-eyed, ivory-skinned and so slender she seemed to live on air. His princess.

Once upon a time.

She moved away from him. "I smell coffee."

"Do you still take it with cream?" he asked.

She nodded.

"Then I'll pour us some while you change."

She looked down at her pink jumper, now stained from grass and roadside mud. "Thank you."

"Are you hungry?"

"No."

He tried a different tack. "Will you eat if I fix us something? I haven't had anything since early this morning."

"Stefan." Contrition was in her voice. "You must be starving. See what you can find. I'll hurry and come down to help."

"Don't worry. I'm sure I can still find my way around."

She frowned, as if she had caught a trace of bitterness. "When you left I didn't sweep the house clean and start all over again. Most things are exactly where they used to be."

"When *I* left?"

"*You* left. No matter how it was accomplished."

"I'll be in the kitchen."

He took stock when he got there. He had been back to the house many times since the night Lindsey had asked him to leave. Back to see his children, stiff, formal visits when nine-year-old Geoff moved restlessly around the living room and six-year-old Mandy trotted out project after project that she had worked on to please him. But he didn't remember having come this far inside in the past year, into the very heart of the house where meals were cooked and stories told over the kitchen table.

Memories flowed over him as he stood in the doorway. Potted herbs and seashells still decorated every windowsill, and children's artwork covered every spare inch of wall and refrigerator. Glistening apples, dried flowers and Lindsey's prized Depression glass spilled color into the corners of the room. The fragrance of coffee entwined with the sprawling foliage of a rose geranium and pomanders made from oranges studded with cloves.

He was home, and yet he wasn't—and never could be again.

In the refrigerator he found a bouquet of flowers, and under them the freshest vegetables and fruits of the summer that was just beginning. He took out eggs, brown eggs Lindsey must have bought from a farmer, and homemade preserves in a cut-glass jar.

He had put together an omelet by the time Lindsey reappeared. Her skirt was brown, with lace peeking out from under the hem, like a Victorian petticoat. Her blouse was the pale, new-leaf green of her eyes, trimmed with her own cross-stitch embroidery.

"So you found everything?" she asked.

"I did. Sit. I'll serve you."

"I've been sitting all day. And you've been standing." She crossed the room and took a grapefruit from a bowl. "Carol didn't go into any detail, but she told me you made history today."

"History? That's doubtful. It was just a new approach to an old problem."

"She said no one had ever had the courage to try surgery on an aneurysm in that particular location and in that particular way."

"The man with courage was the man on the table."

"And you succeeded?"

"I won't know until tomorrow at the earliest."

"So now you're saddled with a crazy woman to keep you from spending the night at the hospital."

"I'm here because I want to be."

"I'm sorry."

He wrapped his fingers tighter around the handle of the pan. He didn't look at her. "You have no reason to be sorry."

"Do you know what I'm sorry for?" Her words were hesitant. "I'm sorry that you're involved in this. You never should have been called. What good is a divorce if it doesn't free you from obligations?"

He asked himself what good a divorce had been at all. Yet that response stuck in his throat. He had left Lindsey and the children because she had asked it of him. He had no reason to think the divorce hadn't been good for her. Until now.

"You're still the mother of my children," he said instead. "I hope we're still friends."

"Did we ever know each other well enough to be friends?" She didn't seem to want an answer. "And being Geoff and Mandy's mother is a gift to me, not a debt you have to repay. No, you shouldn't have been called today. It wasn't fair. I have to work this out on my own."

He turned the omelet. "What is there to work out?"

"I...I don't know."

He chose his words carefully. "I believe everything you've told me, but I'd be lying if I said I believed it happened the way you think it did. I think there's more here than we know yet, and whatever it is, you've got to pay absolute attention to your health for a while."

"There *is* more than we know, more than both of us know. Isn't that the point? I encountered something outside our entire store of human knowledge." Her voice faltered. "I can understand why this sounds crazy. I can understand why you're skeptical. But just for once, can you listen with your heart? What's logic, anyway, except one particular way to put facts together? And we don't have all the facts."

"We shouldn't talk about this now. You're tired. I'm tired."

She was silent while they took their plates to the round

oak table. He sat where he always had, and from habit she sat beside him. He watched as she picked at her food, and he knew she wasn't even aware that she was. His hand stole to hers, covering it. "Maybe you need sleep more than food."

"Maybe."

Her skin was petal soft. His hand lingered. He hadn't had time to dwell on the things that had happened to her. Now he realized he could have lost her, lost her for the second time. And death was a loss more irrevocable than divorce.

"Whatever happened to you, you're here now. You're alive. You have time to recover. Promise me you'll take the summer off. If you're feeling well enough, you could take the children to your cousin's house in Maine. She'd be thrilled to have you."

"I'd planned to take most of the summer off, anyway." She withdrew her hand and pushed back her chair. "But I'm not going to Maine. I'm going back to Kelleys Island."

He stood at the same moment she did. She didn't turn away; she didn't flinch when he grasped her arm. "No, you're not."

"If nothing really happened there, then there's nothing to worry about."

"Something happened. You were found on the side of the road."

She tried to pull away from him, and he tightened his grip. In all the years of their marriage he had never touched her in anger. Now he had to force himself to drop her arm. "Don't you realize it could have been worse than that? There's no medical care on the island. At best, they could chopper you out if you were sick again. It could be hours before you got treatment, just like it was this morning."

"I was not, *am* not, sick."

"I won't let you do it."

"You have no say." She took her plate to the counter. "I'll have Mandy and Geoff with me. In a few more weeks the summer people will be there in full force. I won't be alone, and I won't go for any more lonely midnight walks. But I have to go back.''

"Why?''

"I don't know.''

So often through the years their arguments had come to this. He felt, as he often had, that he was pounding on a door and the woman on the other side couldn't hear him. He inserted the only key in his possession. "I won't let you take the children.''

"Won't you?'' Her eyes were sad. "Has it come to that then, Stefan? Using the children as weapons?''

"Not as weapons. I'm worried about their safety when you're in this condition.''

"They're safe. We both know it. And what reasonable judge would give them to you if you took me to court? You hardly know them. You have no time to spend with them. Would you take Geoff into surgery with you? Mandy into your office, your laboratory?''

"I didn't see a UFO. That gives me some credibility.''

"I love them. I know them. That gives me more.''

She was both right and wrong. Without a doubt, his attorney could help him gain custody. Without a doubt, even under these circumstances, he didn't deserve it. He searched for another answer. "Let me take some time off. We could take the children somewhere together.''

"That would confuse them.''

He saw she had tears in her eyes. He wanted to reach for her but couldn't. He remembered what she had said about being pulled toward a beam of light. Now he felt that same sensation, yet he fought it, just as he always had. Lindsey was his light, but he couldn't let himself be drawn to her blinding center.

"There's nothing I can say, is there?'' he asked at last.

"Nothing.''

"If you do this, I'm coming to the island as often as I can.''

"To check on us?''

"Exactly."

She brushed a tear off her cheek. "You know, I'd like it better if you'd lie. I'd like to hear that you'll be coming because you want to watch your children grow. Because you want to know them."

"You know that wouldn't be a lie."

"But only a tiny part of the truth."

"You're tired. This has drained you totally. Go to bed now. I'll clean up here. I'll be sleeping in Geoff's room if you need me during the night."

She didn't brush away the next tear. "How did it all go so wrong, Stefan?"

He couldn't answer, because he didn't know. Once it had all seemed so right.

"Good night." She moved past him, careful not to touch him.

He didn't turn to watch her go, afraid that he couldn't stop himself from following.

Later, as he turned off the lights, the house, his house, was absolutely silent. In the years when he had lived here it had never been silent. There had always been laughter and music, the sweet, high-pitched chatter of children, the warmth of Lindsey's voice soothing and cajoling.

In Geoff's room he listened to the reassuring buzz of a fish tank. He found the green canister of fish food and sprinkled some under the hood; then he wandered around the room examining the flotsam of a little boy's life. He lifted the ceramic statue of a dolphin and rolled it around in his hands. For a moment he thought that Lindsey had molded it. Everything she designed or crafted breathed with life. The dolphin seemed to strain against his hand, seeking the reassurance of ocean depths. He turned it over and encountered his son's initials, etched in the clay.

I'd like to hear that you'll be coming because you want to watch your children grow.

He put the dolphin back on the desk and telephoned the

hospital to see how his patient was doing. Then, carefully, he removed his clothes and hung them on the back of a chair. He was as exhausted as he had ever been in his life.

But he didn't fall asleep easily.

Chapter 2

The colors reached beyond the spectrum of the rainbow. The light was pure and soft, yet bright enough to force Lindsey to shade her eyes. A star had come to earth, its blinding brilliance subdued and adjusted so that it wouldn't inadvertently incinerate an earth creature who might see it.

But she had seen it. She had bathed in the many-colored light, allowed it to draw her to its core. And once there, she had opened her mind and her heart willingly.

There had been apologies. She could feel them deep inside her, although she couldn't remember that words had been spoken. There had been no plan for the star to contact anything living. But even the most intricate calculation could not take into account the random actions of those who breathed.

She had laughed, a child's unfettered laugh. She was more random than most of those who breathed, she had admitted. She was sorry, too, for the difficulty, but not really sorry at all.

No, she could not return with them. She could not return,

could not remain forever bathed in the glorious light, in the hope, the joy, the center. There were her children.

And Stefan.

"Stefan." She fought her way back, calling his name. "Stefan."

"I'm here. You're all right. You're all right, Lindsey. Open your eyes."

They wouldn't open, even at his command. She felt herself being drawn away from him, drawn once again toward the light. She fought against it, even as she apologized silently for not following.

"Open your eyes!"

She did. The light was still there, floating like rainbow sunbeams. Spectrum by spectrum it disappeared until only sunshine lit the room. Something blocked her throat. Tears. Then she began to sob.

She felt her cheek resting on a familiar bare, hair-roughened chest. She felt the warmth of Stefan's arms surrounding her. "Are you in pain?" he asked.

"Yes."

"Where? Tell me where."

"Nowhere you can see." She burrowed her cheek into his flesh. He slid his fingers down her arm, stopping at the pulse point on her wrist.

"Do you know where you are?"

"In my bed."

"Do you know what day it is?"

"I don't care."

"Does your head hurt?"

"You're making it hurt." She tried to free herself, but his arms surrounded her again.

"I'm not trying to upset you. I wanted to be sure you were only having a dream."

"It wasn't a dream." She tried to hang on to the moments now fading so quickly. "Not a dream. I was there again."

"Where?"

"On the island. I saw the light. I was drawn through the

air.'' She tried to remember more, but even as she spoke, the memories disappeared. She felt emptied, as if those precious moments had once more been taken from her.

"Anything else?"

"No." She struggled to sit up, and this time he let her. "Why are you in here?"

He gave her the box of tissues before he responded. They were pastel, as was everything in the room except the heavy mahogany furniture. Like all the rooms in the house, this one had been a compromise between their tastes. Unlike their marriage, it had been a surprising success.

"I came in several times through the night. I woke up a little while ago to check on you again. Before I even got to the bedroom door I heard you calling me."

"I wasn't calling you."

"You were."

"I don't remember."

"You were deeply asleep. You frightened me when I couldn't wake you."

"I was exhausted. Yesterday was exhausting."

"You've always been a light sleeper. When the children were babies you knew when they were awake before they'd made a sound."

"I was young."

"You're still young."

She wiped her eyes. She cried easily. She laughed as easily, loved as easily. She had never been ashamed of that, but now she wished she had choked back her tears.

"I know you're worried," she said, choosing her words carefully. "I appreciate that. But please, please don't be. For both our sakes."

His hand cupped her cheek. His eyes searched hers. "Why not?"

"Because I can't bear it." She swallowed hard. He was so close, but she needed only a moment to remember how far away he really was and always had been. The poignantly familiar things about Stefan could not make up for what had always been missing from their relationship. The rugged line of his unshaven jaw, the sleepy, morning smell of his skin, the way his flesh warmed and molded to hers. None of those things could be as important as what they had never had.

His eyes didn't waver. "I said 'I do.' I never said 'I don't.'"

"You need to say 'I don't.' *We* need to. Nothing's changed."

"I was never sure anything needed to."

"I know."

He dropped his hands, then paused a moment, as if schooling himself to be more objective. "How do you feel now?"

She knew he was asking about her health. It was strange that he would phrase the question that way, when discussing feelings was foreign to him. "Awake. Hungry." The second was a lie.

He didn't seem to want to leave her. "You should sleep in today. My mother's bringing the children home—"

"You've called her?"

"She called a little earlier."

"What time is it?"

"Almost nine. Geoff and Mandy have been up since six terrorizing her."

"I never sleep this late."

"Neither do I."

"You should be at the hospital. Your patient, how is he?"

"Awake. Hungry."

She smiled. His smiles were all too rare, but he favored her with one now, and her defenses quivered. "Thank you for staying last night."

"My pleasure."

"Hardly."

"Well, I'll admit to having had better nights." His fingers danced along the flowered cover. "Anyway, my mother is bringing the children home in a little while. She volunteered to stay and watch over things while you rest."

"I don't think so."

Lindsey had always appreciated Stefan's mother, although the two women couldn't have been more different. Hilda Daniels lived in a world of equations and formulas. A retired physics professor, she now devoted her hours to condensing and simplifying the principles of her beloved science for the layman. The surprising thing about the project was that she had finally noticed that the rest of the world wasn't as educated or brilliant as she was. She'd had enormous success with her first book and was hard at work on her second.

Hilda did not bake cookies, and she didn't own an apron. She liked children in their place, which in her considered opinion should be the library or the classroom. Her house was filled with priceless art objects, the bombastic overtures of Wagner and philosophical conversation. She loved her grandchildren, just as she loved her son, but neither Hilda nor Stefan's recently deceased father Samuel, whose research on DNA had been world-renowned, had ever accommodated to a child's needs. Geoff and Mandy loved and admired their grandmother, but they preferred their visits with her to be short.

Stefan stood. "I'm sure she'd be happy to stay."

"I'm sure she would be, too. But she'd be happier to go back home and work on new ways to explain the theory of relativity."

"Are you going to tell her what happened to you?"

"Yes."

"She won't understand."

"I'm sure you're right." Lindsey swung her feet over the bedside. She remembered how exposed she had felt yesterday in a thin hospital gown. At least this morning she was in her own night clothes and Stefan was wearing less than he'd been then. But she still felt odd, even though she was covered to her thighs by a violet T-shirt. There was an intimacy about being in the bedroom where they had shared so many impassioned encounters, an intimacy about bare chests and bare legs and hair that hadn't been combed.

"Who else are you going to tell?" Stefan asked.

"Anybody who wants to listen." She went to the closet for her robe, burying herself in its satin folds before she turned. "I don't have anything to be ashamed of. Why should I keep this secret?"

"Because almost everybody will react the way I have."

She appreciated his honesty. "I've survived your reaction."

"This could become public knowledge."

She hadn't had time to think about that. She frowned, imagining what life might be like if it did. "Tabloids? Television talk shows?"

He smoothed the covers, his hand lingering where Lindsey had been. "The sleaziest of them."

"They would find out that we'd been married. That would embarrass you, wouldn't it?"

"Would it embarrass you?"

"Our marriage? Or the publicity?"

"I'm the one who moved out. It might appear that I left you because I thought you were coming apart."

"Perhaps that's not so far from the truth."

"Lind...sey."

"You know I always react when you say my name that way, don't you? You make me feel like a little girl who's failed you somehow."

"I have never thought of you as a little girl."

She felt color rising in her cheeks. She was covered now, but Stefan was not. He wore the same pants he'd worn last night, but he'd yet to put on his shirt. He was tanned—she was glad to see he was getting outside the hospital occasionally—and fit—she was equally glad to see he was taking care of himself.

His body had always fascinated her. He had an athlete's build and an athlete's obsession with nutrition and exercise. The combination subtracted years from his thirty-nine and

sent heartbeats racing in the women who had thrown themselves across his path in the year since their divorce. She
knew about the other women, not because Stefan had ever
mentioned them, but because so-called friends of theirs had
always found a way to tell her. She had begun to solve that
problem by finding new friends.

She looked out the window. "I don't want you to be hurt
by this. The encounter happened to me, not to you, but I
know the publicity could make you uncomfortable. I won't
spout off, Stefan. If I talk to anyone, I'll be discreet."

He seemed to want to say more, but the slam of a car
door interrupted. She heard Mandy's happy shrieks. "The
Munchkins are here," she said. "I'll go open up for them.
You'd better get dressed before you come down. As it is,
I'm not sure Hilda will understand why you're not starched
and pressed."

"I'm surprised you kept that robe."

She looked down. The robe had been a gift to her in their
last year of marriage. Stefan had seen it in the window of
a lingerie boutique. The fabric rippled from shoulder to floor
in dark-flowered femininity, an ode to the soft curves of the
female form. She had hardly believed he had noticed it in
the window, much less gone inside such a store to buy it.

He had given it to her after the children were asleep. He'd
made a fire in their bedroom fireplace, a rare pleasure, because he had seldom been at home in the evenings. Then
he had settled her there to warm herself while he'd gone to
the closet to take out the box. She had opened it, and the
satin had spilled into her lap as if alive. He had undressed
her slowly until her skin was fire-warmed ivory and his
hands a darker adornment. Then he had settled the robe over
her shoulders before…

"Did you think I would give away everything that reminded me of you?" she asked. She realized she was
smoothing her hand over the robe's satiny surface, and she
put it in her pocket before she met his eyes. "I would have
nothing left."

"I still have your photograph in my office. The one in the silver frame."

She stared at him. The revelation was so unlike him that she could find no response.

"Did you think I would give away everything that reminded me of you?" When she didn't answer he turned. "I'll get the door. You change." He left the room. She heard him in Geoff's room, probably getting his shirt. Then she heard him on the stairs. Finally she heard Mandy and Geoff's greetings as he opened the door.

"I know how it sounds, Hilda." Lindsey helped herself to another cup of coffee. Her former mother-in-law had brewed a pot as Lindsey dressed, but she had only poured each adult one scant cup. She had strong opinions about caffeine and addictions of any sort. Hilda had little patience with anything that smacked of weakness.

"There are so many ways to explain something of this nature."

Lindsey knew Hilda was trying to be kind. She *was* kind; there was nothing malicious about Hilda Daniels. Her moral principles were as straight as her spine. She knew what was right, and she lived her life accordingly. And at this moment, she obviously felt that kindness was the only response to Lindsey's story.

Lindsey took her cup back to the table and sat down. "Do you believe it's possible that it happened the way I say it did?"

Hilda frowned. "There are laws, universal laws. Lights that pull you into their center? I've never heard of this."

"Do we understand all those universal laws? Or is it possible that there's more we have to learn?"

"We understand enough to doubt that certain things are possible."

"Then you think I imagined it?"

"What does Stefan say?"

"As little as he can get away with." Lindsey didn't add,

"as always," although the words formed on her tongue. She doubted that Hilda had ever understood why she had wanted a divorce. Hilda had created her son in her own image. She probably couldn't imagine why Lindsey had found him lacking in any way.

"So what do you do now?" Hilda asked.

Lindsey knew the entire episode had been disposed of with those words. What would she do now?

"I'm going to spend the summer on the island. I've completed the orders I had. I need a change of scenery for some new inspiration."

Lindsey designed and marketed needlework patterns. In the past two years some of her designs had been purchased by a major manufacturer for distribution in craft stores all over the country. The income had been welcome, since she had not wanted to touch the investments that had been her share of the divorce settlement.

"And you think this is wise? Going back there after what happened to you?"

"Whatever happened to me, I want to go."

"I showed Daddy the report I wrote." Mandy came into the kitchen and hurled herself at her mother. Lindsey had just enough time to set down her coffee before Mandy landed in her lap.

Stefan followed. "It's very good. Her writing has improved."

"If it improves any more it will look like a computer printout." Lindsey kissed her daughter on the top of her head, her lips touching the flawless white line dissecting Mandy's scalp. Hilda had parted Mandy's fine brown hair and braided it into two tight braids.

"I told him my multiplication tables, too."

"They don't do multiplication in first grade." Geoff stood in the doorway, restlessly kicking his toe against the wood trim.

"Yes they do! My teacher said it would keep me quiet."

"Well, it didn't work!"

"I am quiet in class!"

"Everyone in first grade should know their tables," Hilda said. "If the school doesn't think so, then she should be in a better school."

"She's in a good school. A very good school." Lindsey had been through the argument about public versus private schools so many times that her voice was calm. The schools in suburban Cleveland were excellent, but Hilda believed that her grandchildren should be in private academies, training for brilliant futures. Lindsey believed her children should be right where they were, learning something about the real world along with arithmetic and spelling. Stefan had allowed her to make the decision.

"I still don't know mine," Geoff said. "I always forget my sevens and eights. And when I come to seven times eight, my head hurts."

"Fifty-six," Mandy said.

Hilda didn't smile. Lindsey didn't think she understood her daughter-in-law or grandson any more than her son did. Years before, she had discovered that Lindsey wasn't going to allow her to reshape Geoff into someone he didn't want to be. She still loved her grandson, but now that he was nine, in some elusive way, she seemed to have given up on him.

Silently Lindsey applauded Stefan for pouring himself a second cup of coffee and emptying the pot. "Did Geoff show you his painting of the lake?" she asked him.

"No. Why don't you run up and get it?" Stefan asked. He didn't turn.

Lindsey watched as her son's brown eyes, so like his father's, flicked around the room. He looked everywhere, except at Stefan. "I don't know where it is."

"It's hanging on the wall by your bed," Lindsey said.

"Not anymore. I moved it."

"Oh."

Geoff pushed a lock of blond hair off his forehead. It fell again as soon as he moved his hand. His hair was the silky blond of hers; his features, particularly his mouth, were more like his father's. He was tall for his age, fine-boned and slender. He was a striking little boy; he would be a handsome man.

"How is your baseball team doing?" Stefan asked. "You haven't told me anything about it lately."

"I don't know. I quit."

This time Stefan turned. "You quit?"

"I didn't like it."

"But you need the activity. You need to be part of a team."

"I ride my bike all over the neighborhood." Geoff ran the toe of his sneaker along the floorboards. "Me and my friends are building a clubhouse at Adam's. His dad's letting us use his tools."

"That's nice, but sports are important. You learn to work with others. You develop your body."

"I think Geoff's trying to tell you he's doing those things without playing baseball," Lindsey said.

"It's not the same."

"It's *not* the same. It's more fun," Geoff said. "The clubhouse is in the trees. We pretend it's a castle. It doesn't have a roof, but we like to see the sky, anyway."

"That way no flying knights can surprise them," Lindsey said. She winked at her son to show him that she understood.

"If you don't like baseball, there's soccer and flag football," Stefan said. "Next fall we'll see about getting you on another team."

Geoff didn't argue. But from the set of his mouth, Lindsey knew that Stefan was going to be in for a battle. The thought didn't displease her. Perhaps a confrontation of wills was what Geoff and Stefan needed to make them understand each other a little better.

The doorbell rang, and Mandy slid off her lap to answer it.

"Were you expecting anybody?" Stefan asked.

"No. Maybe it's Mrs. Charles."

"I doubt it. She called earlier while you were still sleeping to tell you that she'd be over after lunch."

"Perhaps I should go." Hilda stood. "If you need me, Lindsey, call. Please. I would be happy to come and watch the children."

Lindsey could only imagine what her house would look like if Hilda spent a day there. Every piece of furniture, every vase and knickknack, every one of the children's toys, would be cleaned, ordered and lined up symmetrically. The kitchen cupboards would be divided neatly among the four food groups. Every leftover in the refrigerator would be properly labeled.

She stood, too, and embraced Hilda. Her chin rested on Hilda's steel gray hair. "You're a dear for taking them yesterday," she said. "And I'll call you if I need you. But you go home and get to work now. I'm feeling fine."

For a moment she believed it herself. Here, in her own house, surrounded by her family, she felt no different than she ever had. The vanished hours on Kelleys Island seemed like a tall tale invented by the town fathers to keep tourists away. Those moonlit hours had vanished for someone else, not her. She was the person she had always been. Still confused, perhaps, by her feelings for the man who was no longer her husband. Fiercely proud and protective of her children. Accepting and fond of the woman who had once been her mother-in-law. She was Lindsey Daniels, nothing more.

"Mommy, there's a man with a video camera at the door." Mandy came into the kitchen, her eyes glowing with childish excitement. "He wants to know if you live here. He says you saw a spaceship. Did you see one?"

"A spaceship? What did it look like?" Geoff asked, crossing the room to her side. "Were there Martians on board?"

Lindsey drew her children to her. Her eyes met Stefan's.

And she knew that she was no longer just Lindsey Daniels, mother, ex-wife, daughter-in-law. She was someone more. Much more.

And everything in her life had changed.

Chapter 3

A cool, wet spring had painted Kelleys Island the emerald green of that distant island country still peopled by Kelleys of all sizes and descriptions. Kelleys Island shared little else with Ireland, however. Four miles north of Marblehead, Ohio, and twenty miles south of the Canadian mainland, the 2,800 acre Lake Erie island was an oasis for summer visitors. Accessible only by boat or airplane, laid-back tourism was the island's major business. When the visitors went home in the fall, Kelleys was populated by just over one hundred hardy full-time residents.

Three weeks after the solitary trip to the island that had ended in such mystery, Lindsey wished it was even more remote.

"Why couldn't we tell anybody where we were going?" Mandy asked for the fifth time.

Lindsey held on to the ferry railing. The lake was gray and the waves were high. Clouds were moving faster than the ferry, and she expected a storm to catch up with them sometime after they docked.

"Don't you ever listen, dork?" Geoff asked his sister. "We couldn't tell anybody because we didn't want to be followed."

"I like talking to people from the newspaper. And the pretty lady from television signed her picture for me."

"Mom doesn't like you talking to them. Neither does Dad."

"Why didn't we go somewhere else, then? Somewhere far away. Like Hawaii."

The question was a good one. Lindsey wasn't sure why they were on a boat heading back to the scene of the incident…encounter…sighting…panic attack. She had heard it called all those things and worse in the weeks since she had been found by the roadside. She was no ordinary citizen, she had once been the wife of Stefan Daniels, a neurosurgeon already distinguished in his field. Someone at one of the hospitals, someone who obviously appreciated the irony of such a man having an ex with a brain disorder, had leaked the story to the media.

From that moment on myriad experts in psychology— none of whom had ever spoken with her—gave their professional opinions about her experience. Myriad experts in astronomy and physics—who had never set foot on Kelleys Island—gave their professional opinions about a spaceship landing there. Reporters in television and print clamored to interview her.

Through it all, through opinion and innuendo and lies, Stefan had stood by her. He had defended her intelligence and her sanity. If he had not defended her version of what had occurred, well, Lindsey realized that blind faith was more than she could expect from anyone. Had the tables been turned, she might have had difficulty accepting the same story from him.

"I hope," she answered Mandy, "that nobody will know we've come here. And if they do find out, I hope they'll decide it's not worth coming all this way to try to get an interview."

"Grandmother says the story is dying down," Geoff said.

"I think she's right."

"Ever since those men came out and said there was no sign that any kind of spaceship had landed in that field."

Lindsey stared at the waves. "I knew nothing would be found, Geoff. Whoever, whatever, I saw was an accident. The people on the ship didn't expect to be seen, and they didn't want to be. They would have been careful not to leave any traces."

"I believe you."

She turned and ruffled his hair. "I know you do. And don't think I'm not grateful."

"How grateful?"

"Not grateful enough to raise your allowance."

"Darn."

"Besides, there's no place to spend it here, anyway," Mandy said.

"Your brother can always find a place to spend money." Lindsey hugged both her children as the ferry docked. Then together they went down to the main deck to check on their van.

Half an hour later they drove the short distance to the cottage. During the summer months a ferry ran at least every hour to and from the island until nightfall. But most of the day-trippers taking the ferry either biked or rented golf carts to travel the nearly fifty miles of paved roads. Lindsey brought her van loaded with supplies for the summer, but once it was parked beside the cottage, she usually left it there until it was time to take the ferry back. The charm of the island was its tranquility and slow rhythms.

She had been charmed by the island from the first day she had set foot there. Four years ago she had brought Geoff to spend a day biking and sketching, and that evening on the way back to the ferry they had passed the cottage on a side road on the western half of the island. The sun was setting, and the sky was an artist's palette of colors. The cottage, white and Victorian, trapped the sun's fiery display in its multipaned windows as if starved for color and life. The yard was overgrown, with lilac bushes towering to the roof and a garden of perennials choked with weeds.

Unable to get the picture out of her mind, Lindsey asked about the cottage at the ferry landing. She was told that it was owned by an old woman named Emma Johnston. Emma was in a nursing home in Sandusky now, but she refused to sell. Yes, the man at the landing knew which nursing home it was. No, Emma wouldn't mind a visitor; she probably had precious few. Some people thought that visitors were the reason she had hung on to the cottage for so long. That way she was guaranteed chats with a couple of potential buyers each summer.

Lindsey traveled to Sandusky the next morning to introduce herself. Emma was hard of hearing, but her voice still boomed with enthusiasm. She liked to talk, and Lindsey liked to listen. They took to each other immediately. Four visits later, Emma sold the cottage to Lindsey. Two weeks after the sale, Lindsey and Carol, Stefan's right hand, transported Emma by special ambulance to the island for a final trip. From a wheelchair Emma instructed Lindsey in the care of everything in the yard, told her the history of each of the cottage's antiques, and related stories of people long since gone who had lived and loved there. At the end of the day, back in Sandusky, she squeezed Lindsey's hand in gratitude. Two months later she died in her sleep.

For Lindsey, the cottage immediately seemed like a second home. The children were equally as fond of it. But it had never really belonged to Stefan, although his name had also appeared on the deed. He had been too busy to spend more than a day or two there each summer.

"Who's that?" Mandy pointed out the window at a man digging in a flower bed at the corner of their lane. The flower bed belonged to the house closest to theirs, but the equivalent of half a city block separated them. From their cottage nothing but trees was visible.

Lindsey raised her hand in greeting as she turned down the lane. "I don't know."

The man raised his hand in answer. Lindsey got a glance of blond hair and broad shoulders before he was out of sight.

"What happened to the Randolphs?" Geoff rolled his window down and stuck his head out as far as he could to look behind him.

"They were just renting. Looks like this man and his family have the place now. Maybe the Randolphs will come later."

"I didn't like the Randolphs. They didn't have any boys."

"I liked them," Mandy said. "They didn't have any boys."

"Maybe there'll be a boy and girl for each of you this year." Lindsey pulled into the driveway. "But before you go check, we've got some unpacking to do."

They hauled box after box out of the van. Since the few stores on the island only carried basics, Lindsey had brought enough food and supplies for the summer. While the children unpacked their clothes she filled the chest freezer and refrigerator and restocked the shelves with canned goods and staples.

The seven-room cottage seemed dearly familiar, aired and dusted and ready to be occupied. She had worked to ready it on that day weeks before when she had come to stay here alone, but now she tried not to think about that. On the trip from the ferry she had not passed the field where she had seen the lights, and she didn't intend to go there until she was feeling more courageous. What courage she had once possessed was gone now, sucked dry by accusations and interrogations. Little by little she had lost the feeling of well-being that had been such a precious gift.

Mandy skipped into the kitchen. "Somebody's been in my room."

"You sound just like Baby Bear." Lindsey turned her

head to smile at her daughter. "Did somebody break your chair and eat your porridge, too?"

"Somebody really has been there, Mommy."

"Well, I was in there last time I came. I opened windows and vacuumed and dusted."

"Somebody moved my clothes around. My shorts are in my top drawer now, and my shirts are in my second drawer."

Lindsey tried to remember if she had opened Mandy's drawers. She couldn't think of a reason why she might have. Mandy had left little behind last August, only a few summer things that had been large enough that she could wear them this summer, too.

"You've probably just forgotten where you put them." Lindsey held out a banana from a box she was unloading, and Mandy took it.

"I didn't forget. I wasn't tall enough to reach the top drawer last summer."

"Then I must have moved things around."

"But you don't remember?"

Lindsey didn't want to tell Mandy that there were large chunks of time during that particular twenty-four hours that she didn't remember at all. "There was a lot to do, and I worked at high-speed. I probably rearranged everything."

"The games in the living room, too? Scrabble's on the bottom now. It's never on the bottom because we play it most."

Lindsey vaguely remembered dusting the boxes of board games, but not rearranging them. There would have been no point. "There's nothing to worry about, sweetheart. Now, if you notice that something's missing, then we should worry."

"My stuffed bunny is missing some of his stuffing."

"Well, I hate to say it, but that's probably mice."

"Mice!" Mandy made a face.

"Field mice. But don't worry. I'm sure they prefer living outdoors when the weather's warm."

"Maybe we should catch some. For pets." Geoff came into the kitchen carrying a deflated basketball. "There's no air in this anymore."

"It must have a slow leak," Lindsey said, handing him a banana, too.

"There's no air in my football, either. Can we catch some mice? Please?"

"No. Field mice were meant to live in fields, not in cages."

"Then can we have a dog?"

"Dogs were meant to live in somebody else's house."

"You like dogs."

She did like dogs; Geoff had her number. Stefan was the prime reason they had never owned one. Dogs were whimsical creatures that barked when people were trying to sleep, and chewed on slippers and table legs. They had to be taken for walks at odd moments, and they demanded affection when it was least convenient. It wasn't that Stefan had insisted that everything be orderly and trouble-free. It was just that when the world wasn't that way, he didn't entirely comprehend it. She had never felt brave enough to introduce the unknown of a dog into the equation of their lives.

"Please?" Mandy asked, adding her plea to her brother's.

"It might be nice," Lindsey admitted. "But not for the summer. There's no place to get one here. Maybe after school starts."

"If we had one now, it could protect us."

Geoff didn't have to spell out what they might need protection from. Lindsey gave up trying to create order in the cupboards. She crossed the room and gave Geoff a big hug. "This is a very safe place to be. Safer than any city. I know what happened to me was strange, but I wasn't hurt at all. Nothing and nobody is going to hurt you, either."

He squirmed a little, as if to point out that nine was awfully old for such goings-on. But he didn't move out of her arms. Nine was also a time when a mother's hug—if nobody important was watching—still had appeal.

"Somebody's at the front door." Mandy dropped her banana peel in the trash and took off through the cottage.

"Mandy, wait!" Lindsey hurried after her. Something clutched in her chest. She had never been afraid on the island before. Now, despite her reassurance to Geoff, there were a host of reasons to worry, ranging from pushy reporters to aliens.

"Tell E.T. to phone home," Geoff called from the kitchen.

"Let me see who it is before you open the door," Lindsey said. She went to the window and brushed aside a sheer drape to peek out at the front porch. The man they had seen at the end of the lane was waiting patiently.

"Go ahead."

Mandy threw open the door with enthusiasm. "Hi. Are you our new neighbor?"

He smiled. "I'll be living in the house at the end of the road for the summer."

"What happened to the Randolphs?"

He looked puzzled. "Randolphs?"

"The people who lived there last summer."

"I guess they didn't want to come back."

"Do you have kids?"

"Enough questions, Mandy." Lindsey went to Mandy's side and put a hand on her shoulder. "Come in. I'm Lindsey Daniels, and this is Mandy." She heard a noise behind her and saw that Geoff had followed. She introduced him, too.

"I'm Alden Fitzpatrick." Alden stepped inside and held out his hand. Lindsey shook it; his hand swallowed hers.

"I don't know anybody named Alden," Mandy said, when Alden offered her his hand.

He shook Geoff's, too, before he answered. "Is it so unusual, then?"

"It's unusual enough to be interesting," Lindsey said. "Is it a family name?"

He hesitated. "No."

"Do you have kids?" Geoff asked.

"I guess you're going to have to tell them." Lindsey admired him as they spoke. Alden Fitzpatrick was a handsome man. The glimpse she'd had of him had not prepared her for the real thing. He was tall and broad-shouldered. His face was defined by strong bones, with a chin that pointed out clearly that he was someone to be taken seriously. His hair was a thatch of bronze curls and his eyes a clear lake blue. When he smiled his eyes turned bluer still.

"Kids? Children? No."

"Darn." Mandy shook her head. "Are you going to stay all summer?"

"Mandy!" Lindsey pulled the little girl to stand beside her again. Her fingers pressed into Mandy's shoulder in warning.

Alden laughed. "I'll bet you wanted somebody to play with."

"Do you have a dog?" Geoff asked.

Alden hesitated. "Nope. Afraid not."

"What can we do for you, Mr. Fitzpatrick?" Lindsey asked.

"Nothing, really. I just wanted to introduce myself."

Lindsey wondered if that was really all he had wanted to do. As they'd talked his clear blue eyes had taken in everything around him. He had no children, not even a dog. Yet he was spending the summer on a quiet island in Lake Erie when most men his age—she judged him to be in his early thirties—would have been busy clawing their way up the corporate ladder or, at the least, vacationing with golf clubs or scuba gear. She was not by nature suspicious, but the last weeks had taught her to be cautious.

"I'm glad you came over," she said. "Are you enjoying the island so far?"

"It's a lovely place."

She noted the way he hesitated a moment or two each time just before he spoke. She'd once had a friend with a slight stutter, and the best way he'd found to combat it had been to rehearse exactly what he was going to say before speaking. She wondered if Alden had a similar problem, or if his hesitation was more the action of someone carefully trying to avoid telling the truth.

"Is this a vacation for you?" she asked more boldly.

"Vacation?" He smiled broadly. "Well, it's definitely a change from what I usually do."

"And what's that?"

"I'm a physician."

"Really? The children's father is a neurosurgeon. Do you specialize?"

He seemed to find that an odd question. "Specialize? No, I take any patients who need me."

"Then you're a general practitioner," Geoff said.

"From what I can tell, any kind of doctor's at a premium here on the island. So if you need me for anything this summer, just call."

Lindsey was surprised. "That's very kind. Most doctors don't want to treat patients while they're on vacation."

"I might forget how if I don't practice."

Lindsey couldn't help herself. She answered his smile with one of her own. "Stefan, that's the children's father, never finds the time to get away. How on earth can you manage a whole summer off?"

"Well, I'm really here to do some studying. And there were others who could take over my practice while I'm gone."

"Couldn't somebody take over for Dad sometimes?" Geoff asked.

Lindsey imagined that idea had never occurred to Geoff before. Stefan and work had always seemed wedded for better or worse. Alden was spreading subversive doctrine.

"Your father has a different kind of practice," Lindsey explained, aware that making excuses for Stefan wasn't going to work for too many more years.

Alden fingered the doorknob. His hands reminded Lindsey of Stefan's, long-fingered and broad. "I'll be going. But I just wanted to tell the children that somebody built a house in a big tree a hundred yards from my front door. I'm too big to spend much time in it. I thought maybe they'd like to claim it as their own for the summer.''

''A tree house?'' Geoff's eyes widened. ''I don't remember a tree house!''

Lindsey didn't remember one, either. She wondered how they could have missed it the previous summer.

''I've been up to look at it,'' Alden said. ''It's sturdy, and not too high to be worried about. Why don't you come have a look at it later?''

''Can we?'' Geoff and Mandy asked together.

''I don't see why not.'' But despite her words, Lindsey could think of some very real reasons not to let them.

What if Alden wasn't who he claimed to be? What if he was pretending to be friendly because what he really wanted was a story? She couldn't imagine any reporter going to such extreme lengths to win her trust. After all, there were so-called UFO sightings on a regular basis. Her story had been less sensational than that of the man from Iowa who'd claimed that when he'd been taken on board an alien vessel recently, he'd run into Elvis and Abraham Lincoln.

Still, she'd learned firsthand that the media preyed heavily on anyone with a claim to fame. She was Stefan's ex-wife, and she'd had some success nationally with her needlework. Therefore she was more interesting than an Iowa farmer or the old woman from New Mexico who had recently encountered aliens that looked like—in her own words—giant green tomatoes with celery stick legs.

''Well, I'll be home all day. I'll see you when I see you,'' Alden told the children. He turned his attention to Lindsey. ''I'm glad to have met you. Call on me if you need anything.''

''You do the same,'' she said politely. ''It's a small island. People take care of each other here.'' She meant the last as a warning, but if he understood, he didn't show it.

''That's the way it should be.'' He said goodbye to the children and shook her hand once more. Then he was gone.

*   *   *

Emma Johnston had never married. Instead, her flowers and shrubs had gotten the care she might have given children if she'd had them. Lindsey loved everything about the cottage, but the patio and English country garden behind it had completely captured her heart. She enjoyed taking care of Emma's garden—she never thought of it any other way. She had carefully taken notes about each plant in addition to Emma's instructions for watering and fertilizing them. Along with groceries and supplies, each summer she brought flats of annuals to intersperse with the perennials just making their debut in the warming ground.

By late afternoon she had unpacked and settled in. The children, after a lecture on how to behave around strangers, had gone to inspect Alden's tree house. Since there were still several hours of daylight left, Lindsey decided to go outside and begin planting the blue ageratum that by the height of summer would spill its lacy flowers along the border of the brick patio.

Half a flat later she lost interest. There was plenty of time to plant, but now the sky was fast darkening with the storm that had been threatening since they left the ferry. She loved storms, the wild display of power and beauty that man could not create himself. She considered walking through the woods to the lake to watch it build, but she didn't want the children coming back to an empty house. Instead she went in to make a cup of tea, then brought it outside to drink while she sat on a wooden bench on the patio to watch the clouds gather.

Since coming back to the island she had forced her mind away from the night when she had encountered the beings from another galaxy. Now, enthralled by the mystery of distant lightning, she could no longer push those memories away. So little would come into focus, yet she felt no frustration. She knew, without knowing how, that she was not supposed to have remembered anything. And she was not supposed to have ended up by the roadside. Nothing had happened exactly as it was supposed to from the moment she had seen the lights in the field.

And where were the beings now? What distant star were they exploring? What had they learned from their visit here?

A light rain began to fall, but, engrossed in her thoughts, she ignored it. She had been part of something miraculous, something so far beyond human comprehension that suspicion was the only natural response to expect from others. For hours, or perhaps only minutes, she had been part of something that words could not describe. And now she felt as if she were part of nothing. She was the mother of two wonderful children; she was an artist. But at that moment she was only terribly, terribly lonely, as if something precious had disappeared from her life.

The rain fell harder, and she could no longer pretend it was going to pass over. The children were at Alden's, and she needed to get them home before the full fury of the storm broke. She rose and followed the brick pathway to the road.

By the time she reached it the rain was falling harder still. She was beginning to feel chilled; in moments her clothes were as wet as the ground at her feet. She shaded her eyes to see if the children had started home, but she couldn't see more than twenty yards in front of her. She called their names and picked up her pace.

She was halfway to Alden's when she heard a car engine. Surprised, she stepped to the grass. A Peugeot appeared through the thick curtain of rain. A door opened, and a familiar voice shouted at her to get in.

Gratefully she obeyed. "Stefan? What on earth are you doing here?"

"Rescuing my children and my wife."

She didn't point out that the second was no longer true. "Well, we're grateful." She turned to look at Geoff and Mandy, subdued and soaked on the back seat. "Why didn't you start home before the storm hit? I told you if the sky got darker you were to come straight home."

"But we couldn't see the sky through the trees." Mandy squirmed uncomfortably. "And we forgot."

"Not a very good thing to forget. A tree house is no place to be in a storm."

"That's what Alden said. He came and got us when the rain started. He was taking us back to his house when Dad saw us."

"Who is that man?" Stefan asked. "And what were Geoff and Mandy doing at his house in a thunderstorm?"

Lindsey understood Stefan well enough to know that his voice got quieter, his words more measured, when he was worried or upset. "He's our new neighbor," she said. Her own anger surprised her, replacing her gratitude. "He told the children they could play in a tree house down the road from his house. It's on his property. And there was no thunderstorm when they left. I don't keep them inside if the skies get dark. Getting wet has never killed anybody."

"Lightning has."

"They'd been told to come home if the weather got worse."

"Well, I'm glad I came along when I did."

"I'm glad, too, but everything would have been fine if you hadn't. Alden had the children with him, and I was on my way to get them."

"You're soaked. You need to take care of yourself now."

"Now? As opposed to before I was found on the roadside not too far from here? Did that somehow make me vulnerable to disease?" Lindsey looked straight ahead. "What are you doing here, anyway? Why are you on the island?"

Stefan pulled into the driveway and turned off the engine. "My attorney has a cottage on the other side. He's not going to be coming out often this summer, and he's invited me to use it whenever I want. He keeps this car here."

She didn't point out that he had never wanted to use their own cottage while it had still belonged to him. The children were listening, and she had already said too much.

"Please come in," she said. "I'll make some cocoa."

"With marshmallows?" Mandy asked.

"You bet," Lindsey said. "But first, you have to dry off and change."

Geoff spoke for the first time since Lindsey had gotten into the car. "Are we going to be allowed to go back to Alden's? The tree house is great. It's big. And it's got a table and chairs. It's even got shelves to put things on."

"Only if you can remember to come home when you're supposed to." She glanced at Stefan and saw that he didn't approve of her answer, but she didn't defend herself. She didn't linger after the children slammed their doors. She followed them, not waiting to see if Stefan would follow, too. Inside she went to her room and stripped off her clothes. Once dry, she pulled on a skirt and blouse and went downstairs.

She found Stefan in the kitchen. He had carefully laid out four mugs, four brightly colored mugs with their names painted on them. She realized that she had never stored his away. Almost as if she had been waiting for him to come back.

"You don't have any right to be critical," she said, before he could question her again. "I've never let anything happen to Geoff and Mandy, and nothing's any different now. But kids don't always do what they're told. If you knew them better, you'd understand that."

He looked up. His expression didn't change. "Who are you angry at, Lindsey?"

She realized that she didn't know. She was so seldom angry that the experience was almost too new to comprehend. She didn't, couldn't, answer.

"You know I think you're a good mother. If I didn't, I would have fought you for custody."

"I'm sorry." She crossed to the cupboard and took down the cocoa.

"Are you upset because I'm here?"

"You're checking up on me."

He didn't deny it. "I wanted to see if you were settled

in all right. I knew if I'd offered to help, you would have refused.''

"There was a time when I would have given almost anything just to get you out here.''

"I know.''

"Alden's a doctor, too. A general practitioner. He's here for the summer to do some studying.''

"Strange, don't you think, that he can take a whole summer off like that?''

"You saw him. He doesn't look like an ax murderer to me.''

"He could be from the media.''

"Don't you think I've thought of that?'' She set the cocoa on the counter and took a deep breath. "I'm sorry. I really don't know what's wrong with me today.''

"Will you be upset with me if I make a guess?''

She shook her head. He moved behind her, so close she could feel his warmth through her cotton blouse, though he didn't touch her. "I'd guess,'' he said, "that coming here, even though you felt drawn to do it, isn't an easy thing for you. It has to stir up memories.''

"It does, but not the kind you think.''

"No?''

She turned. He was just inches from her, but he didn't move away. "Not bad memories, Stefan. Good ones. Memories of the few times we were here together. Memories of watching the children grow each summer. Memories of Emma Johnston and her funny antiques and wonderful garden.'' She put her hand over her heart. "Memories here.''

"And memories of the last time you came?''

"Those, too. You can't understand this. Nobody can. But those memories are beautiful. So beautiful. And now I'm losing them. Everyday I lose a little more. And Emma's gone. And you're gone.''

"I'm right here.''

"No. You never were. That was an illusion. I just feel so

empty." She patted her chest again. "Do you know, *can* you know, what I mean?"

"Don't you think I've ever been lonely?"

"I don't know."

"I can't believe that."

"Can't you? When did you ever tell me you were? You always had your work, your books, your conversations with your colleagues. When did you have the time to be lonely?"

He didn't answer.

"I don't blame you." She turned away from him. "Maybe it's all my fault. Maybe I just want more than anybody can give me. Maybe I'm just too needy."

He put his hands on her shoulders.

"Why do I feel so empty?" she asked.

His fingers stroked the side of her neck. Up, then back. Slowly, so slowly. "I have studying to do this summer, too. Just like your neighbor. I'll be here often."

She wanted to tell him not to touch her, yet she didn't want him to know what his touch could still do to her. "You don't have to come. I'll be fine. We'll be fine."

"I want to. I need to come." He paused. For a moment she thought he was finished. Then he added, "I've got to get to know my children. You've been right about that."

Tears filled her eyes. She wasn't sure if they were triggered by his hands or words. "Really?"

"Yes." He began to knead her shoulders. His hands, a surgeon's hands, healed and soothed. And aroused. "I need suggestions. I don't even know how to begin."

"Just show them you love them."

He laughed softly, and his breath warmed her ear. "It's always been that easy for you."

"They want a dog." She wasn't sure where the words had come from. But they had been spoken before she could think better of them.

"A dog?"

"Yes."

"That's a good idea. I always wanted a dog."

She faced him again, forcing his hands to his sides. "You wanted a dog?"

He sent her one of his fleeting smiles. "I must have. What little boy doesn't?"

"Did you ever have one?"

"In Hilda Daniels's house?"

"Why didn't you ever suggest that we get one, then?"

"I didn't know you liked dogs. You never said anything."

"You never asked!"

He stared at her, his eyes inscrutable. Moments went by. Finally he shook his head. The movement was almost imperceptible. "What kind of dog do they want?"

"They'd be happy with anything you got them, I'm sure."

"A dog would be good protection out here."

"Geoff said that, too. He's definitely your son."

"Is he? I always wondered." He smiled again to assure her he was joking.

"But there's never been any doubt about Mandy, has there? She's so much like you, it's uncanny."

"And you love her anyway?"

Her answer was so forceful, it surprised them both. "With all my heart."

They stared at each other.

Mandy broke the spell. "Where's my cocoa?" She barreled into the room, skirted her father's legs and threw herself at her mother.

Shaken, Lindsey stooped and lifted her daughter until Mandy was between her and Stefan. "Did you interrupt adults this way when you were little?" she asked him.

"You weren't my mother," he said. "I didn't dare."

"Grandmother says my manners need improving," Mandy said.

"I like your manners fine," Stefan assured her.

Mandy's eyes widened. Then, tentatively, she held out

her arms. Stefan took her, and she hugged him. Then she scrambled down. "I've got to get the marshmallows."

Lindsey watched the expression on Stefan's face. The changes were subtle, so very subtle. But she imagined he would look much the same if a truck knocked him fifty yards into the middle lane of a freeway.

She didn't dare examine the fact that the loneliness that had so overwhelmed her only moments before had disappeared like the storm outside.

Chapter 4

Lindsey stood beside the windswept field and gazed across its length to the woods beyond. Her sketch pad rested on a fence post, and her hand hovered over it. But it had hovered there for minutes, and nothing had yet appeared on the paper.

She could not remember the last time she'd been here. No images rose from the green grass to taunt her; no colored lights twirled through her imagination. She stared at the field, and it was like staring at a place she had never seen before. If she had encountered another life form here, if her own life had been forever transformed on this spot, surely something would seem special. But as she stared she felt nothing. The field was wide and green, and there was nothing else to see.

"Aren't you going to draw?" Mandy asked. "See, I made a picture of that tree."

Lindsey looked down at her daughter's drawing. The tree was in plain sight at the edge of the field, and Mandy had captured it nicely. There was a fluid sweep of ground across half the paper, then the tree bending against the wind. The drawing, like the field itself, gave Lindsey the same barren feeling she had experienced on her first day back on the island.

In the three weeks since she and the children had been living here, she had experienced that feeling often.

"That's very good, Mandy. Let's find something else to draw." She closed her own pad and turned her back on that strange night in May.

"Shouldn't we get Geoff?"

Lindsey looked at her watch. "We have a little time, but maybe we should head back. Geoff can show us what he and Alden have done."

"I wanted to help them build the fence."

"I know you did. But Alden just needed one helper, and Geoff is bigger. I bet he lets you help the next time."

"Geoff is bigger, but I'm smarter."

"Sorry, but no, Mandy. You and Geoff are different, that's all. You learn differently. You're good at different things."

"I get *excellents* in school."

"And that's good. I'm glad you like to learn."

"Geoff doesn't."

"Geoff likes to learn, too. But Geoff likes to learn best when he's not in school."

"That doesn't make any sense."

"It might when you're older."

"I wish I was the biggest."

"I know you do." Lindsey bent and kissed the top of Mandy's head. "But you don't have to be the biggest or the smartest for me to love you. You just have to be Mandy."

Mandy giggled. "I am Mandy, silly. I can't be anybody else."

"That's a big relief."

The bike trip back to the cottage took twenty minutes. The afternoon promised to be warm, but late morning was still pleasant, cooled by wind off the lake and clouds drifting over the sun. They turned into Alden's drive and stood their bikes against a tree. Then they went to find Alden and Geoff.

The fence had been Geoff's idea from the beginning. On one of Geoff's visits to the tree house, Alden had told him that he was planting a vegetable garden. He had invited the little boy to see the plot he was spading in a sunny patch of lawn at the back of the house. Geoff's enthusiasm had mirrored Alden's own. Together, the two males had laid out rows and planned exactly what to plant. Neither had the slightest idea what he was doing; neither cared in the slightest, either.

Mandy had only been peripherally interested until talk of a fence began. The first green bean seedlings had been mowed to the ground by tiny rabbit teeth. The sunflowers had quickly met the same fate. Lindsey had gone to pick up the children at Alden's house one day after the sunflower massacre to find the three of them sitting at the garden's edge watching two baby rabbits chew their way through the second planting of beans.

"You don't seem to have the hang of this," Lindsey had told them, shooing the baby bunnies back into the woods, where Mrs. Rabbit was undoubtedly preparing chamomile tea for them.

"I took an oath to do no harm," Alden said. "It was never specified to whom or what."

Geoff had come up with the idea of a fence that night. The next day he had drawn up a design after riding his bike into town to see what materials were available. Alden had been as enthusiastic about the fence as he had been about the garden.

Alden was a man who understood children.

"Do you think the plants will grow now?" Mandy asked.

"If Alden and Geoff aren't too soft-hearted to weed."

"I can weed," Mandy said.

Lindsey smiled. "You're ruthless. You're just what they need."

"They don't want me. They wouldn't let me build the fence."

Lindsey had a theory about that. Alden seemed to sense Geoff's need for a man in his life. Although she still didn't trust Alden's explanation of why he was spending the summer on the island, she couldn't help but like him. In addition to being one of the most attractive men she had ever met, he was a gentle man, sensitive to everything around him. He had befriended Geoff at a time in the boy's life when he was searching for role models. Despite her misgivings, at the moment she couldn't think of a better one...except Geoff's own father.

She soothed Mandy's hurt feelings. "Alden told me that he was counting on you to help him look for wild strawberries tomorrow."

"He says I have eyes like an eagle."

"High praise."

They found Geoff and Alden inside Alden's house drinking lemonade. Alden was listening as Geoff explained how to win at his favorite home video game. He stood when they walked into the kitchen, and gave Lindsey one of his warm, easy smiles. Then he patted the chair next to him for Mandy. "Lemonade?" he asked.

They sat, and he filled glasses for them while Geoff chatted on. "Well, it sounds pretty tricky," he said, when Geoff had finished. "I don't know if I'd be up to it."

"Alden has never played a video game. Never!" Geoff told his mother.

"Now, that was supposed to be our secret," Alden said.

"I thought there wasn't a male alive who hadn't gotten hooked." Lindsey set her lemonade down after several polite sips. She could swear that Alden's version of lemonade had no sugar in it. She watched Geoff and Mandy try to struggle through their portions. It was a mark of their affection for him.

"Dad doesn't play, either," Geoff said.

Lindsey stood. "And speaking of your father, he's going

to be here pretty soon, so we'd better get back home. Are you two going to show us the fence before we go?''

The children gratefully set down their lemonade glasses; then Alden and Geoff led the way to the garden.

The fence was a masterpiece of post and wire mesh; the gate was sheer artistry.

''Geoff, this was your idea?'' Lindsey asked. ''It's wonderful.'' She stared at the design. Thin wooden slats crisscrossed more wooden slats in a complicated pattern of triangles and squares. There was nothing ordinary about it. And there was nothing ordinary about her reaction. She was enthralled.

''Part of it was my idea,'' Geoff said proudly. ''And part of it was Alden's.''

Lindsey stood at another angle. Just as she'd suspected, the design looked different now. ''It reminds me of something. I can't think what.''

''It makes me dizzy,'' Mandy said.

''Well, I like it,'' Geoff said.

''I spent a year in Paris while I was in college,'' Lindsey told Alden. ''I was interested in sculpture. Maybe this reminds me of something I saw there.''

''Parisian sculpture?'' Alden put his hand on Geoff's shoulder. ''Apparently we're more talented than we thought.''

''I wish I could remember what....'' Lindsey shrugged. ''But my memory isn't as great as it used to be.''

''No?'' Alden sounded interested. ''What makes you say that?''

She caught herself just before she started to tell him about her experience in the field. It was increasingly hard to believe that Alden might be after a story. But she was sensitive to nuance, and he had seemed particularly interested in her comment. Perhaps he had recognized it as the perfect lead-in to an interview of sorts. And she didn't want to find herself in a newspaper headline again.

''I think I just have more to remember these days,'' she

said. She reached for Mandy's hand. "We've got to go now. Thanks a lot for letting Geoff spend the morning here."

"Geoff's always welcome," Alden said. "And Mandy, too." He smiled and touched Lindsey's arm. His hand lingered for a long moment before it dropped back to his side. "And, of course, their mother."

The dog was a mutt. Not purebred, not registered, licensed or defleaed. Not even cute. It had the droopy ears and sad eyes of a basset hound, the matted, kinky fur of an ungroomed poodle and the appetite of King Kong.

Stefan fed the dog another in a long series of fast-food hamburgers. It finished in one gulp, then belched, wagging a mangy tail throughout the whole process.

"That dog botherin' you?" A young man who had been diligently wiping the tables on the restaurant patio came over to Stefan's table.

"No. Is he supposed to?"

The man frowned. "What?"

"I thought this might be a new marketing technique. I've bought him four hamburgers so far."

"Manager called the pound. Dog's been hanging around for days. Some guy in an old truck dropped him off. Manager's tired of him botherin' people. Not sanitary. You know?"

Stefan knew. He also knew what would happen to the dog once he passed through the animal shelter's doors. "Poor fellow." The dog wagged his tail harder. He moved closer to Stefan, stretched out on the ground at his feet and put his head on his paws.

"Dogs, they're a dime a dozen," the young man said philosophically before he headed back inside.

"Thrown out like an old shoe, huh, Kong?" Stefan asked the dog. "What happened? Did you eat too much? Bark? Get fleas on the rug?"

Kong rolled over and waved all four legs in the air. Stefan saw that his paws were way out of proportion to the rest of his body. He was a young dog, already a large dog. He would be a huge dog when he was finished growing—something he would probably never get to do. "Did you bite somebody? Get in fights over pretty little girl dogs?"

The paws waved harder.

"I can't take you home," Stefan apologized. "I'm sorry, but I really can't." He realized he was talking to a dog in a public place, but he couldn't seem to stop himself. "I live in an apartment, and they won't let me keep you there. My children want a dog, but not one like you."

He thought of the careful research he had done. In the last weeks he'd read volumes on breeds and listed the best possibilities for children and the care requirements. He had visited pet stores and breeders and watched puppies romp. He had made notes on their temperament, their relationships to their siblings and their relative sizes. Just five days before, he had put down a large deposit on a cocker spaniel with blood lines purer than Britain's royal heir. The puppy would be ready to take home at the end of the month. He was going to tell Geoff and Mandy today when he got to the cottage.

"I'm sorry," Stefan apologized. "I really am."

Kong rolled over again. He sat up and stared directly into Stefan's eyes. His tongue lolled halfway to his chest.

If Stefan hadn't known it was impossible, he would have said the dog was smiling.

Stefan knocked on the front door of the cottage. He heard shouts from the back of the house, but he didn't open the door. The house had once belonged to him, but it no longer did. He was a guest now, and guests waited for doors to be answered.

Something rubbed against his leg, but he didn't look down. He knew only too well what it was.

The door opened. "Stefan, you're late. I thought you'd be here an hour—" Lindsey looked down. She looked up. "Stefan?"

"I had nothing to do with this."

"Nothing?" Lindsey stooped. The ugliest dog she had ever seen lunged forward and almost knocked her on her bottom.

"Down, Kong!" Stefan dragged the dog back with the new collar he'd bought him on the way. It was the largest size that the drugstore had stocked, and in another month it would be too tight.

"Kong?" Lindsey brushed off her skirt as she stood. "Kong?" She couldn't help herself. She started to laugh.

"You can name him anything you want. Anything."

"Me? Why me? This isn't my dog."

"Dad?" Geoff stopped three feet from the merriment. His eyes widened. "What's that?"

Stefan understood why Geoff had to ask. "A dog. A stray. They were going to take him to the pound." He didn't add that he had barely gotten the dog in his car before an evil-looking man had driven up in a truck with three howling captives in cages. He and Kong had escaped just in time.

"The pound?" Lindsey's smile turned to something else. Something sad and wistful. Stefan hoped it was the beginning of acceptance. He released Kong's collar, and the dog started for Geoff. To Geoff's credit, he didn't retreat.

"He stinks!" Geoff wrapped his arms around Kong's neck anyway.

"There's got to be a stronger word than stink," Lindsey said.

"I stopped and bought flea shampoo for him and—"

"Fleas? Stefan, what have you done to me?"

"And medication."

"Is he sick?"

"Just a precaution against parasites."

"Parasites?"

Stefan had the grace to look away. He watched Geoff bury his face in Kong's matted fur. "I would have taken him to the vet if I could have. But it's Sunday, and I didn't pick him up in Cleveland. I picked him up on the way. I'll make an appointment in Sandusky for early next week. And I'll find somebody to come out here and get him and take him in for shots and an exam.''

"Darn right you will."

"You said the children would like a dog."

"I must have been out of my mind."

Something about the way she said it made him look at her. She was smiling again. He remembered too well how it felt to be bathed in this kind of warmth. As always, she looked lovely. Her dress was the color of lilacs, with a huge white collar that draped over her shoulders. Her hair was drawn back from her forehead with a silver band. And her smile. Her fairy princess smile.

"I must have been out of my mind, too," he said quietly.

"And into your heart," she said. "Your warm, sensitive heart."

"I just didn't want him to suffer."

"I think he may suffer from an excess of love if he lives here."

"If?"

"Can we keep him?" Geoff asked. His sentence was punctuated by a squeal from Mandy, who came skidding through the hallway. "He's beautiful!"

"I don't think I'm going to have much to say about it," Lindsey said.

She stepped aside, and Stefan skirted the heap of children and reeking dog. He tried to bring some order to the ensuing chaos. "Geoff, the shampoo's in the car. You and Mandy are going to have to learn to take care of him. He's your dog now."

"What's his name?" Mandy demanded.

"He doesn't have—"

"Kong," Lindsey said firmly.

"Like Hong Kong?"

Lindsey looked at Stefan. "More like King Kong. Right?"

"They can call him anything they want," Stefan said.

"Kong." Geoff lifted his head. "I like it."

"Prince," Mandy argued.

"Prince?" Geoff made a face. "Not my dog."

"He's not your dog! He's my dog, too!"

"Shall we let them fight?" Lindsey asked. She took Stefan's arm. He looked bewildered. He had never understood that children sometimes resorted to primitive tactics. "They'll work it out."

"I had another dog all picked out."

She dragged him toward the kitchen. "Did you?"

"A cocker. A purebred. You don't want two dogs, do you?"

"I'm not even sure I want this one."

"I'm sorry I've done this to you."

"Are you really? I don't think so. I think you're pathetically grateful I'm taking him. I think you've been completely knocked off your pins." She pushed him toward a kitchen chair. "Sit. I'll get you some coffee."

"He could go to the pound."

"Sure he could."

"Maybe somebody would adopt him."

"Nobody in their right mind."

"The children seem happy with him."

Lindsey measured mocha java beans into an antique grinder she had bought at a flea market. "I went back to the field today." She fell silent, staring down at the grinder. She didn't know where the words had come from.

Stefan watched her carefully, all thoughts of the dog forgotten. "Did you?"

"There was nothing there that seemed familiar."

"And you thought there might be?"

She nodded and began to grind.

Lindsey had always made the mundane tasks of daily living into ceremonies. Now Stefan watched her with the coffee. She didn't hurry. Her arms moved in time to her own internal music. Her body swayed with the rhythm. Something hot and long-repressed streaked through him. He remembered all too well the feel of that swaying body beneath his.

His voice was sharper than he'd intended. "What did you expect? A sign that you'd really seen something from another world?"

"Maybe." She could smell the aroma of the beans now. She stopped grinding, but she held the mill against her possessively. "I thought there would be something."

"Don't you think you'll be happier if you try to put it behind you?"

"Will I? Have you had so much experience with cases like mine?" She remembered that she was supposed to be making coffee. She set the mill on the counter and stood on tiptoe to reach for a filter.

"I wish you would let me do a really thorough workup, Lindsey."

"I know you do. But there's no reason to. Nothing showed up on the tests that were done the day I was brought in."

"There are other tests."

"And no reason to do them." She didn't tell him about the deep sense of loneliness she'd been experiencing or the absentmindedness. How could it help to tell him that she was suffering emotionally from the effects of all she had undergone?

"You're feeling well? No headaches? No odd sensations?"

She smiled despite herself. "If I'd known how much attention you'd pay to this, I would have been looking for UFOs every night of our marriage." She stopped smiling when she saw his expression change. She had meant the words as a joke, but she saw that they had resurrected bitterness.

"I'm sorry. I was just teasing, but I guess we haven't come far enough for that, have we?"

He didn't answer.

"Did you ever guess how hard it was going to be to pull

this off?'' she asked at last. She poured boiling water over the grounds and watched the coffee drip slowly in the hour-glass-shaped pot. It would be worth the trouble when it was finished.

"Pull what off?"

"A friendly divorce. People think marriage is hard. They don't realize divorce is every bit as difficult."

"Only if you're trying to be civilized."

"Are we?"

"I don't know. I'm just trying to get through it one day at a time."

She stared at him. The words were as much a revelation of his feelings as any he'd ever spoken. "You've never said it was difficult, Stefan. It wasn't much of a change for you, was it? You can live closer to the hospital now. You don't have to feel torn if you want to work nights."

"What do you want me to say?"

"Whatever you want to." She turned away and fussed with the coffeepot, pouring more hot water over the grounds.

"Are you sure you want to hear an honest answer?"

She considered. "I don't know."

"I didn't think so."

Geoff ran into the kitchen, the dog and Mandy at his heels. Geoff stopped, and Mandy and the dog stopped, too. But not in time. There was a pile up, ending in a writhing mass of dog fur and children's limbs.

Geoff was the first to untangle himself. "Can we show him to Alden? Can we take Kong over there?"

"Kong?" Lindsey asked.

"Prince Kong the First," Mandy said. "But we're going to call him Kong unless he's bad."

"Can we show him to Alden?" Geoff repeated.

Lindsey looked at Stefan. "Your father just got here, guys. Don't run out on him yet."

"Just for a minute?"

"There's a leash in the bag with the flea shampoo," Stefan said. "Better put him on it, or he might run away. He doesn't know you're his family yet."

"Then we can go?"

Stefan nodded. The children took off the way they had come. In a minute there was a resounding slam of the front door.

"I'm sorry," Lindsey said. "They're just excited. They have to show somebody, and Alden's the only person around. And he's been so good to them."

All the warmth Stefan had felt since arriving with Kong turned to ice. "Has he?"

"He's a very kind man, and he likes children. I've told him repeatedly to send the kids home if they bother him, but he never does."

"Do you think it's a good idea for them to spend so much time with someone you really don't know?"

"How well do we really know anybody?" She leaned against the counter and folded her arms. "You can be married to somebody for years and not know him. You can meet a stranger and feel like you've known him forever."

"You can't really believe that."

"Sometimes I do."

"And you feel like you've known this Alden forever?"

She turned back to the coffee and covered the grounds with water one last time. "Alden shows what he's feeling. That makes it easy to know him."

"Easy to know what he *wants* you to know."

"I know what you're saying. I'm not a pushover. I wonder about him, too. For someone who's supposed to be spending his summer studying, he has an enormous amount of free time. But it's hard not to trust him."

"Is trust all we're talking about?"

"What do you mean?"

He couldn't make himself say more.

Lindsey waited. When he didn't answer, she didn't push. She had learned long ago that the more she begged Stefan to communicate, the less he shared. She watched the coffee fill the pot, and when it was finished she poured them both some.

She brought the cups to the table. "Anyway, I'm sure the kids will be back in a few minutes. They've been looking forward to you coming all morning. And now that you've brought them a dog..."

"Little enough."

Something about the way he said the words tore at her heart. She sat beside him and tentatively touched his arm. His skin was as warm as the expression in her eyes. "It shows them you love them."

"Can anyone doubt that?"

She sat back and picked up her cup. "Are you going to help them give that monster a bath?"

He sipped his coffee, his gaze locked with hers. There was nothing he could say about the knot of emotion inside him. He had always suspected that Lindsey had the skill to unravel it, but he knew he had never given her the chance to try. During their marriage she had asked him repeatedly to tell her what he was feeling. She had never understood that his feelings had no names.

They sat in silence until the children came back, dragging Kong. "He wasn't there," Mandy said. "He's gone someplace."

Stefan rose when they came into the room. He took his cup and Lindsey's to the sink. "Are you ready to give Kong a bath?" he asked. "I'll help."

Geoff jerked Kong to a halt. "You're going to help?"

"I think it might take the three of us. I don't think he's used to baths."

Mandy stopped an arm's length from her father. "Where?"

"In the lake. You and Geoff change into your suits. Then we'll take him over to the beach and throw him in."

Mandy squealed with delight.

"Go get your suits on."

The children didn't need another invitation. They took off up the stairs at a run, with Kong following behind.

"In the lake?" Lindsey stood, too. "It's chilly today."

"Weren't you the one who said that water never hurt anyone?"

"Shall I expect the three of you for dinner?"

He heard the invitation but knew better than to accept it. He knew the correlation between longing and time spent with Lindsey. "I'll take them to my place for dinner. There's a fireplace. We can roast hot dogs."

She felt the chill of loneliness and wondered if this was what Stefan experienced when he knew he had a night in an empty apartment to look forward to. She told herself she was being silly. Stefan never found the time to be lonely.

"Then it looks like I have the evening off." She forced a smile. "I'm going to be very lazy."

"It'll be good for you."

For a moment she wondered if he was telling her more than he seemed. Perhaps he wanted her to know what he felt when he was separated from his family. Again she told herself she was being silly. "Have a good time with them."

"I will."

Geoff and Mandy came back into the kitchen, pulling up straps and tightening strings. Kong launched himself at Stefan, front paws nearly reaching Stefan's shoulders. Stefan rubbed his ears, then firmly pushed him to the ground.

"He doesn't have any manners," Mandy apologized.

"I like his manners fine. For now," Stefan said. "Is everybody ready?"

Lindsey watched the Peugeot pull out of the driveway. The house was still, and loneliness closed around her. Loneliness and loss were becoming familiar, but there was no comfort in her acquaintance with them. She knew when the sound of the car died away that she could not stay in the house.

Chapter 5

"I thought that was you."

Lindsey turned and saw Alden striding across the road. It wasn't the first time she had noticed the fluid perfection of his walk. He moved like a wave in the ocean, utterly boneless and free. His body was glorious, lean-hipped, broad-shouldered and muscular. She knew other women must have watched him move, must have added up the blue of his eyes, the bronze of his hair and the thoroughly masculine jut of his chin. And she doubted that any of them had found him wanting in any way.

"Hello." She turned back to the field, embarrassed to have been caught there. She tried to think of an excuse to be standing and staring at nothing.

"Do you want to be alone?" he asked. "I was just passing by. I can keep going."

"No. I'm about to leave anyway."

"If you're heading back home, I'll walk with you."

"You're walking?"

"I've heard it's good for you."

She smiled. No longer did the slight hesitancy before his replies bother her. She was fairly sure that it signalled uncertainty of one kind or another, not calculation. As handsome and charming as Alden Fitzpatrick was, he still seemed less than sure of himself.

"Were you sketching?" he asked, gesturing to the pad she had tucked under her arm.

"Trying to."

"That's a pretty barren landscape."

"Apparently so. I've tried twice today, and I haven't gotten anything worthwhile on paper."

"Would you like to show me?"

"No."

"I'm sorry. Was I being pushy?"

"I don't know. Were you?"

"I don't know, either."

She sighed. "Alden, are you really who you say you are? Because if you have another reason to be my friend or make friends with my children, I'd like to know what it is."

They walked a distance before he answered. "I am who I say I am."

"Well, that's good."

"And I like your children. And you."

"That's good, too."

"What other reason could I have?"

She considered whether to tell him or not. Her experience at the field was no secret. Kelleys Island buzzed with it. She had been to town twice since settling in, and both times she had been asked to recount her story for friendly townspeople. No one meant any harm. They were, in fact, completely behind her. She had brought excitement to an island renowned for the lack of it.

"Haven't you heard about me and what happened in that field?" she asked. "Someone must have told you."

"No one's told me anything."

"In May I was at the cottage, getting it ready for the summer. I took a walk after dark. It was a beautiful night.

Stars were everywhere. I walked along this road, and I came to the field where you just found me. And then I saw lights.''

"Lights?"

"Yes.'' She told the rest in one rush. He seemed to be listening with an open mind. "And then I woke up the next morning on the side of the road with two very worried residents bending over me.''

"You must have been frightened.''

His response was a welcome relief. "A little.''

"And confused.''

"Everyone else was confused. I knew what had happened to me. At least, I knew some of the basics. Everyone else thought I'd lost my mind.''

"It's very difficult for people to believe anything they haven't seen themselves.''

"Well, what do you believe? Am I crazy?''

"No.''

"So you believe there might be life out there?'' She lifted her palm to the sky.

"If we don't believe in things we don't see, then we can't discover anything new.''

"I wish everybody felt like you do.''

"And they don't?''

She shook her head.

"I'm sorry.''

He sounded it. He sounded genuinely sad that she'd had a difficult time. She told herself that he could very well be sympathizing to get her to talk more. But she didn't believe it.

"What were you hoping to find back there at the field?'' he asked.

"Answers.'' The conversation was veering toward new, unpublished material. Nothing she had told him so far was news. But she had spoken to no one except Stefan about her feelings. In the tabloids, emotion could be stretched into a story.

"Did you find any?"

"Not a one."

"Answers are rarely where you look for them."

"I have no idea where else I should look."

If he had an answer, he didn't give it to her. Instead, and to her relief, he changed the subject. "Do you mind if I ask where the children are?"

"They're with their father. He got them a dog. They went over to show it to you this afternoon, but you weren't home."

"I'll look forward to that pleasure later." They were almost at his house before he spoke again. "Why don't you stay here and have dinner with me?"

"I don't want to impose."

"You're lonely, Lindsey."

"How do you know?"

He seemed puzzled for a moment. He hesitated longer than usual. "It's obvious to me," he said at last.

"I suppose I don't hide my feelings very well."

He smiled. His smile was dazzling and utterly genuine. "Why should you? What would be the point?"

"It can keep you from getting hurt."

"I'm not going to hurt you."

She believed him, although he was obviously a man who could easily get close enough to a woman to try. She watched his eyes turn a deeper shade of blue as he waited for her answer. Something stirred inside her. He was kind, he was concerned and he was the most extraordinary specimen of manhood she had ever seen. He was also here, when she needed his companionship.

"Maybe another time," she said, denying herself his comfort.

"You never explained why you asked if I was the man I said I was."

"I've wondered if you have ulterior motives for getting to know me."

"Ulterior motives?"

"Well, do you?"

"Isn't it rare to find a man without an ulterior motive when a woman is as attractive as you?"

She realized he was flirting. She met his eyes and saw nothing there but warmth and concern. She smiled. "You're very good at evading an answer."

"How about this one? I like you, and I want to get to know you better. I've got no suspicious motives of any kind."

"And you're not going to hurt me," she finished for him.

"Exactly."

She wondered what it would be like to take him at face value. In the year since her divorce she had avoided men. She had not met one who didn't somehow remind her of Stefan. And she hadn't needed that pain.

There was nothing about Alden that was like Stefan at all. And, oddly, that brought its own kind of pain.

"I'll take a rain check."

He hesitated. "All right. Another time."

He turned toward his house, but she stopped him. "Alden?"

"Change your mind?"

"I've never asked you where you're from."

"Why do you ask now?"

"Your accent."

"Make a guess."

"That's just it. I can't. I'm good at accents. But you don't seem to have one." She mulled over her own words. "Have you moved a lot?"

"Yes."

"So, where is your practice?"

"North, south, east and west." He let her hang for a moment. "I fill in wherever I'm needed," he explained.

"You substitute?"

"I enjoy traveling. I work all over, move when the urge strikes."

"So that's why you can take the summer off."

"Exactly."

"An itinerant doctor."

"At your service."

She raised her hand in goodbye. Halfway home she realized that he had not answered even one of her questions head on. Alden Fitzpatrick might be a handsome, thoughtful man, but she wasn't certain that handsome and thoughtful were all he was. She had been wise not to let down her guard with him. She would be wise to remember it the next time, too.

The early evening was silent, with only the ticking of the mantel clock to break the stillness. Lindsey made herself a sandwich from bread she had baked earlier in the day and took it out on the patio. There were enough clouds streaking the horizon to promise a beautiful sunset, and when she'd finished eating, she followed a path to the lake to watch.

She rarely missed sunset or sunrise. Sometimes she thought they were the only things that bound her to time. They started and ended her days, and on those occasions when she couldn't celebrate them, she felt distinctly disoriented.

When she reached the lake she realized she had been right about this sunset. The sky shimmered with orange and gold streaked by fingers of purple. She lowered herself to a stone bench to enjoy the view. No one else was about, for which she was grateful. The sky was as still as her house had been. Even the ducks flying across the horizon made no sound.

She wondered if Stefan and the children were enjoying the sunset at his house. Stefan had rarely paused more than a moment or two for anything as sentimental as dawn or twilight.

Except once. Once.

She wondered why she was thinking of that evening now. Since the divorce she had carefully tried to store away all memories of her days as Stefan's lover or wife. She had hoped that someday she could remember those times with no sadness. But not now. Not yet. She had not prepared herself for this piercing sweetness, this crystalline memory that cut straight through all her protective layers and filled her with feelings she had also tried to store away.

The evening was the one when they had met. And the sunset? She remembered now, against her will. The sunset had been the most beautiful she had ever seen.

She had been a senior at last, after three years of floating through college. Those years had been filled with dance, art and poetry. Her major had been eclectic and experimental, guaranteed to leave her a more creative person, but a creative person with no firm employment opportunities. That hadn't mattered at all. She had been filled with dreams and energy and life. She had been a lark set free from demanding parents who had used her love and vitality to feed their own immaturity. Now, safely away from home, she had begun to soar.

The college was a small one in Michigan, a place where students called professors by their first names and professors took desks in the classroom and waved students to the front to teach. In the dormitories there were discussions into the wee hours of every morning, organized protests and impromptu concerts. There were signs in the cafeteria railing against sugar, meat and white flour, signs on the restroom doors declaring them to be unisex and politically correct. Lindsey had absorbed it all, lived and loved and drunk it in with the thirst of a lifetime.

Then she had met Stefan.

In early October, sunset had begun to edge closer toward the end of her final class of each day, and she found she had less and less time to get to the part of campus where she could best see it. She'd had a dance class that evening, and she was still wearing her leotard when she hurried along the pathway to her favorite view.

The sky was a dark blue, the Prussian blue of her favorite childhood crayon. The path climbed, but she was tireless.

Dance class always exhilarated her. She would never be a professional, nor had that ever been her goal, but she felt music inside her, just as she felt colors when she painted, shapes when she sculpted and words when she composed poetry.

No one else was on the path. The weather was turning cold—another reason to move quickly—and the other students had gone back to dorms or on to the cafeteria. She didn't mind being alone. The campus was relatively safe, and she was fearless. Sunset itself was a protection. She couldn't imagine anyone able to commit an act of violence when the sun was streaking the horizon.

Her favorite spot for viewing was a knoll overlooking a valley of houses and a strong sweep of sky. Valley was an exaggeration. The terrain around the college wasn't really hilly, but the knoll was the highest place for miles. This particular part of the county had not been highly developed. She could ignore the houses dotting the fields below, stand on the knoll and pretend she was the only person in the universe.

When she reached the knoll, the sky was growing darker still. A wide strip of brilliant gold colored the horizon, and shafts of sunlight spun away from it to shatter the sky. No one else was there to see it. She threw her books onto a bench and ran to the railing.

Something told her that this was the last sunset she might see for a while. Tonight the sunset had begun without her, and tomorrow and the next day it would begin earlier. She held her breath and tried to absorb each particle of light, each color and shape and pattern. The sky was a kaleidoscope, changing subtly as she watched. And when she could watch silently no more, when she was completely filled with the sunset's beauty, she began to dance.

At first she wore her sweater, but as her body warmed, she threw it to the ground beside the fence. She twirled and leaped and held out her hands in supplication to the setting sun, begging it to stay a little longer. Her hair swept her back, then cascaded over her breasts as she shook her head. She kicked, and her toes pointed toward heaven; she leapt and she felt as if she could fly.

She finished at last, chest heaving, perspiration clammy in the rapidly chilling air. She spun for one more look at the sunset, and at that moment she saw what she had not seen before.

A man.

"I'm sorry," he said. "I'm sure that was meant to be very private."

She stared for a moment. Then she picked up her sweater and buried her face in it. When she looked up she smiled— because this was a man who was easy to smile at. "If I'd known I had an audience, I would have tried even harder."

"I don't know how you could have."

"Were you there long?"

"Long enough to wish I'd been here longer."

"Are you an admirer of sunsets?"

"Of sunsets?" His gaze drifted subtly over her, the faintest of caresses. "Not particularly. Of beautiful women?" He shrugged.

She felt as if she'd been touched. She felt as if his hands, not his eyes, had moved over her body. "Are you a student here?"

"I'm in my last year of medical school, across town at the university."

"So you're seeing if this place is as crazy as outsiders think?"

"I'm meeting someone. I parked off campus, and I was taking a short cut."

She wanted to ask if the someone was male or female. Instead she held out her hand. He took it in his, and the warmth of his touch was like an embrace. "I'm Lindsey Parker."

"Stefan Daniels." He didn't drop her hand. He transferred it, then reached for her other hand, too, and examined it closely.

"Are you going to tell my fortune?"

"Mine. You're not married, and you're not engaged—unless your intended is too poor to afford a ring."

"I'm free as a bird."

"When I watched you dance, I thought you were a bird. I thought you were going to take flight and leave me anchored to the ground."

"If I could fly, I'd take you with me. Would you want to go?"

"Probably not."

"Hmmm… That's too bad."

He threaded his fingers through hers. Enchanted, she let him. "Some of us weren't meant to soar."

"Why not?"

"We want to understand everything here, I guess, before we take off for more unknowns."

"And that's why you want to be a doctor?"

"That's why."

"Are you on your way to understanding everything?"

He pulled her a little closer. She went. "I just found one more thing I want to understand better."

"Then I'll help. I'm just twenty-one. I'll graduate with a bachelor of fine arts at the end of this year. I want to make my living creating, but I don't know how."

"And the rest?"

"Rest?"

"The personal."

She smiled a daring smile. She felt daring. "I have a dozen boyfriends but presently no lovers. The past three years have been the best of my life. After I graduate I want to live on every continent—"

"Simultaneously?"

"If I can."

"I almost believe you could manage it."

"I want to experience everything. Everything!"

"Everything good?"

"Yes, and some of the pain, too. I want to know what other people feel. I want to feel it, too."

"I want to *stop* their pain."

She gazed into his eyes. Even then, in those first crucial moments together, she could see how different they were. She wasn't discouraged, though. "Two halves of a whole," she said softly.

With obvious reluctance, he dropped her hands. "Will you have dinner with me tonight?"

"Weren't you meeting somebody?"

"I'm just delivering papers to one of the professors here from one of mine. They're working on a research project together."

"Will I have time to shower and change?"

He smiled. It was the first smile he had given her, and it was as promising as the sunset. "I wish you wouldn't change."

She compromised. While he delivered his papers, she showered and put on a burgundy leotard with a calf-length suede-cloth skirt and tights. She pulled her hair back from her face with a gray satin ribbon and wore embroidered shoes that could have passed for ballet slippers. By the time he arrived at her dormitory, she was waiting in the parlor.

They had pizza, his loaded with pepperoni, hers with mushrooms, since she had given up eating meat the day she realized where it came from. They talked until the restaurant closed, then found another that stayed open all night. Over coffee and pie he told her about his successful parents and his childhood. She read between the lines and understood that he was a remarkably gifted young man who took his education seriously and his mission to heal even more so. She also heard loneliness, the loneliness of a child who had developed so quickly that he'd gone on to other things as his peers enjoyed the pleasures of childhood and adolescence. The loneliness of a man who needed more than study and discipline to become the person he was meant to be.

She told him her own lonely childhood, about the divorced parents who had depended on her for emotional support and sustenance until they remarried. She told him about the teachers, the girl scout leaders and dance instructors who had helped her through her own crises when her parents became busy with their new loves. She confided the dreams she indulged in now that she was free to pursue them.

They talked of books they both liked, films that had moved them, music they listened to. They didn't agree on anything. She loved Debussy, Billy Joel and classic Bob Dylan. He loved Handel, Dave Brubeck and anything on the harpsichord. He read philosophy; she read Gothics. He had walked out of *Annie Hall,* her favorite movie of all time.

He didn't touch her again until he walked her back to her dormitory. They had talked all night, and the sun was just beginning to light the horizon when they climbed the outside stairwell of her dorm to the roof to watch the dawn.

"I come up here as often as I can," she said.

"Do you ever sleep?"

"I really don't need much."

"You should be in medical school."

"Am I going to see you again?" She faced him instead of the sunrise. "Or are we too different? Do I scare you or intrigue you more?"

"I could ask you the same."

"But you didn't."

He opened his arms, and she went into them willingly. She had never been as excited by a man. He was self-confident and brilliant. He needed nothing from her except exactly what she wanted to give. She ran her hands up his sides, under his open coat, then clasped them around his neck. She stared into his eyes as he pulled her closer. In the first light of dawn she knew that a lifetime together would not be long enough to know him.

If he ever let her.

Just before he kissed her, she felt the faintest thread of alarm. Already, what she felt for him was powerful. She sensed that there might be no turning back if he kissed her. And they were so different. Perhaps too much so.

What barriers there were tumbled when she felt his lips on hers. His mouth was as hungry, as relentless, as she had somehow known it would be. Her body melted against his, and she could feel his heat pour into her. She learned the feel of him, the taste, the essence. She learned how much he wanted her and how careful he would be when he finally took what he craved.

He ended the kiss. She didn't know if she would have had the control.

"The sun's up," he said.

"Yes." She leaned her head against his shoulder.

He held her close, but not too tightly. "We'd better end this now, if we're going to."

"Yes."

"Are we going to?"

She realized he was leaving the decision to her. "What do you want, Stefan?"

His hand brushed a strand of hair back from her cheek. "To see you again."

She smiled. She suspected that was as much of a hint at his emotions as she was going to get. "Then you will."

They shared another kiss, a kiss even more impassioned than the first. Then she stayed on the roof as he took the stairs at a run until he was back on the ground. She leaned over the railing and watched him emerge. He gave one wave, then turned and started across campus.

She stayed on the roof until he was no longer visible and the sky was filled with the promise of a brand new day. Then she danced a tribute to dawn.

The sun was gone when Lindsey made her way slowly back to the cottage. Without street or house lights to soften the night, darkness on Kelleys Island was a black curtain. She stumbled once, but hardly noticed. Her head was aching, and she couldn't have hurried if she'd had to. Her body felt strangely heavy and sluggish. She was still remembering that first night with Stefan, that joyous night of discovery and sensation. How could something that had held such promise have ended so sadly?

She looked toward the heavens, but there was no answer there. In the years of her marriage she had learned about loneliness, but she had never known this hollow emptiness, this feeling that she was completely alone in the universe.

Inside the cottage she turned on lights and turned down the children's beds. She found old blankets and made a bed for Kong on the floor in the hall between their rooms.

When she was finished and she could find nothing else to do, she sat on the front porch and gave in to tears.

Chapter 6

Kong was clean and at least temporarily without fleas. Mandy had made a bow out of an old tie, and Geoff had patiently combed out every one of the mats in Kong's mottled fur. He was still the most pathetic excuse for a dog that Stefan had ever seen.

Quite obviously the children didn't think so.

"He's beautiful now," Mandy said from the back seat of the car, resting her cheek against Kong's side.

The response from Kong's other side was muffled. Stefan tried to interpret, factoring in a high margin for error. Geoff's words had sounded suspiciously like "Mmmmph tho."

"What did you say?"

"Mom will think so," Geoff repeated more audibly.

"I hope so." Stefan turned into the lane leading to the cottage. He hadn't intended to keep the children so late, and he hoped Lindsey hadn't been worried. Normally his rare times with Geoff and Mandy bordered on the stiff and formal. He talked; they listened. He took them somewhere, the zoo, the symphony, the art museum, and they watched and listened dutifully. Usually he returned them home before supper.

Today had been nothing like that. He hadn't been called on to relate to them at all. Even the symphony had required that he make small talk during intermission, but today his children had been perfectly content to talk to each other and to Kong. When they'd addressed Stefan at all it had been to ask for his help scrubbing or training the dog.

None of them had worried about what to say; no one had given a thought to what to do. The afternoon had centered around Kong. He imagined that this was the kind of gentle, easygoing day that most families shared frequently.

Except that he and Geoff and Mandy hadn't really been a family. Not quite.

"Mom's out on the porch," Geoff said.

Stefan saw that his son was right. Lindsey was sitting on the porch swing, moonlight reflecting off the corn-silk blond of her hair. He parked in the driveway and let the children greet her first. She cooed over the dog and assured Geoff and Mandy that she thought he was magnificent. Then she shooed them inside to get ready for bed.

The screen door slammed shut behind the children and dog, and Lindsey turned toward Stefan. Fireflies winked in the air between them. He knew he should just say goodnight and go, but he couldn't make himself.

"You look exhausted," she said. She smiled, and he felt it somewhere deep inside him.

"You do, too." He moved closer. She did look tired, and that was rare. She had boundless energy. Even during his residency, she had slept less than he. "Are you feeling all right?"

"I thought you had the day off, Dr. Daniels."

"Old habits." He moved closer. She looked as if she had been crying. He felt alarm. Perhaps he was imagining it. "Lindsey, I'm not trying to pry. I know I don't have that right. But are you okay? Is anything wrong?"

She lowered herself to the swing again. That in itself was strange. Usually she would be upstairs with the children, coaxing and laughing until they were in bed for the night. "I'm fine. I guess I just had too much time to think tonight."

He was at her side without planning to be there. "May I sit?"

She moved over in answer. He sat beside her, careful not to touch her. They had sat like this only rarely during their years together. But each one of those times came back to him now, like the brightest moments of a past he had little to show for.

"Our first apartment had a porch swing," he said. "Remember? There was just one. All the residents and their wives used to fight to see who could get to it first on a warm summer night."

"I remember. We were never first."

"Then there was the swing at Patterson's house."

She didn't answer. The swing rocked gently. He let her set the pace.

"I was thinking about the night we met," she said at last. "Earlier. Before you came. I was down at the beach watching the sunset."

He was sure he hadn't forgotten one moment of that night, but he wasn't going to tell her. "Was it a good sunset?"

"Lovely. I felt…" She didn't finish.

He rested his arm along the back of the swing, still careful not to touch her. "You've hardly changed since that night."

"Yes I have."

"Mommy?" Mandy came out on the porch dressed in a long cotton nightgown. "Geoff says Kong gets to sleep with him!"

Lindsey rose and started toward the door. "I'll talk to him."

Stefan rose, too. "I'd better be going."

"You don't have to." Lindsey turned. "Stay a little while."

He wasn't certain if he was imagining the intensity behind the polite phrase. "Are you sure?"

"Whatever you want. If you're in a hurry to get back, I don't want to keep you."

"I'm not in a hurry."

"Then I'll put some coffee on for us. Sit and relax."

He settled himself back in the swing. He heard the clatter of Mandy's feet on the stairs, then the pleasant murmur of voices from the second floor. He could almost pretend that the house was his again, that Lindsey was putting the children to bed and that soon he would be going upstairs to their own bed and her arms.

She had been thinking about the night they met.

He wondered why. When she had asked him for the divorce, he had assumed she would lock away all memories of the good times they had shared. Wasn't that the way it was done? Wasn't that how people survived the dismantling of the most intimate of relationships? For the first six months after the divorce he had hardly been able to be in the same room with her. He had not been able to face the pain. And memories? Well, he'd struggled to keep memories in their place, snugly tucked in the appropriate region of the brain. He had disciplined them with hard work and longer and longer hours of devotion to his patients and research.

But had the inevitable happened for them both? Could even the most rigid discipline collapse? He wasn't sure facing memory or pain was going to be easier, even now. And what about Lindsey? He was sure she'd been crying. How much more could she take before shattering into a thousand tiny pieces?

The swing rocked back and forth beneath him. He wished that he hadn't brought up another porch swing. She had been right; they had rarely sat in the swing at their first apartment, because he had been too busy. But there had been another one.

Patterson's swing. He remembered all too clearly one night soon after he and Lindsey had met. He had been twenty-four and so taken with the woman beside him that he could think of little but touching her. He tried to file the memory away, but it was as solid, as immobile, as a mountain. Was this what Lindsey had come up against at the beach? Were they doomed now by a past they had once shared?

He wondered about discipline and self-preservation. But in the end, with the voices of his children woven with Lindsey's own, he stopped wondering. He could only remember.

"I'm glad that for once we get to make dinner without your roommates around. It's awfully nice of Patterson to let you have the key to his apartment when he's not here."

"Somebody has to feed his fish." Stefan watched Lindsey stroll slowly through the bedroom-living room of his best friend's efficiency, touching everything, lifting things and handling them for the sheer sensory joy of it.

There was lots to touch. Patterson was a collector, an eccentric lover of both the mundane and the bizarre. Stacked on every surface were ashtrays—one from each state—although Patterson railed constantly against the evils of tobacco. The walls were cluttered with collages of everyday items. One was an assortment of household cleaner labels, another cancelled checks. On a shelf in the corner there were statues of hula dancers. In the opposite corner was a stuffed pelican dressed in a rhinestone-studded tutu. In deference to the approaching Christmas holiday, a gaudy plastic star decorated his head.

Fish lined the walls of this room and the kitchen in aquariums both large and small. They were all goldfish, all the same plain gold, all the same size down to a centimeter. Patterson knew each of their names and insisted each had a different personality.

Patterson planned to become a psychiatrist.

"This place drives you crazy. Right?" Lindsey spun around and gave Stefan a spontaneous hug.

He wasn't sure what he had done to deserve her affection, but he let himself indulge, anyway. He loved the feel of Lindsey's lithe body against his. Holding her was like holding music, like holding light itself. More and more he found himself thinking about holding her when he was supposed to be concentrating on other things.

"This place is crazy. Patterson's crazy," he said.

"Wonderfully so. He's alive."

"You haven't even met him."

"Is that my fault?" She pushed him away so she could look at him. "You don't introduce me to your friends. Are you ashamed of me?"

"Ashamed?"

"Well, are you?"

"Are you kidding? I just have no intention of sharing you, that's all. I've already had to fight off my roommates. If my friends met you, I might not see you again."

She sent him a teasing half smile. "Really? And why not? Do you think you're so expendable?"

He knew what he was. Single-minded, dedicated, passionate-seeker-of-truth. And he knew what he wasn't. Warm, expressive, spontaneous. Those things were beyond his reach. They had been exorcised in his childhood, and he rarely missed them...except at moments like this, when he wished he could be everything for the woman staring at him.

"I don't want to scare you away," he said.

Her smile disappeared. "What makes you think you hold so little attraction for me?"

He wasn't sure how they had gotten so serious. They had only been dating for two months, and then only when their crowded schedules meshed. His head told him that relationships grew slowly, that courtship was a time to carefully check all the little things that could make or break a marriage. The rest of his anatomy told him to embrace the woman in front of him and never, never let her go.

"Well?" he asked.

She put her hands on her hips. "Well what?"

"Well, are you attracted?"

"Haven't you been able to tell?"

He realized he was enjoying this. "Maybe I need an education. What are the signs?"

She seemed to be enjoying their conversation, too. She had the most delicious repertoire of smiles. She could say anything she wanted with them. Smiles never came easily for him. Now he bathed in the glory of one of hers.

"Let's see." She pretended to think. "My pulse quickens."

"Does it?" He reached for her hand and slid his index finger to the pulse point at her wrist. "I don't have anything to compare it to."

"My temperature rises when we're together."

"Your cheeks are flushed."

"I go out with you every time you ask."

"You turned me down last Friday."

"I had a prior engagement."

"You had a date."

"Well, I wished all night I was with you."

He lifted her hand to his cheek. She wasn't smiling now. "My pulse rises and my temperature quickens," he said. "And I think about you when I shouldn't."

"Stefan." She framed his face with her hands. He could feel each separate finger against his skin. "I'm afraid we're in this together."

He laughed. The sound came from somewhere deep inside him, from that secret prison where smiles were held captive. He kissed first one palm, then the other. And he knew that if he didn't get out of Patterson's room with the big, tempting double bed in the corner, he was going to make love to her right now. Somehow the kitchen, where they had planned to make dinner together, didn't seem quite far enough away.

"Let me show you the swing." He took her hand and started through the room.

"Swing? Isn't it a little cold for a swing?"

"Wait and see."

He led her through the kitchen into a dank, cold hallway. Then he opened a door. "Patterson's secret hideaway."

She clapped her hands. "Who would have thought it?"

The swing hung from the ceiling of a tiny glassed-in porch. Through a thick cover of evergreens, the room was tinted by moonlight. The apartment was one quarter of an old brick Colonial, and it had its share of the house's idiosyncracies. The sunroom was one of them.

Lindsey preceded him. "I can't believe it. It's heated."

"He collects plants, too."

"I can tell. It's practically a greenhouse."

"Begonias. And he never gets a bloom out of them."

Lindsey ignored the plants cluttering everything but a narrow path. She maneuvered the short distance and plopped down to test the swing. "Stefan, it's wonderful. Come here and sit with me."

He joined her. The swing was just wide enough for two. Just. He rested his hip against hers and felt her breast brush his arm as she put her hand on his shoulder.

"Look, it's snowing." She pointed in the direction of a streetlamp that illuminated snow drifting in soft, fragile clouds.

"It's supposed to snow most of the night."

"I love winter."

"And summer, spring and fall. What don't you love?"

"Cynics."

"I'm not a cynic. I love your enthusiasm."

"Do you?" She rested her head against his shoulder. "Do you know what I love about you?"

Something gripped his throat. For a moment he couldn't speak. "What?"

"Well, it's a long list. Do you have time?"

"We might starve before you finish."

"I'll take the chance."

"Don't say I didn't warn you."

She kissed his shoulder. He could feel it burn through his sweater. "I love the way you think about everything. Nothing comes quickly or easily. You consider everything, and you're so, so careful. You want to be absolutely sure. It would pain you forever to think you might have hurt someone or been dishonest, even unintentionally."

"I sound repressed."

"That I haven't noticed. You have trouble keeping your hands off me. I love that, too."

He put his arm around her. "Do you?"

"And I love the way you choose your words. If you say something to me, I know you mean it. I can trust you completely."

"I'm not sure I'm that safe."

"I can manage you."

"Can you?"

"Want to see?"

He wasn't sure. He was eaten up by the strongest emotion he had ever felt. His control was disappearing at a remarkable speed. He was afraid to get caught in Lindsey's spell, afraid for both of them.

He felt her then, and he turned, too. His body seemed to belong to someone else. It refused to obey the commands he issued.

"Lind…sey." He said her name, slowly, carefully. It was as much a warning as he could give her.

"Stef…an." She smiled just before she pulled his head to hers, just before her lips sought his.

She tasted like fire, like music and light and all things elemental. Her lips moved over his as if she were afraid she would miss something new, something even better. He crushed her against him, longing for everything all at once. He understood her desire to embrace life in its fullest. She

was life, and he wanted all of her. Nothing separate. Nothing
held back.

She moved against him, rubbing her chest against his until he was on fire everywhere that her soft breasts touched.
She laughed, a low, throaty woman's laugh, when he tried
to hold her still. Her lips sought his ear, the curve of his
jaw, the hollow of his throat. And she swayed against him,
pliant, sensuous, relentless.

In a moment his hands were under her sweater, sliding
over the warmth of her skin. Flesh melted against flesh. His
fingers absorbed her heat, the satin texture of her back. He
knew he was trembling, but he didn't care. That passion
could be this intense, this immediate, was a revelation to
him. She was not the first woman he had touched this way;
she would not be the first woman he would have. But in
that moment he knew this was another kind of first, and in
the most important of ways, she would stand alone in his
life.

She wasn't wearing anything under the sweater except a
silky, taunting camisole. Her breasts were unfettered for his
touch. She moaned softly as he circled them. Slowly, increasingly aware of his ability to please her, he circled them.

"Stef...an."

This time he laughed. He was triumphant, filled with his
own power. His hand moved closer to her breasts, then
closer still. Finally he let himself explore them. She kissed
him as he did, murmuring nothing and everything against
his lips. He hadn't known that breasts could feel like velvet,
that the shape of a woman's curves could turn him into a
man he didn't know. He explored the hardening nubs of her
nipples, the valley between, the rapid beat of her heart. He
caressed her, and each movement, each new inch, was a
glorious torment.

He wasn't even sure what was happening when she
slipped off her sweater. He had to let her go to do it, and
he felt a new rush of exquisite agony. Then in the moonlight

he saw the pearly glow of her skin and knew that the camisole had gone, too.

She was beautiful, so perfect, so luminous. For a moment he wanted time to stop; he wanted to capture her this way forever. Then time moved on, desire rushed over him, and he bent his head to taste what she had so freely bared.

She tasted the way she looked, the way she felt. Perfect, warm, fragrant, quintessentially woman. He heard her murmur, felt her arch against him. Her breasts were small and perfect, and he explored them with his tongue, curling it around each nipple. She sighed and thrust herself forward, offering more. He took her between his lips and tugged. She murmured again, a plea for yet more. He lifted her skirt, and his hands splayed against her hips. His hands sank lower still and felt her most intimate heat through the fabric of her panties.

She arched again, and for a moment he didn't understand. She tensed and cried out once, then once more. And finally he knew.

He clasped her against him as she shook with the power of release. Blood roared in his ears. He had brought her to this with so little. He had known how responsive she was, how thoroughly, wonderfully sensual, but he had never dared to hope she would be this aroused by him. That lovemaking could reach such a tumultuous, instantaneous peak seemed impossible. But it hadn't been impossible. It hadn't.

He whispered her name. Her arms tightened around him; then he felt his sweater being drawn over his head. He had already been reduced to instinct and emotion. He wanted to stop her; he would have killed anyone who tried. He shut his eyes and felt her unbuttoning his shirt. Then he felt her hands against his bare chest.

"Your turn," she said softly. He could feel her words deep inside him. He was as hard as he ever remembered being, and she hadn't even touched him there.

Not yet.

"Didn't you know?" she asked. "Didn't you know what you could do to me?"

He didn't, couldn't, answer. Her lips grazed his chest. He knew that Lindsey and he were invisible, that the dark and evergreens hid them from view. But he felt completely exposed, to this woman, to the world. He was a fraud who pretended he lived in his head. And now his head and all thinking parts of him had disappeared.

His jeans came unsnapped with one flick of her hand. Her hand, her graceful, expressive hand, closed over him. Through his briefs he could feel the heat of her fingers. He moaned.

"Good," she said. "Moan for me, Stefan. Like I moaned for you."

He held her still and kissed her. Her lips were soft against his. They grew softer still as the kiss went on and on. But her hands never stopped. She moved under the briefs and played with him, toyed with him relentlessly. Fire rushed through his veins. How could he be so hot, how could he burn for her, when snow was falling and nothing but glass kept them from it?

She ended that kiss and trailed a new path of kisses down his neck. Slowly, so slowly, while her hand moved faster. Her lips touched one nipple. Her breath warmed it; her teeth grazed it. She laughed a little, and he felt the laugh follow the fire's path.

He arched, just as she had. Then he called her name. Her hand moved slower, slower, then not at all.

He took a moment by himself in the bathroom. When he returned to the porch he pulled her against him to rest. He felt clean, purified by the roaring blaze and its aftermath. Her hair rested against his cheek. She smelled like violets and infinitely satisfied woman. He wrapped his arms around her. Beneath them the swing rocked lazily.

"Yes. I can manage you," she said at last.

"And who's going to manage you?" he asked.

She snuggled more securely against him, like a cat

stretching blissfully. "I knew it would be like that. Just that easy. Didn't you?"

"You'd thought about it?"

"Constantly."

Satisfaction was pierced by something warmer and quite familiar once more. His arms tightened. "Constantly?"

"Yes."

"About this?"

"Not exactly this."

He knew *exactly* what she meant. "About making love."

"Together. Naked. All night long."

"How did I find you?"

"You almost tripped over me." She lifted her face to his. "I'd been waiting for you." She caressed his cheek. "I'd been waiting for you, Stefan, but I didn't know it. There have been other men. I didn't wait alone. But they weren't important. When I wasn't with them, I didn't think of them at all. And they never made me sing inside, the way you do."

He stared at her. He understood what she was saying. There had been other men, but she had not responded to them the way she had responded to him tonight. He wanted to assure her that she was different, too. That no one, no one at all, had ever made him lose control the way she did. But he didn't know how to say the words without sounding foolish. Without feeling foolish.

"Thank you for waiting" was all he could say.

She smiled. "And I suppose we'll wait a little longer before we make love, won't we? You're such a careful man."

"Am I?" He really wasn't sure anymore.

"Yes." She kissed him, as if his caution pleased her. As if he pleased her.

He clasped her to him again, and for a long time they lounged in each other's arms and watched the snow fall in silence.

* * *

"I have your coffee." Lindsey stood in front of Stefan holding out the mug with his name on it.

He took it, and it surprised him that his hands didn't tremble. So caught up in memory had he been that for a moment the fireflies resembled falling snow.

"Our relationship can be measured from one cup of coffee to the next." He moved over to give her more room to sit.

She settled herself beside him. "We're not even supposed to have a relationship."

"We have two children we share."

"They couldn't stop babbling about Kong. They're thrilled that you gave him to them."

"We had a good afternoon."

"Did you? I'm so glad. They need you."

He wondered if she could possibly need him, too. Were there other men now who filled the space he had left in her life? He wasn't sure how wide or deep that space had been, but he did know that there would be any number of men willing to insert themselves into it.

They had never talked about those faceless, nameless others who haunted him. She was no longer his wife. She had every right to have relationships, but the thought of another man's hands on her body turned him to stone. The divorce decree had not wiped away his claim to her. That was written on his soul, and no lawyers, no laws or judges, could change the way he felt.

"Do you ever think about getting married again?" she asked.

He wondered if she had guessed his thoughts. "Do you?"

"You always turned questions around that way. Like a simple answer was too much of a peek into what you were thinking."

"You didn't always criticize me for it."

"No. That came later, didn't it? When I got desperate." He set his mug on the porch floor. "I should go."

She laid her hand on his arm. "No. Stay. I'm sorry, Stefan. I guess we're going to have to work at being divorced the way we didn't work at being married.''

"I don't think about getting married again.'' He sat back, but he left the coffee where he'd put it. He was going to have enough trouble sleeping tonight.

"Really?"

"Why are you surprised?"

She debated continuing this. She wasn't sure where they were going, but she was absolutely sure where they shouldn't. She was vulnerable tonight, and she thought maybe Stefan was, too. Tears rose to her eyes. For the second time that evening. She swallowed.

"Our friends love to tell me how many women you have in your life now,'' she said, keeping the tears from her voice.

"What friends?"

"It doesn't matter."

"It does. Why would anyone be so intentionally cruel?"

"Cruel? It's not supposed to be cruel. We're divorced. I suppose they think I'm interested.''

"Cruel."

She sighed. "You have a right to whatever kind of personal life you want and need. So do I. I just didn't expect it to bother me.''

"Didn't you?"

"I guess I never thought about it. Everything hurt so much at the end, I couldn't think about more pain farther down the road.''

"Why are you bringing this up now?"

"I don't know. Maybe you're right. Maybe I am going crazy.''

"I never said I thought you were crazy." He turned to face her. "I've never even thought it.''

"I see lights in the sky that aren't there. Suddenly I believe in UFOs when I never did before. I cry at the drop of a hat." She swallowed tears again. "I ask you stupid, personal questions."

"There are no other women in my life. I've taken colleagues to functions where I was expected to put in an appearance. I tried dating twice and hated it. I tried to imagine myself in bed with both women, and it was a nightmare."

She stared at him. "Stefan."

He ran his hand through his hair. "Did you want to hear that, Lindsey? Was that what you were after?" He got up and went to the railing. The sky was a blanket of stars, all light-years away. It didn't matter. He felt smothered by them. "I haven't slept with anyone since our divorce. I can't get over the feeling that I'd be unfaithful to you if I did."

"How could I have hurt you so much? How could you have hurt me?"

"It doesn't matter. We can't go back."

"No."

"Well, there's my answer." He faced her. "Let's hear yours. Do you think about getting married again?"

"No."

"There must be men in your life."

"No one important."

He remembered, had remembered already, another night so many years before when she had told him the same thing. He wished that they were back on Patterson's porch. He wished that he could somehow live the last years over again with a different result.

"I haven't slept with anyone else, either," she said. "We're a pair, aren't we?" She rose and joined him at the railing. "We can't have this conversation again."

"We shouldn't have had it at all."

"I had no right to ask you anything. You're free. I'm free."

"Free?" He lifted her left hand. "There's no ring on your finger anymore. You're free of less than an ounce of precious metal, and so am I. But what else are we free from?

Pain? Everyone tells me that will go away. But mine doesn't seem to.''

Her eyes filled, and nothing she could do would force the tears away. "I never wanted to hurt you."

"Our intentions have always been honorable, haven't they? And it didn't matter." He didn't drop her hand, couldn't seem to make himself. And he knew his intentions at that moment were anything except honorable.

"Maybe you should go," she said. But she didn't pull her hand away, even though her cheeks were wet.

"What about Alden Fitzpatrick?"

"Alden?"

"Is something developing there? Geoff and Mandy talked about him all afternoon."

"Alden's a very warm, very considerate man who also happens to like our children."

"And you're lonely and vulnerable."

She knew she should be offended. Stefan was no longer her husband, and even when he had been, he had rarely offered advice. But she was not upset. She wanted to touch him. She wanted to reassure him that no one was stealing his place in the hearts of their children. She wanted to soothe the pain he talked about and the pain he couldn't even acknowledge.

But she couldn't.

"I am lonely and vulnerable," she said. "And if I weren't, we wouldn't be standing here this way, would we?"

"No? Is that all this is?"

"That's all. And it's more than it should be."

"Can you say you feel nothing for me now? Can you say that yet?"

She shut her eyes. Tears squeezed between the lids. "I will never be able to say that."

"Lindsey." He took her in his arms. She leaned against him and knew that if she didn't break free quickly, she might never be able to again.

He lowered his head and kissed her tears. She felt like something precious, something frighteningly fragile and precious, in his arms. For a moment she bent her body to him, curved it into the harder places of his and told him without a word how well they would still fit together.

Then she broke away. She backed up against the railing, her eyes wide. And scared. "You'd better go now."

Stefan knew she was right, but he didn't want to go. He wanted to forget all the things he knew, all the things he believed. He wanted to sweep away her doubts, carry her to her bedroom, *their* room, and make love to her until all her defenses were gone and she was his again.

He wanted to be someone other than the man he was.

"I'll be back next weekend."

She nodded.

"I'm sorry."

She nodded again.

He left her standing there. She was still standing there when he drove away.

Chapter 7

Mandy spread a slice of Lindsey's homemade bread with peanut butter, evenly covering the surface to every edge. "Cut the cucumbers thin."

"Please."

"Please." Mandy stood back and examined her work of art. "I'm ready for another."

"I'm ready for another, please."

"You are, too?" Mandy giggled.

Lindsey smiled at her, although it was hard to smile at anyone this morning. "When you're a surgeon like your father, you won't have to say *please* in the operating room. But until then, you do."

"I forget sometimes. But I'm only six."

"Six going on thirty." Lindsey ruffled Mandy's hair to show that she wasn't mad. "No cucumbers on Geoff's. He'll take bananas."

"Honey." Geoff came into the room with Kong trailing behind him. "And chocolate chips."

"Nice try." Lindsey got the honey out of the cupboard; the chocolate chips stayed behind.

"Aren't you done yet?" Geoff asked. "We've been waiting and waiting."

"We'd get done faster if you'd help."

Geoff thought that over. "I can wait some more."

"Wash the apples, please."

Geoff grumbled, but he complied. Lindsey watched him polish them to a high sheen, then stack them into an impromptu apple sculpture.

"Kong barked at every squirrel we saw on our walk," he said as he topped his creation with a banana. "He's a good watchdog."

"I'm glad. We won't have to worry about a squirrel attack."

"He barked at people, too."

"Did you take him to Alden's?"

"He wasn't there."

Lindsey looked up and saw Alden pass by the open window on his way to their back door. She waited for Kong, the superior watchdog, to set up a howl but he just sat there, tongue lolling.

"Alden's here now," she told Geoff. "Open the door for him, would you?"

Geoff flung the door open. Only then, at the sound of Alden's greeting, did Kong react. As Lindsey watched in horror, Kong launched himself at Alden, teeth bared, ears flat against his head. He looked like he was out for murder, and although he was only half-grown, he was large enough to try.

"Kong!" She started after him, but Geoff had reacted first. He threw himself on top of the dog and grabbed his collar. Kong stopped just short of Alden. When he realized he couldn't reach him, he began to bark wildly.

"Stop it, Kong!" Lindsey reached the dog's side and grabbed his collar, too, just in case the dog proved too much for Geoff to handle.

Alden stooped calmly in the doorway and began to speak softly. Lindsey couldn't catch his words over Kong's barking, but little by little the dog began to calm.

Finally Kong was silent. Still watching him, Alden rose and held out his hand. Kong growled. Alden murmured softly and moved closer.

"Watch out," Lindsey said. "We really don't know anything about this dog." She realized how true that was. They had brought him into their home knowing nothing about him. For the first time she wondered if they'd made a big mistake. Stefan's mistake.

"I startled him," Alden said. "He's fine now." He stood directly in front of Kong, reached down and rubbed his ears. Lindsey could feel the tension in the dog's body, but gradually he seemed to relax. "You can let go of him now," Alden said. "Right, boy? We're going to be friends."

Kong whined.

"Do you know him?" Geoff asked. "I mean, he was a stray. Did you know him before he came here?"

"No."

"He seemed mad at you."

"I took him by surprise. Dogs like to be warned."

"I don't think he's very bright," Lindsey said. "I saw you coming. I don't know why he didn't figure it out."

"He's a smart dog," Mandy said. She threw her arms around Kong, and he licked her face.

"So, he's the new family member," Alden said.

Lindsey smiled, glad the furor had ended. "Afraid so. May I get you a cup of coffee? We're making sandwiches to take to the beach. The children convinced me the water's warm enough to swim in. They were there yesterday with their father."

"It's perfect. I've been swimming everyday."

"Mommy doesn't like cold water," Mandy said.

"But I make myself go in anyway, don't I?" She poured Alden coffee and watched him settle himself at the kitchen table. Mandy crawled up into his lap as if she always sat there. Lindsey started to protest, but she saw from Alden's expression that he didn't mind.

She set the coffee in front of him. "Would you like to go to the beach with us? It's easy enough to make more sandwiches." She hadn't even finished asking the question when she began to wonder why she had. She was still hurting from her encounter with Stefan last night. She was too confused, too unsure of her feelings for her ex-husband to encourage another man in any way.

Yet, what was she risking? She and Alden would be with her children. And Kong was enough of a diversion to keep the conversation from getting personal. If she was honest with herself, she would have to admit that she had sensed a certain amount of interest from Alden. But he had never been forward. He had been warm and concerned. Was she going to run from every man who possessed the qualities she had so longed for in Stefan?

"I was going to go later, anyway," he said. "You've got enough to do making sandwiches for these appetites on legs you've got here."

"Don't be silly. What's one sandwich more or less?"

"We can build sand castles," Mandy said. "Geoff builds better castles than anybody in the world."

"Jeez, Mandy," Geoff said. "Don't scare Alden away."

"You're sure?" Alden asked.

Lindsey saw compassion in his eyes. For a moment she had the ridiculous sensation that he knew what she'd been thinking. But then, that might not be so ridiculous. Stefan had often told her that everything she felt passed across her face.

And almost nothing that Stefan felt did.

"I'm sure," she said. "Absolutely."

He gently pushed Mandy to her feet and stood. "Then I'd better get my things together. I'll bring cookies. I baked some last night."

"Terrific. We'll pick you up on the way. We're going to

ride our bikes. Why don't you borrow the green bike in our garage? Take it with you now.''

"Sounds good.'' Alden raised his hand in goodbye.

Kong jumped when Alden moved past him, and for a moment his ears flattened, as if he were going to attack again. Then he put his head on his paws and contented himself just following Alden's departure with his eyes.

"It's a beautiful day.'' Lindsey stretched in the sunshine. She hadn't felt well since her encounter with Stefan the night before, but on the beach, with the sun stroking her body and a cool breeze from the lake drifting over her, she could almost forget the headache and fatigue that had plagued her all day.

"It is that.'' Alden lay down beside her. She had prepared herself mentally for the moment when he would disrobe. And she was glad she'd had the time and forethought to make that preparation. Because Alden in a bathing suit was one of the most incredible sights she had ever seen.

Like Stefan, he had an athlete's body—although after watching him swerve precariously on the bicycle for the first half of their ride, his athletic prowess was in doubt. His shoulders were unbelievably broad; his chest was dusted with golden hair; his waist was narrow, and his legs were long and muscular.

Forcing herself to look away, she shaded her eyes with her hand to get a fix on the children's positions. The public beach on the north end of the island was small, and at this time of day the water was shallow for a good distance out. Both children swam, but neither was a strong swimmer. Luckily they were safe here, unless they took unnecessary chances.

Mandy wasn't in the water yet, but Geoff was swimming back and forth in an area not much deeper than his waist. She wondered what game he was playing, what fantasy he was living out. Was he Neptune, god of the sea? A pirate watching for enemy ships? Something had triggered his one-man race.

She spoke her thoughts out loud. "I wonder what Geoff is doing?"

"Practicing," Mandy said. She had come back up to the blanket to get her sand pail. Like her mother, she had to ease into cold water.

"Practicing what?"

"Daddy showed him how to race. He's racing."

"Racing?"

"Daddy said that Geoff should practice so he can get on a swim team."

"Oh."

Mandy ran back down to the water's edge to begin building a castle.

"You don't like the idea of a swimming team?" Alden asked.

"I don't like the idea that Geoff thinks he has to excel at something competitive or academic to make his father love him."

"Does he?"

"I think Stefan loves him now. But Geoff isn't anything like his father, and that confounds Stefan. He thinks his job is to encourage his children toward excellence in every field."

"And you don't?"

"I think his job as a father is simply to let them know that he loves them. Mandy's always showing off for him, and that's easy for her to do, because she's good at the things that are important to him. But Geoff's not, and he feels like he's failing his father. So, usually, he doesn't try to impress him."

"But he's trying now."

"It looks that way."

"Have you told Stefan what you see?"

"How many stars are there in the sky?"

"An exact count?"

"I've told him that many times."

"And that's why you're divorced."

It wasn't a question. He simply understood, and she was grateful to him for that. "He's a good man. I couldn't live with our differences."

"But you wanted to."

"More than anything."

"Does it bother you to talk about it?"

"No. Does it bother you to listen?"

"I'm interested."

Gulls flocked along the beach edge, cawing secret gull messages into the wind. A sailboat came into view and dropped anchor just across from the northernmost point a quarter of a mile away. The day was absolutely normal, a summer day just made to sweep away all vestiges of the year past. Lindsey scooped up a handful of sand and let it dribble through her fingers.

"The night I met Stefan, I told him we were two halves of a whole. I think I fell in love with him that night. He seemed to be everything I wasn't. And he was everything I've told myself I wanted in a man. He was strong, intelligent, cautious. He wanted me, but he didn't need me. I had to take care of my parents a lot when I was growing up. I knew Stefan would never need me to take care of him."

"But you missed it when he didn't?"

"I missed feeling like I was part of his life. He didn't need me to take care of him. He didn't seem to need me for anything. So I had children, and they needed me. For a while that seemed like enough."

She thought of all the nights that had gone by when she hadn't seen Stefan at all. As he had gotten deeper and deeper into his career, he had abandoned her more. He had risen quickly to the top of the pack during his internship and residency. He had been courted by the best hospitals and clinics. He had begun to fill his free hours with research, and that research had made him even more desirable professionally. And less available to her.

"After we came to Cleveland, I thought things would change." The sand was gone. She scooped up another handful. In much the same way she had tried again and again to hold on to her marriage. And every time, no matter how hard she had tried, it had dribbled through her fingers.

"They didn't?"

"No. Stefan seemed to think he had to work even harder. He hardly saw the children. We were living apart, only he didn't seem to notice it. When he was with us, he was pre-occupied. When he did relate to Geoff and Mandy, it was to instruct them in something. He didn't know how to be affectionate with them. Remember when Mandy crawled up into your lap today?"

"Did she?"

"You didn't even notice because it came so naturally to you. Stefan wouldn't have known what to do."

"He doesn't seem cold."

"Oh, he's not. Not at all. I think he's the most emotional man I've ever known. And that's part of what I fell in love with. But he doesn't know how to express anything he's feeling. Finally I just couldn't live that way anymore. I thought if he was free of us, he could concentrate on his career without distraction. Then, when he had time, he could devote it to the children, without recriminations from me. I thought if I set him free, maybe he could be the father the children need."

"And the husband you need?"

His words gave her a start. She stared at him. "No."

"No?"

"When I ended our marriage, I ended it for good. I thought if I could just live through that pain, I could start my life fresh when it was over, and so could he."

"And did it work?"

"I don't think so."

"You still love him?"

The sand was gone again. She didn't pick up another handful. She was sitting next to the most attractive man she had met since her divorce, and she was talking about Stefan. "Love is very complicated," she said huskily.

"Is it?"

"Haven't you found it so?"

"No."

"Have you ever been married, Alden?"

"Married? No."

"Are you another doctor who's married to his career?"

"No. There are women in my life. I have other interests, too. I have friends."

"And you don't want a wife and children?"

He smiled. His gaze was warm. "I'm beginning to think I've missed something very special."

"You'd have to put down roots."

"Well, that seems a small price to pay."

She smiled, too. She was entranced by his eyes. There was something there that she hadn't seen before, something nameless, as deep and secret as forever. "I think you're one of a kind," she said. "You're different from anyone I've known."

"In what way?"

"I'm not sure."

He touched her hair. Just a brief, hesitant touch. Then his hand fell back to the blanket. "I'm not so different. All of us share more than we think. Differences are surface things."

"Mommy? I can't see Geoff."

For a moment Lindsey didn't understand Mandy's words. Then, with her hand shading her eyes, she peered out into the lake. Geoff, probably tired of kicking bottom in the shallow water, was swimming farther out. "I'd better call him back in," she told Alden. "He doesn't swim that well, especially if he's tired."

She walked to the edge of the water to stand with Mandy. "He's heading out into the lake." She pointed so Mandy could see.

"He shouldn't."

"You're right." Lindsey cupped her hands. "Geoff! Get back in here. You're too far out. You can't touch!"

The sun blinded her, and she shaded her eyes again to see if he had turned back. "Geoff!"

One childish arm lifted, then another. Geoff was still swimming his own version of the Olympics.

"Geoff!" Lindsey kicked off her sandals. "I'm going to get him. I don't like him out so far."

"I don't see him anymore."

Lindsey stripped off her shorts. "Shade your eyes."

"I still don't."

Lindsey looked up, and her heart nearly stopped. Geoff had disappeared. Frantically she shaded her eyes, as she'd instructed Mandy. "Geoff!"

He was nowhere in sight.

"No!" She was in the lake swimming before she even felt the shock of the cold water, water that seemed to hold her in place. She could not make herself move fast enough; no speed could be fast enough. She pulled one arm through the water, then the other. She was gaining on the spot where she'd last seen Geoff, but not quickly enough. She realized that she could no longer touch bottom, that the water was even deeper than she'd feared.

And Geoff was still nowhere in sight.

She swam with her head above water now, even though her strokes had to be slower. She prayed for a sign, a ripple, a splash, anything to tell her that she was heading in the right direction. But nothing appeared. She dove underwater and opened her eyes, scanning the depths until her lungs nearly burst, but she could see nothing.

When she surfaced, Alden was to her right, twenty feet away. "I see him," he shouted. "I'm going under."

She started toward him. He disappeared under the water, and before she could reach him, he surfaced holding Geoff.

"I'm taking him to shore." With Geoff floating face up under one of Alden's arms, Alden started in. Even without the handicap of the little boy, Lindsey couldn't keep up. By the time she reached the beach, Alden had Geoff on his back just feet from where the waves were breaking. As she stumbled out of the lake, she heard Geoff start to cough.

"Geoff!" She reached him at the same moment Mandy did.

"Is he going to be all right?" Mandy pleaded.

"He's fine," Alden promised. "Really. Just stand back and let him cough up some water." He turned and twisted the little boy into a position that seemed peculiar to Lindsey, but Geoff heaved up what seemed like lungs full of water and didn't choke on any of it. As she watched, the bluish tinge of his skin turned a healthier pink.

"He's breathing well," Alden said. "Cough it all up, Geoff, and you'll feel better."

Geoff didn't argue. Finally Alden let him go, and Geoff lay back against the sand. His eyes were shut. Alden motioned Lindsey forward. She knelt beside him. "Geoff?" She clasped his hand. "Are you really all right?"

He opened his eyes. Then he began to cry. She propped him against her chest and stroked his hair. "It's all right," she murmured, over and over again. "You're all right."

"I got a cramp."

"You were practicing too hard."

"I wanted to be a star," he choked out. "For Dad."

"You are a star. You're wonderful just the way you are. You don't have to prove anything. Dad loves you."

Geoff didn't answer. He began to cry again, and this time Lindsey couldn't find the words to comfort him.

"Alden flew through the water." Mandy sat at the kitchen table, hugging a cup of cocoa to her chest.

"I'm sure it seemed like he did," Lindsey said.

"How did he find me?" Geoff, pale but otherwise no worse for his experience, held out his cup for a refill. Lindsey poured him more cocoa from the pot in front of her. It was evening, and she had told the story over and over again. But obviously Geoff still needed to hear it.

"He knew where he'd seen you last, and he's a strong swimmer. He got there and went under to look for you. Lucky for us, he found you on the first try."

"He looked like he was flying," Mandy said.

"I'm glad he's such an athlete." Lindsey couldn't tell the children just how glad she was that Alden swam so much better than he rode a bike. She wanted to protect them from the worst of what might have happened. For long moments she had been sure her son was going to drown. She could still hardly believe it. She had taken her eyes off him for only a moment. She was safety conscious. She was always careful, very careful. And Geoff had seemed to be perfectly content where he was.

Her head pounded harder. There had been moments in the water when it had felt as if it were going to explode. Not that the pain had stopped her.

"I was swimming fine, then my leg started to hurt. I tried to kick, and I couldn't. I got scared." Geoff stared into his cocoa.

"I called your father while you took your shower."

Geoff looked up. His eyes filled with tears. "Why? He can't do anything now."

"Because he's your father. And if something happens to you, he wants to know about it." She didn't add that, of course, she had not been able to talk to Stefan himself. She had left a message with his service because he was at the hospital and had left instructions not to be paged unless it was an emergency.

Not even for his own family.

She had lost her temper on the telephone, something she rarely did. It hadn't done any good. The woman on the other end had been firm. Lindsey was not on the list of people who could disturb Dr. Daniels. The woman would be certain to give him the message when he called in. She was sorry Lindsey's son, *Lindsey's son,* had almost drowned. Certainly, if the boy actually had, she would have considered paging the doctor.

Now the whole exchange seemed almost funny, but at the time Lindsey had been furious. Her head had threatened to explode. Tears had flooded her eyes and her voice. And armed with that fury, she had done the unforgivable. She had called Hilda and told her mother-in-law exactly what she thought of her for raising a son like Stefan.

Something was wrong with her.

"He's angry at me, isn't he?" Geoff asked. "He thinks I didn't try hard enough."

"He's not angry. Not at all. He loves you."

"Then why hasn't he called me?"

Because he's probably still in his laboratory.

Lindsey wasn't going to admit that to Geoff. "He will," she said. And she almost believed it.

From the floor at Geoff's feet, Kong gave an enormous belch. The children's laughter broke the tension, and by the time they went upstairs to change for bed, they were almost acting like themselves again.

Lindsey cleared away their dishes while they changed. Her hands still trembled, and she had to concentrate to keep the dishes from rattling.

She wondered how she would have gotten through the afternoon if Alden hadn't been there to help. Certainly Geoff might not have survived. Perhaps she would have found him; perhaps she would have been able to revive him. But Alden had done both of those things almost effortlessly. Then, and almost as important, he had kept her from falling apart, had kept all of them from falling apart with his matter-of-fact serenity and his sensible advice.

He had stayed for supper. He had even helped—although Alden's cooking was almost more of a hindrance. Something always seemed to be missing from whatever he prepared. Lemonade without sugar, rock hard cookies without leavening, and tonight a salad of torn up lettuce and not a drop of dressing until she got some from the refrigerator and put it on the salad herself. She suspected that he was a

man who simply didn't find food important. She wondered
if all his appetites were so casual.

By the time the children were ready to be tucked in, she
was calmer. She knew she had to call Hilda and beg for her
forgiveness. Hilda was no different from most people. She
had raised her only child in the best way she knew how.
She was a good woman, a moral, earnest woman who loved
her family and tried to be there for them. But she was also
a genius, as her husband had been, and that genius had
called both of them in ways and at times that had meant
sacrificing the little boy who'd grown up to be a genius,
too.

Hilda was not to blame. Perhaps Stefan was not to blame,
either. Perhaps she herself was to blame for expecting support, for expecting the simple things like having her name
or the names of her children on the list of people who could
disturb him. She had never been able to disturb him enough.
Wasn't that why she had divorced him?

"Mommy, we're waiting!"

Lindsey realized that she was standing at the bottom of
the stairs, staring at the bannister. For a moment she wasn't
certain she could make the climb to the second floor. She
swayed, or the stairs did—she wasn't certain which. Her
head pounded harder, despite the painkiller she had taken
half an hour before. She was so rarely ill that she didn't
know what to do. She shut her eyes and took deep breaths.
And when she opened them, the stairs were rock-solid again.

She climbed slowly. She kissed Geoff first, tucking a light
blanket under his chin while she tried not to think that she
might have lost him today. In Mandy's room she turned off
lights and opened a window before she kissed her goodnight. Mandy, like Geoff, seemed particularly precious tonight.

Downstairs once more, she poured herself a glass of wine.
If aspirin hadn't helped her head, she could only hope that
relaxing on the porch might. Before she went outside she
tried to force herself to dial Hilda's number, but she

couldn't. Her intentions were the best; she wanted to do what was right. But tomorrow she might feel better able to cope with an apology.

The sky was a canopy of stars again, with not even the trace of a cloud in the sky. For a moment she considered going back inside. Tonight of all nights she needed no reminders of another star-filled night on the island. She could trace too much of what had gone wrong with her life from that night. The headaches had begun soon after, along with the deep sense of loneliness, the longing for Stefan, the anger.

But even as she concluded the list, she knew it wasn't completely true. She had never stopped longing for Stefan. Only after her sighting of the UFO had she begun to admit how devastating the divorce had been for her emotionally. She had needed him, really needed him, and she had been confronted head-on with the fact that he wasn't really there.

The headaches, the lapses in attention, the loneliness, the tears, all were symptoms of depression. She hadn't wanted to face it before, but now it was perfectly clear to her. She had gone through a crisis, and everything since was a response.

And telling herself so didn't change a thing.

She had seen lights in the sky. Colors she couldn't even describe. And there had been friends, new friends, friends so special, so extraordinary, that she still felt their loss. She had seen lights. And she had heard the purr of a motor, not the roar of an airplane engine, but something subtler, something almost musical.

The sky had been filled with music as well as light. She hadn't remembered until that moment. Excitement gripped her. She had remembered something new. And even if it wasn't particularly important, might she not remember more? Maybe there was more, and little by little she could piece together the blank hours in her memory.

From somewhere outside her memory she heard the purr of a motor. For a moment, for one shattering, breath-stealing moment, she wondered if she would see the lights again. Then she saw two lights, headlights, coming down the lane.

Disappointment curled through her, then the resurgence of anger. She recognized the car. It was the Peugeot.

Stefan had finally been disturbed.

She set her glass on the table beside the swing and stood to wait for him. He was out of the car in a shot, up on the porch as fast as she had ever seen him move. "How is he?"

She was not angry enough to toy with him. "Geoff's fine, Stefan. He's asleep now."

"I'm going up to check on him."

"Don't wake him up. He's exhausted. Alden's already examined him, and he says that he didn't suffer any after-effects. He's just a little worse for wear, as you'd expect."

Stefan nodded, then pushed past her. Through the screen door she watched him take the inside stairs two at a time. His face had shown no signs of terror, but she knew him well enough to make that leap. She felt not a trace of pity. She was only glad that for once she was sure that both Geoff's parents cared enormously about him.

She was sipping her wine again when Stefan came back out to the porch. "Did he wake up?" she asked.

"No."

"Tomorrow morning I'll tell him you were here."

"How the hell did this happen?"

She stared at him; then she carefully set her glass down. "That's an excellent question. I would have been happy to discuss it with you on the telephone. Unfortunately, I wasn't given that opportunity."

"I fired my service. The woman on duty was an idiot! Your name is at the top of my permanent list. I'm always supposed to be paged if you call. She checked my daily list. She didn't even think to check the permanent one."

Lindsey needed to hold on to her anger. She wasn't even sure why. "Well, it's nice to hear that you think your children are important enough to be called away from work for.

How did you finally get the message that your son almost died?''

"My mother."

"Oh. I see. They let her through."

"She told them what she thought of them."

"After I told her what I thought of you." Lindsey felt new guilt, but she pushed it away. "And you couldn't call to let me know you'd heard? You couldn't call to talk to your son?"

"I called. Your phone was off the hook. I put it back after I checked on Geoff."

She remembered slamming the phone down after her conversation with Hilda. She obviously hadn't gotten the receiver exactly back in place. She shut her eyes. "I'm sorry, then. That part was my fault."

"I want to know how this happened! You know Geoff doesn't swim that well. He needs lessons and some concentrated practice before he's going to be good enough for you to take your eyes off him. Weren't you watching? Were you and Alden so busy talking that you forgot your own son was in the water?"

Guilt disappeared in a rush. She slapped her hands on her hips. In a moment she was facing him with nothing but inches of moonlight between them. "How dare you! Don't pose as father of the year, Stefan. It doesn't suit you! That little boy almost drowned because of you. He was doing that concentrated practice you're so fond of pushing on him. He was swimming back and forth by the shore, trying to build himself up to please you. You must have shown him how yesterday. Right?"

She went on without giving him time to respond. "Then he got tired of kicking the bottom and started swimming out deeper. I'd been watching him, but he seemed perfectly safe. So I looked away for a few moments. When Mandy told me he was going out deeper, I called him, but he didn't come. I went after him, but by that time, he was in trouble.

In trouble because he was trying to do what he thought his absentee father wanted him to do!''

What control she'd had vanished. She put her hands against his chest and shoved him in emphasis. "In trouble because he was trying to make you love him, you bastard!"

He grasped her arms and held her still. "What are you talking about?"

"Can't you hear me? He was trying to make you love him! He knows he's not the son you wanted. He's not like you. He doesn't care if he competes with anybody. He doesn't care if he wins at anything. He doesn't care if he's the best. He just wants to be Geoff. And you want him to be somebody else!"

He dropped his hands and turned away from her.

She drove her point home. "After he was breathing again he told us he'd wanted to be a star. For you."

"Stop it."

"I'm finished anyway." She rested her head in her hands because she could no longer hold it up.

"How long have you been this angry at me?" he asked quietly.

"I don't know."

"So this is my fault."

"You decide."

He turned back to her. She was rubbing her temples and struggling not to cry.

"He doesn't have to be a star."

"Then tell him!"

"I will. Tomorrow."

"You work tomorrow. You work everyday. How did you get over here, anyway? The ferry doesn't run this time of night."

"A friend flew me over."

She pictured Stefan desperate, distraught and willing to ask someone, anyone, for help. Shame filled her. How could she have doubted he loved Geoff? How could she have allowed herself to get so worked up? She should have known that he hadn't tried to block her phone calls. She never should have blamed him or his mother for something that wasn't their fault.

With her head still in her hands she began to sob. For a moment he didn't touch her; then, tentatively, he put his arms around her. She wanted to push him away; she wanted to fall into his arms and stay there forever. But she was helpless to do either. She sobbed harder, powerless to stop herself.

His arms tightened, and he rocked her gently as she sobbed. "I'm so sorry," he said. "I should have been here with you. You shouldn't have had to go through this alone. Go ahead and cry. I wish I could cry with you."

She cried harder. She felt his cheek against her hair.

"My father was almost always gone," he said. "When he was home, he would teach me things. Sometimes he would take me to work. That was the way I knew him best."

He reached into his pocket for a handkerchief and gave it to her. She snatched it from his hand.

"Let them teach you," she said.

"All right."

She looked up at him at last. For once there was emotion written on his face, but so much that she couldn't analyze exactly what she saw. "I'm sorry," she whispered. "I did need you, and you weren't here!"

"I'll never be more than a phone call away again. I promise."

That wasn't good enough. She looked in his eyes and knew that one phone call away would never be good enough. She had given up on Stefan, given up on their marriage, because to stay with him and share only a tiny part of the man had caused her agony. Now she wondered if a tiny part had been better than nothing, after all.

She wasn't sure who reached for whom, whose lips crossed the moonlit space between them, but in a moment they were locked in an embrace.

She needed him, and for that moment nothing else mat-

tered. His taste, his scent, his touch, were wholly familiar
and right. The tension and sadness that had gripped her for
so many weeks disappeared. Their kiss was a reunion, a
homecoming. If they were two halves, then they were whole
together, whole and real and part of something bigger and
more important than either of them could ever be alone.

He kneaded her back as he kissed her, as if he wanted to
absorb all of her through his fingertips. She curved against
him, craving the feel of his body against hers. He made a
sound deep in his throat, part surrender, part resistance. He
tugged her even closer and pressed her against his hips.

He was as aroused, as ready for her, as he had ever been.
If moonlit nights and loving communion could be aphro-
disiacs, then anger and despair could obviously be the same.
She felt her body prepare for him, felt the rush of heat between her legs, the thrusting of her nipples, the sensitizing
of her skin. She wanted him with as much desperation as
he wanted her.

She wanted him, and what could be wrong with having
him? They were as much married as they had ever been.
They had remained faithful to each other even after their
divorce. They shared a love of their children and a mutual
concern for each other.

But they weren't married. Not anymore.

Her head tipped back as he took her lips more fiercely.
Her lips parted for his tongue. Her hands lifted under his
shirt, and her nails dug into his back.

They were no longer married.

"No!"

At first she thought the voice was her own. She knew
better than to let their lovemaking continue. She had fought
too hard to part from Stefan to pull him back into her life
this way. But the voice was not the small rational one still
hidden somewhere inside her.

Stefan thrust her away. "That's Geoff," he said.

She understood. "Go to him."

She watched him open the screen door. In a moment he was up the stairs. She heard the murmur of his voice.

When she was calm enough, when the rational voice inside her was the loudest amidst the clamor, she followed his path up the stairs.

She found Stefan in Geoff's room. The little boy was still asleep, but now he was pillowed safely against his father's arm.

The nightmare that had made him cry out had gone away.

Chapter 8

Stefan spent the night. He didn't ask permission, since he wasn't sure what Lindsey's answer might be. He just held his son until Geoff was sleeping peacefully again; then he moved to the twin bed across the room.

Geoff's face was the first thing he saw the next morning. Looking at his son had always made Stefan's heart ache with love and pride. But Geoff was as foreign to him as the woman he had loved from the first day he'd seen her. He had never loved either of them any less because he didn't understand them. Rather, having Geoff had been like watching the sun rise and set. He had been awestruck; nothing he had ever learned from a book or a lecture could fully explain such glory.

"What are you doing here?"

Stefan considered his answer carefully as he sat up. "I was worried about you," he said, and thought how woefully inadequate that was.

"Worried?"

Stefan patted the bed beside him. Geoff sat, careful not to touch his father.

"Of course I was worried, Geoff. I had to see for myself that you were really okay."

"I'm okay."

Stefan searched for something else to say. "No aches or pains? No trouble breathing?"

"No."

"You must have been very frightened."

"Alden got me so quick, I didn't have time to be too scared."

Stefan knew he should be feeling nothing but gratitude to Alden Fitzpatrick. He didn't understand his own irrational dislike of the man who had saved his son's life. But the dislike was now more firmly rooted than it had been before.

"Geoff," Stefan rested his hand on his son's knee for a moment, "I never wanted you to practice so hard that you put yourself in danger."

Geoff looked down at his bare feet.

"I thought you'd have fun working on your strokes," Stefan continued. "And later, I thought you might like swimming on a team. But swim team's no fun at all if you drown."

"I like to play in the water."

"And you were swimming so hard yesterday because you thought it would please me?"

"No. I was just playing."

Stefan knew that Geoff didn't want him to feel guilty. He was still just a little boy, but he already understood so much about human nature. Perhaps more than his father. Stefan put his arm around his son's shoulders and pulled him closer. "I know what you were doing. And I'm sorry I made you think it mattered so much to me. I don't care if you swim on a team. I just want you alive and happy."

"I am."

"Let's keep it that way."

"Okay." Geoff didn't pull away, but he didn't lean closer, either.

Stefan sensed that his son wasn't sure what to do. He wondered how their relationship could have come to this. He had intended to take the next ferry back to the mainland once he'd had a chance to talk to Geoff. But now he realized—and wondered why it had taken him so long—that he couldn't. There was something more important to do here.

He rubbed Geoff's shoulder. "I want you to do me a favor today."

"Sure."

"I want you to spend the day with me. I'm always trying to tell you what you should do. Why don't you show me some of the things you like to do?"

"Like what?"

Stefan managed a laugh. "That's the point, isn't it? I don't really know. You'll have to show me."

"You mean stuff like Alden's tree house?"

"Yeah. Stuff like that."

"You wouldn't like it."

"How do you know?"

"Well, there's nothing important about it. You know? I don't learn anything from the stuff I like to do."

"I think you must learn a lot. You're a wonderful boy. You must have gotten that way somehow."

Geoff looked up at him. "Me?"

Stefan hugged him harder. "Who else would I be talking about? Aren't you my son? Geoff Daniels?"

"What about Mandy?"

Stefan didn't have to force his smile. "Mandy will have her chance some other day. She likes to take over, doesn't she?"

"Oh, she's all right. Most of the time."

"Well, I think she's all right, too. Better than that, even. But I think today's just going to be our day."

"Can Kong come?"

"Sure."

"Kong likes to take over, too."

"Well, we won't let him."

Stefan called his office, then showered while Geoff went downstairs to tell his mother their plans. When he got out of the shower he found clean clothes on the sink, his clean clothes, left over from the days when he had lived here, too. He wondered why Lindsey had never returned them. Neatly placed on top of the pile he found a razor and a toothbrush. And when he emerged, he felt like the man who had once jointly owned this cottage.

Downstairs, he tried to think of a way to let Lindsey know he was sorry for the inconvenience and stress he must have caused her by staying overnight. The stress they had caused each other on the front porch was too overwhelming to even consider.

Her smile welcomed him but gave no clues to what she was thinking. Before he could say or signal anything, she handed him a cup of her carefully brewed coffee—the best coffee in the world—and gestured him to the table for a breakfast of whole wheat pancakes.

"Geoff tells me the two of you are going to spend the day together," she said, ruffling her son's hair as she passed his chair.

"If it doesn't interfere with anything you had planned."

"Not at all. I think Mandy and I are going to take the ferry to Put-in-Bay for the day. She has a friend from school who's staying with her grandmother there this week."

Put-in-Bay was the more popular name for South Bass Island, one of the Lake Erie islands that was only a ferry ride away. It was considerably livelier than Kelleys, with a main street that was thronged both day and night.

"Had you planned to take Geoff?" Stefan asked.

Lindsey stacked his plate with pancakes. "I'd planned to drag him along."

Geoff made a face. "Yuck."

"If you're finished," Lindsey told him, "you can take

Kong for a quick walk. Mandy's trying to get him on the leash out in front.''

Geoff pushed back his chair and sprang to his feet, obviously anxious to start this unusual day. "He's too big for her to manage." In a moment he was gone.

Stefan wondered if Lindsey was going to take this opportunity to talk about their behavior last night. It would be like her to bring it out into the open immediately, deal with it and put it behind them. He wasn't sure he was up to any of that, particularly the last.

"How can you take the day off on such short notice?" she asked instead.

"I wasn't scheduled for surgery today. I had meetings, but none of them were important."

"You don't lie very well."

"I'm not lying about surgery." He looked up and saw she was smiling at him. "This was important," he said. "I need to spend the day with my son."

"You're right." She turned away.

"Thank you for understanding…everything."

"I don't understand everything. But I do understand why you stayed last night. It was all right."

"I'm not planning to make a habit out of it."

"You can't. It's confusing to the children."

He wondered if that was the only reason she minded. But he couldn't bring himself to ask. "Geoff's going to show me what he likes to do."

"Prepare yourself. You're bound to spend some time lying on your back staring at the clouds."

"When I could be back at the hospital listening to Alpert's lecture on suboccipital craniectomies?"

"You'll see brains and networks of arteries and nerves in the sky. Geoff will see unicorns and elves."

"And what would you see?"

"Spaceships, probably. Colored lights. Friendship."

"That night still seems absolutely real to you, doesn't it?"

"Only to me, obviously." She leaned against the counter and sipped her coffee. "I remembered something else last night, just before you came. Something new."

"What?"

"Music. I heard music that night. The sky was filled with it." She hummed a little, then stopped. "I can't get it right. Not nearly. I've been trying all morning."

He put down his fork. "Have you had any other experiences like that? Colored lights? Music? Blackouts?"

She sighed. "Why? Are you afraid it's a recurring pattern? Some sort of seizures?"

"Then you've wondered about that, too?"

"No. It was mentioned as a possibility when I was at the hospital, but it doesn't make sense to me."

"Some epileptics have very specific sensations right before a seizure. They smell unpleasant odors or hear strange sounds. Their vision is distorted. After a seizure they feel completely relaxed, and they fall asleep."

"Do they wake up and claim they've seen a UFO?"

"Every case is different."

"Well, in your experience, how many believe they were taken aboard a spaceship while they were having those seizures?"

"None."

She smiled. "I rest my case."

He was glad to see she wasn't angry. "I'll rest mine."

"For the moment." She didn't wait for a response. "I called your mother this morning and apologized."

"I'm glad."

"She told me she was sorry I'd divorced you."

Stefan was surprised. He was one of the few people who understood how deeply his mother's feelings ran; conversely, he also understood why she was usually unable to express them. Her attention to detail, to schedule and discipline, was her way of coping with emotions too overpowering to be logical. So she covered them up.

"She always loved you," he said. "She still does."

"I never felt like I met her standards."

"You exceeded them."

Geoff, Mandy and Kong pelted through the front door and arrived in the kitchen in a three-way tie. "How come Geoff gets to spend the day with you and I don't?" Mandy demanded. She stopped short of her father and shook a finger at him.

"Would you like to spend a day with me?"

Mandy looked away from him. Asked so directly, she didn't seem to know how to answer.

Stefan put his hand on her arm and drew her to him. "Well, I'd like to spend a day with you. Next time it'll be your turn."

"When?"

He laughed. "Do you have your appointment calendar handy?"

"I have a calendar in my room. Would you like to see it?"

"I'd like that very much."

"I mark off every day. Before I go to bed. I never miss."

"I always did that when I was a little boy."

"Sometimes it makes me sad. Did it ever make you sad?"

Stefan drew her closer and put his arms around her. "If it did, I wasn't as smart as you are. I didn't notice."

"Sometimes there are things that Mom doesn't think I should do." Geoff stared up at the clouds.

Stefan had made one discovery already in the three-hour island tour that his son had arranged for him. If he responded to a statement such as that one with his usual explanation or advice, Geoff would say no more. But if he just said something simple, something with no implied judgment, Geoff would keep talking.

"Like what?"

"Like carve things. Use a knife. You know."

Stefan knew a test when he heard one. "Moms worry. Actually, for that matter, Dads worry, too."

"I'm real careful."

"I'm glad."

"Well, one thing's for sure. I must have got it from you." Stefan laughed. "Just don't tell me you're carving up brains. Not without a little training."

"I'll never carve up anything alive!" Geoff made a retching sound common to all boys under twelve.

"Suppose you tell me what you do carve up?"

"Tree roots."

"With or without the trees attached?"

"Without. Roots that wash up on the shore. I collect them. Branches, too. But roots are best."

Stefan weighed the mental picture of his son with a machete hacking roots and branches—fingers and toes—against his desire to gain Geoff's trust. "What do you carve from them?"

"Would you like to see?"

"I was hoping you'd ask."

"You can't tell Mom."

"I can't lie to her, Geoff. She would never lie to me."

"I thought when people got divorced they didn't care about stuff like that anymore."

"I care."

"Brandon Riley's parents are divorced, and they yell at each other all the time. Brandon's mother won't even let his father stand on the porch. He has to stand in the yard and yell for Brandon when he comes to get him for the weekend."

"Your mother and I are still friends."

"Then why are you divorced?"

"Sometimes even best friends have trouble living together."

"That's what Mom says, too."

Stefan was glad that at least he and Lindsey had their stories straight. "Are you going to show me the roots?"

Geoff sat up. "Maybe you don't have to tell Mom unless she asks. I mean, if she says, did Geoff show you anything he carved with a knife, you'd have to say yes. But maybe you could just forget to mention the roots if she asks what we did today. That's not exactly lying, is it?"

"It is. Exactly."

"Oh."

Stefan sat up, too. "But I could point out to her that you still have all your fingers. And if you show me how well you use a knife and what safety rules you follow, I could mention that, too."

"You'd do that?"

"I don't know. I'll have to see how careful you are, won't I?"

"Thanks, Dad."

Stefan squeezed his shoulder. "Anytime." He pulled Geoff closer for a moment. "Anytime."

"You aren't going to believe it until Geoff gets up the nerve to show them to you." The children were in bed for the night, and Stefan was about to head back to his attorney's cottage. But first he knew he had to discuss Geoff's carvings with Lindsey.

He accepted a drink from her. Along with his clothes, some of his favorite Scotch was still on hand at the cottage. That perplexed him.

"Villages of gnomes and trolls?"

"Elves and dwarfs and hobbits. He could probably take them to craft shows and pay for his college education."

"He's been hiding them from me. I don't like that."

"He felt compelled, Lindsey. He saw those roots, those branches, and he saw whole villages of tiny little people. They just begged him to be let out."

"And so he used his cub scout knife to set them free."

"He learned the basics of wood carving from his den leader. I don't think he ever really set out to do something that he knew you'd disapprove of. But he just felt he had to.''

''He tried to talk to me about it once. I wasn't in the mood to listen. I kept seeing him minus a finger.''

''He's very careful. But he needs better equipment now. He's been sharpening his knife, but there's only so much he can do with it. He'll be safer if he has better tools.''

''It's not a child's hobby.''

''He's promised he'll only carve under supervision. I told him I'll watch him whenever I'm around.''

''How often will that be?''

Stefan dropped to a bench next to Lindsey's garden. The sun had set, but there were enough stars and a full moon to illuminate the flower beds. Moonflowers bloomed on a trellis, and night-blooming stock scented the moonlight. Lindsey wove her way between beds to light half a dozen torches that sent thin trails of smoke skyward.

She waited while Stefan searched for an answer. ''Don't come out of guilt,'' she said, when it was clear he was still searching. ''They don't need a reluctant father any more than they need an absent one.''

As always, it surprised him when she didn't understand his struggle. ''I don't want to be either. But how often do you want me here? We're not married anymore. We can't pretend things haven't changed.''

''No. But if you saw twice as much of the children as you did when we were married, it still wouldn't be enough. And it wouldn't be a problem, because you'd still hardly ever be here.''

''When we were married, you rarely criticized.''

''When we were married, I was a fool.''

''What does that mean?''

''It means that I shouldn't have waited until the very end to speak up about the things that bothered me. Like your being gone all the time. And about the distance you kept even when you were with us.''

''Distance?''

"You weren't part of the family, Stefan. Don't you realize it now? You watched us from a distance. You were never really there."

"I was building a career. For all of us. I was busy, but I never took time for myself. I either worked, or I was with you and the children. You never had any reason to worry about the things that some wives do."

"I think if you'd been unfaithful I could have fought for our marriage and won. But as it was, I couldn't fight anything. You weren't there to fight with or for."

The time was long past for confessions, but he still felt he owed her a small one. "I know I worked too hard."

She was surprised he would admit that much. She sat beside him on the bench and touched his knee, removing her hand quickly when she realized what she'd done. "I guess that doesn't matter now. What matters is that you still have time to be the father your children need. See them as often as you want. If you don't want to see them here or at our house, take them somewhere. But talk to them, like you talked to Geoff today. It's so important."

"*Our* house?"

She tried to smile. "Old habits are hard to break."

"Habits like being married? I'm curious, Lindsey. Have you asked yourself why you still have my things around here?"

"No."

He leaned toward her. "Maybe you should."

She turned away, determined to avoid that discussion. "It's hot enough tonight to pretend we're in the tropics. That's probably why I lit the torches. I hardly ever bother."

"It reminds me of another garden."

She had been trying to change the subject. Now she realized exactly where she had led them. Had she done it on purpose? Had she remembered a certain garden, a certain night when hope was alive and love still flourished? A night when they had talked about their differences and convinced themselves that what they shared was more important?

"That was a long time ago," she said. "Too long ago to think about now."

"Then you never think about it? Sometimes I shut my eyes and I see you at twenty-one. You're wearing a sundress. Blue. Pale blue, with silver threads running through it. And you have gardenias in your hair."

"Divorce doesn't wipe away memories, does it? It should."

"And I wore?"

"I don't remember." And she tried not to.

"A shirt you'd made me. No collar. Long flowing sleeves. And embroidery around the opening at the front. Ivy, I think."

Despite herself she smiled a little. "You were so uncomfortable. I could tell you wanted to wear a tie with it."

"I still have it."

"No."

"I do. Packed away in the spare bedroom of my apartment."

She was moved by his admission, although she didn't want to be. "That night's long past."

"Tonight it doesn't seem so long ago."

It didn't seem so long ago to her, either. She could shut her eyes and remember every detail. She didn't shut her eyes, but as Stefan fell silent, the memories were there between them.

Spring break of Lindsey's senior year had come on the tail of a series of snowstorms that lasted for nearly a week. Fed up with snow, ice and a boyfriend who was often too busy to see her, she had boarded a plane. Her mother and stepfather had a house in Key West that they weren't using at the moment, and she had gotten permission to stay there for the week-long holiday. She had invited Stefan to come with her, but he had refused. He was mired in studying and projects he didn't want to abandon. She felt abandoned instead.

Her mother's house was a collection of shining surfaces. Glass, terrazzo, marble, stainless steel. All reflected light from wide, unadorned windows. Although her mother and stepfather had been in Europe for a month on business, a housekeeper still came every morning to polish and primp. Lindsey walked through the sparsely furnished rooms and wished that she had stayed at school.

She spent her first day in Florida soaking up sun and swimming in the huge pool that took up most of the backyard. Neighbors had a barbecue that evening, and from a moonlit lounge chair she listened to the friendly give and take of the large happy family behind the wooden privacy fence.

The next morning she shopped, just to get away from the silence of the house. She watched mothers with their children, teenagers clustered in noisy groups on street corners, young men and women strolling hand in hand. Finally she realized that she preferred silence to the loneliness of being on the outside.

That afternoon she was halfway through a novel she had found on her mother's bookshelf when the doorbell rang. She wasn't expecting anyone, but even a delivery man might be more interesting than the book. When she opened the door and saw Stefan, she knew that missing him had been the reason for all her dissatisfaction.

She was in his arms before he could draw another breath. "I thought you weren't coming!"

He held her tightly against him and murmured into her hair, "I missed you. I wasn't getting anything done anyway."

"Because you missed me?"

"What do you think?" Then he kissed her. Hard.

"I think I was at least part of the cause," she said, when she could speak again.

"Is anybody else here?"

"The housekeeper's gone."

"No one else? No girlfriend you invited at the last minute? No boyfriend stashed away?"

"He went out the back way when he heard the doorbell."

"Lock the back door for the rest of my stay." He stepped inside, and his gaze flicked over the barren landscape. "This house isn't you."

"My mother and I don't see eye to eye on much."

"I'm sorry I won't be meeting her."

"No, you're not."

His gaze found hers and held it as he framed her face with his hands. "How do you always know what I'm thinking?"

"You give me plenty of practice in guessing. You never tell me yourself."

"What am I thinking now?"

"That you're hungry."

He smiled, one of those rare smiles capable of eroding all her good sense. "Close."

She knew what he was really hungry for, and she also knew the time wasn't right. Not quite yet. She covered his hands with hers and drew them down between them as a barrier. "And that you want to change your clothes and take a swim while I get you a snack and some tea."

"I do?"

"Yes."

He withdrew reluctantly. "All right. But I'm taking you out to dinner later. Somewhere nice."

"I know just the place."

The remainder of the afternoon drifted by on long looks, smiles and slow, sweet kisses. Despite Stefan's flirting, both of them were waiting for something. They had not made love in the nearly six months that they had known each other. Their schedules were busy, and it wasn't often that they'd had time and privacy. On those rare occasions when they had, they had taken each other to the brink of lovemaking, but never beyond. As different as they were, both of them sensed the importance of their relationship. They were equally afraid of commitment and ruining what they had already built together.

That evening Lindsey dressed for dinner with great care. She had never been to the restaurant she had chosen, but she knew its reputation. It was candlelight on a brick patio overlooking extensive tropical gardens. It was the sound of waves crashing against the beach and slow jazz from a talented trio. It was moonlight and the fragrance of roses and jasmine. It was romance.

Stefan was waiting by the time she emerged. When she found he was wearing the shirt she had given him for Christmas, she hardly knew what to say.

"You look great." She watched the way his gaze roamed over her. He didn't have to tell her what he thought about the way she looked.

He held out a handful of gardenias. "I thought you might like to wear these."

"They're gorgeous. But where did you get them? There aren't any in Mother's yard."

His expression went from wolfish to sheepish. "I went for a walk around the neighborhood while you were getting ready."

"And?"

"I really didn't think the yard six doors down would miss them. It was filled with flowers."

She laughed. Stefan was the most honorable person she had ever met. She knew what picking someone else's gardenias had cost him.

"And there was a For Sale sign in the yard," he added. "I don't think anyone's living there now, or I would have asked."

"I'm sure you're right."

He smiled. "I had to have them, no matter what. But I'm waiting for a knock at the door."

"The gardenia cops?"

"Exactly."

She kissed him, and the perfume of gardenias enveloped them.

"We'd better leave if we're still planning to," he said.

"We have all night together."

He held her tighter before he finally let her go.

Dinner was everything she had hoped it would be. The night was warm, with a light breeze that carried the scent of the gardens and the ocean to their table. By torchlight Stefan ate pompano with a delicate wine sauce and Lindsey an artistic presentation of fresh vegetables. Holding hands over dessert, they fed each other strawberries dipped in dark chocolate and sips of espresso.

Afterwards, she still wasn't ready to go home. "I need to walk," she said after Stefan had paid the bill. "Let's wander a little."

He slid her shawl over her shoulders and held out his hand. They strolled through the terrace and down toward the beach, weaving their way along pathways lined with roses and hibiscus.

"I'm so glad you came," Lindsey said, standing where she could see the ocean.

Stefan put his arm around her. "I am, too."

She held herself away from him and decided that the time had come for total honesty. "I was going to try to forget you."

"I know."

She was surprised. "You do?"

"I'm not completely insensitive."

"I never thought you were."

"It's crossed your mind at times."

"You're confused. I read minds. You're training to operate on them."

"You confuse me. And you distract me."

"Good."

He turned her a little so he could see her face. "I've never given this much thought, but when I have, I've thought that I'd marry a woman like me."

"Someone who runs her life by the clock and matches your brilliance? Someone who understands perfectly why you have to push yourself twenty out of every twenty-four hours?"

"Life's not long enough."

"And there's so much you want to know. You didn't count on me or anyone like me, did you?"

"No."

They walked a little farther in silence. At the end of the terrace there was a cypress gazebo, starkly simple and geometric in design. Entwined amidst the cypress slats were lushly blooming bougainvillea vines.

Lindsey touched a cluster of scarlet blossoms. "What would the gazebo be like without the flowers?" she asked. "I wonder, would you like it better if it was bare?"

"Of course not."

"And without the gazebo for structure, the vines would run wild. There would be a thicket here. No view. No place to sit."

"So I'm the gazebo and you're the bougainvillea?"

She touched his cheek. "You have to decide if you want to learn the things I can teach you, Stefan. I don't want to change you, but I don't want to change, either. I'll confuse and distract you forever if you let me. If you don't let me, if you hang on to this relationship but you isolate yourself, then we'll only hurt each other."

"I'm not sure I understand."

"I'm not sure you do, either." She dropped her hand. "I love you. I have right from the beginning." She had told him that in many different ways, but she had never said the words so directly. She watched his expression, but he hid whatever he was feeling.

"You love me," he said at last, "but you were going to try to forget me?"

"We're on the brink of something here. Don't you feel it? We're reaching a point where it's going to be hard, so very, very hard, to go back again. I love you. I don't want to hurt you. Not for anything. And I don't want to be hurt. But maybe we should do the hurting now. Maybe we shouldn't go any further.''

''And maybe we should.''

She closed her eyes. She felt his hands on her shoulders, then his lips on hers. She had given warning. As the scents of salt air, flowers and the man she loved filled her, she abandoned all caution. She had given Stefan his chance to back away. And he had refused to take it.

''I knew that night we were making a mistake,'' she said. The scents of a different garden filled her, but the man, and his power to hurt her were the same.

''No, you didn't. You were full of hope. And so was I.''

She edged away from him and stood. ''I was full of hormones. I wanted you.''

''You wanted more than sex. So did I.''

''What did you want?'' She faced him. ''What did you ever want that I could give you? I couldn't give you order or calm. The perfect wife would have given you those. She would have cooked your meals, cleaned your house, raised quiet, intelligent children who never bothered you. She would have advanced your career and made no emotional demands. I told you that night I could never be that wife.''

''That should tell you something.''

''And I'm supposed to deduce an answer? You can't tell me that much?''

''I wanted what you had to give me.''

''But you never took it!''

He stood, too. ''Is that what you wanted, Lindsey? Is that where I failed you? I didn't take enough? Maybe my memories are distorted, but I thought you said we divorced because I didn't *give* you enough.''

''You gave me everything material. You gave me nothing of yourself, and you wouldn't take anything I offered.''

''I took this.'' He pulled her to him before she could protest and covered her lips with his. She didn't even pretend to struggle. She was no protesting maiden. She wanted this as much as he did, as much as she had that night in Key West. She would always want Stefan, and nothing, not years or logic or the pain they had brought each other, could change that.

He thrust her away. "You divorced me because you never learned to compromise! You wanted everything, and when you couldn't have it all, you wanted out!"

"I divorced you because I loved you too much to bear it!"

He stared at her. "What's that supposed to mean?"

"I love you—loved you—too much. Can you know what it's like to live with someone, hoping everyday that he'll love you just a little bit, too?"

"I loved you."

"So you said. Occasionally. But your love was like an oasis in the desert, Stefan. An oasis with a brick wall surrounding it. And I couldn't climb that wall, even though I knew that everything I needed to go on living was on the other side. I couldn't climb it, no matter how hard I struggled or what route I took."

His voice was quiet and measured. "When you reached out for me in the middle of the night, I was there. I was always there."

She turned away. "Don't."

"And I could be there again."

"Our marriage didn't work."

"And our divorce isn't working any better. You still want me. I want you. We could be a family again. We could hold each other again." He put his arms around her waist. "We could try again."

"What would be different?" She held herself stiffly. She had kissed him, but she wouldn't lean against him. "What?"

"We could try harder."

"I couldn't."

"Then you don't want me anymore? You don't dream

sometimes that we're back together? You don't think of me sometimes late at night when you can't get to sleep because your body aches with desire?''

''Don't, Stefan.''

He turned her toward him. ''Just tell me you don't love me anymore. Tell me that when you said you loved me a moment ago, it was just a slip of the tongue. Tell me, make me believe it, and I'll never bring this up again.''

She wanted to form the words, but she couldn't lie. ''I think you'd better go now.''

He lifted her chin so she was forced to look at him. ''I'm real, Lindsey. No colored lights in the sky, no unearthly music, no visions of perfection and unity. I'm just a man. But I'm here. You can touch me, see me, hear me. And I want you back in my life. Until death do us part.''

''What I saw that night had nothing to do with you!''

''You have always wanted more than this world and the people in it could give you.''

''I just wanted love.''

''So you found it in a vision one night. But that vision wasn't real. I am.'' He kissed her again.

This time she resisted. She knew how easy it would be to give in to him. And she couldn't, no matter how vulnerable she was. ''I want you to go, Stefan.''

''No, you don't.''

''Go!'' She pushed him away.

''You can't say you don't love me anymore. You can't say it, can you?''

''Why ask me now? Why did you wait so long to ask for another chance?''

''I believed you when you said you wanted a divorce.''

''How logical.''

''And now I don't.''

''I always wanted you. And I never had you. And I never will, because you won't give yourself to me.''

''I'm standing right here.'' He touched her cheek.

His fingertips were warm. She closed her eyes, but she

knew the exact instant that the warmth was withdrawn. She stood in the garden and listened until she heard the sound of his car driving away.

Chapter 9

In the week after the talk in the garden, Lindsey arose every morning before dawn. Sleep eluded her, along with peace of mind. On the eighth morning, through a thick, dreamlike fog, she heard her bedroom door open; then she heard a giggle.

She turned on her side and saw Mandy standing beside her bed. Her tongue resisted forming words. She struggled. "How long have you been up, sweetheart?"

"You're a sleepyhead!"

"You're right." She saw that her bedside clock said ten. She was horrified, but too sick to do anything about it.

"We made you breakfast."

"Cereal and toast," Geoff said, following his sister into the bedroom. "And orange juice."

"You made orange juice, too?" Lindsey knew she had to sit up to let the children see how much she appreciated their thoughtfulness. With difficulty she pushed herself upright. The room spun, just as she had suspected it would. She gritted her teeth and waited. Eventually it stopped.

Geoff leaned over the bed in assessment. "Are you feeling all right?"

"Afraid not. That's why I slept so late."

"Do you need a doctor? Should we call Alden?"

"No. I've just caught some bug or other."

"A lightning bug?" Mandy asked.

Lindsey managed a laugh. "No, but it feels like lightning
in my head."

"She means she's got the flu or something. You know,
like you did last Christmas when you couldn't go to school
and be in your play," Geoff explained.

"Alden could fix it!"

Lindsey held out her hand for the juice. "I don't need
anybody to fix anything, sweetheart. I just need to rest. I'll
probably have to stay in bed most of today. Can you two
take care of each other?"

The idea excited them. They exchanged a volley of suggestions on just how to go about that as they presented Lindsey with soggy cornflakes and perfect toast. By the time the
discussion was finished, it was obvious that Lindsey's illness rated with Christmas and birthdays as something to
celebrate.

It rated lower for Lindsey. She wasn't surprised she was
ill. While shopping for milk and bread in town she had
heard that a number of people on the island were suffering
from summer colds. Her own resistance had probably been
lowered by the busy schedule she had kept with the children.
In the last week they had taken their van back to the mainland to spend two days at Cedar Point, a nearby amusement
park. They had spent one day sailing with friends who lived
on the east side of the island, two more entertaining friends
from Rocky River. They had picked a gallon of blackberries,
ridden their bicycles and taken Kong for endless walks. All,
she suspected, to put the specter of Geoff disappearing into
the lake out of their minds.

And to keep Stefan and the change in their relationship
out of hers.

"This is the best breakfast I've ever eaten," she told the children in between choking down bits and pieces of the toast.

Mandy stood by her right shoulder and watched. "Then how come you're not eating very much?"

"I think that's all I can manage for now." Lindsey handed her dishes back to Geoff and hoped he would remove the leftover food as swiftly as possible. She was feeling even worse than she had feared.

"Can we get you anything else?" he asked.

"I think I'll just rest some more. Leave my door open so I can hear what's going on. Okay?"

"You don't have to worry about us."

"Oh, I know. But just in case, remember the rules." She tried to remember them herself. "No cooking...or using knives to cut anything. No fighting. And don't go anywhere...unless you get my permission." She shut her eyes as the room began to spin again.

The rest of the morning was a haze. She woke up periodically, sometimes to find Mandy or Geoff gazing down at her, sometimes alone. Once she tried to take a few sips of water but found she could barely hold the cup.

Sometime later, it could have been minutes or hours, she heard Kong's ferocious barking. She wondered how one dog could sound like an entire pack of wolves. While she was still slowly forming that thought she heard Alden's voice.

"How are you feeling?"

She felt a cool hand on her forehead. "What are you doing here?"

"Geoff came over to tell me you were sick."

"I told him...not to bother you. I'm getting a cold."

"Is that so?"

"I'm hardly ever sick. I guess...I was due for something."

"Maybe. Why don't you open your mouth and let me take a look?"

She felt too ill to argue. She stuck out her tongue and grunted.

"I'm going to look in your eyes."

"If I can keep them open." She managed to while he flashed something in them for a few seconds.

"Had any headaches?"

"On and off."

"How long?"

"Early June or so."

"Have you had a checkup?"

She thought of the endless hours in the hospital emergency room after her encounter. "A thorough one."

"After that incident you told me about?"

"That's right."

"And they didn't find anything?"

"They found out I'm not a very good patient."

"I see."

"Alden, I'm going to be...fine. I just need some rest."

"I've got something that should help."

"I don't like to take anything. I'd rather...let my body cure itself."

"How sick do you feel?"

"Miserable."

"Let your body cure itself with a little help, then."

"You're relentless."

"And you may be sicker than you think."

"What's wrong with me?"

He hesitated longer than usual. "Probably nothing serious. But it's not something that's going to turn into a few simple sneezes and coughs. You've got a high fever, and I think you're anemic, among other things. Have you been pushing yourself too hard?"

"A little. But I'm never sick."

"You are now. Let me give you something to make you feel better."

She didn't have any strength left to resist. "All right. If

it will make me get over this faster. I don't like leaving…Geoff and Mandy unsupervised.''

He turned his back to her and bent over for his bag. ''They told me you have friends on the other side of the island. Let me call and see if they'll take the children for you tonight. I'll take them if your friends can't, but I think you'll get more rest if they're not so close by.''

''I don't want to put anybody out.''

''Put them out?''

''You know…cause trouble. Disturb them.''

''Right.''

She had a sudden brainstorm, which was surprising, since her brain didn't seem to be functioning quite right. ''Was English your first language, Alden?''

''No.''

''That explains it.''

''What?''

''The reason…you hesitate before you speak. You're translating, aren't you?''

''You're very perceptive.''

Her head began to throb again. She snuggled down into her pillow and shut her eyes. Sometime later she felt Alden lift her arm. There was the faintest prick, so faint that she didn't even open her eyes to see what he was doing. ''The children can stay here. I'm going to be fine.''

''Just think about something pleasant, Lindsey. You'll go to sleep now. And when you wake up, you'll already be starting to feel better.''

''Good news.''

''And I'll be sure Geoff and Mandy are taken care of tonight.''

''Thanks.'' She wanted to open her eyes, but her lids seemed heavier by the moment. She just managed to murmur goodbye before she fell asleep.

Stefan had only met Alden once, and the introduction had been in the middle of a driving thunderstorm. But between

Geoff and Mandy's endless commentary and Lindsey's glowing reports, he felt he knew the man well.

And he didn't like him.

He was too rational not to understand his own animosity. Alden had effortlessly earned the affection from Stefan's wife and children that Stefan had always longed for. From what Stefan knew of him, everything was effortless to Alden. He was a physician, too, but he seemed bound by none of the restrictions that hobbled Stefan. He changed positions when it suited him, took summers off if he needed the rest, even refused to specialize so that he could enjoy the diversity of general practice.

Or at least that was what he'd told Lindsey.

Stefan knew that once more he should be grateful to Alden. He had taken care of Lindsey, even to the point of arranging child-care for her so that she could rest more comfortably. But deep down Stefan was no more grateful than he had been when Alden saved Geoff's life.

It was late afternoon before his ferry arrived on Kelleys Island. In order to take the ferry at all he had turned over two patients to the resident on call and blackened his own name professionally. In the last month he had taken more personal time than he could remember taking in all his years at the hospital combined. His reputation as someone who could be counted on night or day—never mind his private life—was in shreds, and he didn't much care.

When the ferry docked he walked to his attorney's house to get the Peugeot. In minutes he was knocking on Alden Fitzpatrick's door.

The man who answered only vaguely resembled Geoff and Mandy's soaked-to-the-skin rescuer. This Alden was undeniably good-looking, and his smile was friendly.

Stefan held out his hand. "I'm Stefan Daniels, Geoff and Mandy's father. We met a few weeks ago."

Alden shook his hand. "Right. Geoff said he'd spoken to you this morning."

"I called just to see how he was. I'm glad I did."

"Come in." Alden stepped back to let Stefan pass.

Alden's cottage was small and painfully neat. There was no evidence of children here, no small artistic touches like those Lindsey left in her wake. There was, in fact, little evidence that anyone lived here at all. It reminded Stefan of his own apartment. At least they had that much in common.

"I don't want to keep you," Stefan said.

"I just made some coffee. Would you like some?"

"All right." Stefan followed Alden into the kitchen, which was as empty of warmth as the rest of the cottage.

The coffee was strong and bitter, too strong for Stefan's taste. He took three polite sips. Alden drank his without making a face.

Stefan set his cup on the counter. "I'm on my way to see Lindsey. I just wanted to find out what you thought about her illness."

"She should be feeling better by now."

"Oh?"

"I gave her something to make her rest easier."

"What?"

"Something I've devised."

"I don't know if I like the sound of that."

"I've studied oriental medicine extensively. There are many more ways of treating illness than most Western physicians understand."

"I'd prefer you didn't experiment on my family."

"You'll find her improved." Alden poured himself more coffee and topped off Stefan's cup. "You won't find her well, though."

"What do you mean?"

Alden hesitated. Stefan had already noticed a chronic hesitation each time Alden spoke. But this time he seemed to be struggling with exactly what to say—or how to say it. "I believe this is not just a simple virus," he said at last.

"Exactly what do you think is going on?"

"I'm not really qualified to give it a name. But I think she should be seen by someone who is."

"Damn it, man, what are you talking about?"

"I only did a brief exam. But there seems to be a degeneration of sorts. Examine her yourself and you'll see what I mean."

"Degeneration?"

"Degeneration. Deterioration. That's as specific as I can get."

"Where did you train?"

Alden smiled. "In places where we didn't pretend to understand something if we weren't absolutely sure we did."

Stefan stared into Alden's eyes and felt strangely chastened. "I'd better go take a look myself."

"I think that would be wise."

"I haven't thanked you for seeing her. Or for saving my son's life."

"You haven't thanked me because you wish it hadn't been me. You love them very much, don't you?"

"My feelings are my own business."

"Of course. But you don't feel resentment just because I sense your love for your family, do you?"

"How do you feel about them?"

Alden's expression changed. Subtly. "Worried."

Stefan felt a chill. He reached for his coffee and took one final sip. Foolishly, his hands, a neurosurgeon's hands, weren't quite steady. "I hope you're worried for nothing."

"There's much we could teach each other. Do you realize it?"

"No."

"I've studied extensively, but there are things I still don't understand. You've studied extensively, but there are areas and philosophies of medicine that you've never touched on."

"I'm a highly trained specialist. I can't understand everything."

"No."

"And I don't waste my time on the unproven."

"You might consider how much that limits you."

There was something, some fact, some reality, just out of Stefan's reach. He felt it, sensed it throughout his body in a way that was strange for him. But he couldn't imagine what it could be. He set his cup on the saucer. With a final nod to Alden, he left the cottage.

When Lindsey awoke, it was growing dark outside. The last hours seemed like a dream. She wasn't sure Alden had really been there, or that he had given her a shot to make her feel better. But she did feel better. Much better, although certainly not back to normal.

She listened for the sounds of the children's voices, but the house was quiet. She turned over to see what time it was and found a note beside the clock along with a thermos of ice water. The children were across the island and would be back tomorrow afternoon. They had even taken Kong with them.

She sat up slowly to pour some water, and the room didn't spin. There was no reason to worry about Geoff and Mandy. The family they were staying with had children near their ages. Everyone would have a good time, and she could return the favor when she felt well again. Now she could just concentrate on getting better.

Half an hour later she had managed to shower and change into a knit jumpsuit. She was contemplating a trip downstairs for something to eat when she heard the front door open.

"Alden?"

"Wrong doctor."

"Stefan? What on earth are you doing here?"

He took the stairs two at a time. "What are you doing out of bed?"

"I was about to go downstairs and rummage for food."

"Don't try it. I'll make you something and bring it up."

She wanted to protest, opened her mouth to do it, in fact.

But she realized before she could utter a word just how wonderful eating upstairs would be. "Great. Thanks."

Stefan had expected an argument. But the woman in front of him was too pale and unsteady for one. She looked as if the breeze from an open window might knock her off her feet. He touched her cheek with the back of his hand. "How do you feel?"

"You must know or you wouldn't be here."

"I called earlier just to see how things were. Geoff told me you were sick. I saw Alden on the way over here."

"There was no need to worry you. It's just the beginning of a cold."

"You're not hot."

"Good."

"Alden tells me he gave you something."

"Whatever it was worked."

"Don't let him give you anything else."

"Why? Don't you want me to get well?"

He smiled. After Alden's warning he was so glad to see her on her feet that his emotions had ballooned. "He's vague, to say the least, about his credentials. I just don't want him dosing you with eye of newt and bat wing serum."

"If that's what he gave me, I highly recommend it."

"Then I'll see if I can rustle up something like it in the kitchen."

"Thanks, but vegetable soup will be fine. There's some in the cupboard."

"And toast?"

"One piece. No butter."

"Done. Can you make it back to the bedroom by yourself?"

"Easily."

"I'll see you there."

She settled herself back in bed and shut her eyes. The sounds drifting up the stairs from the kitchen were pleasant ones. Stefan had not cooked often during their marriage, but she could remember times, sweet, rare times, when he had stayed home for a stolen weekend or a few stolen hours. Then he had cooked specialties that he remembered from his childhood, Hilda's sauerkraut and dumplings, or chicken paprikash that even she, the lifelong vegetarian, hadn't been able to resist.

She remembered one particular meal so clearly that now she could almost smell it cooking. The similarities were obvious. She had lain in bed, just as she was doing now, and listened to Stefan in the kitchen. But the differences were just as obvious. It was a Florida morning she remembered, the morning after she and Stefan had made love for the first time.

And the night before? She remembered that, too. It wasn't surprising that those memories would surface now, because her resistance had never been lower.

Maybe there was no point in trying to forget what she never could, anyway. Her years with Stefan had been a large portion of her life. Pretending they weren't important hadn't changed her feelings; remembering wouldn't, either. But that didn't matter now, anyway. She was powerless to bridle the memory. Powerless and reluctant.

After their talk in the restaurant garden, Stefan had taken the long way home. Once they stopped the car to stroll hand in hand along a public beach. She took off her shoes and insisted he take off his, too. The water was cool, and they waded and splashed like children.

Stefan found her a shell, a perfect, pearly pink spiral that neither of them could identify. She found a starfish for him, but he sent it sailing back into deep water because it was still alive. As she watched it twirl through the air she knew, irrevocably, that it was too late to stop loving him.

Back at her mother's house he opened a bottle of champagne. They toasted each other with their arms entwined.

"To standby flights to Florida," she said. "And to the man who stood by."

"To the man who doesn't intend to stand by any longer."

She smiled slowly. Very, very slowly. "No?"

"Finish your champagne."

She did. Very, very slowly.

He waited, betraying no frustration. When she had finished, he took her glass and set it on the counter. "Let's take a swim."

"Now?"

"That's right."

"You're not waterlogged from this afternoon?"

"No."

"Let me get my suit."

"No."

"I see."

"Good." He took her hand.

Outside, the same moon that had transformed the white sand beach into an endless stretch of glistening opal transformed the tropical plantings and pool into a South Seas lagoon. Sheltered by thick stands of bamboo and palm against a cypress fence, the lagoon was completely private.

At the water's edge, Stefan dropped Lindsey's hand. She faced him and smiled her most provocative smile. "Who's first?"

"You."

She felt not the slightest trace of awkwardness. She reached for the top button of her dress, but Stefan arrived there first. He smoothed his hands along her collarbone; then his thumbs dipped lower, tracing the soft skin along her shoulder straps.

Her hands fell to her sides. She watched his face. He was the explorer now; the man determined to learn all he could. One strap slid over her shoulder, then the next. His hands dipped lower.

The first button was set free. She could feel the evening breeze against her skin, cooling each inch of flesh as he abandoned it. The second button fell free, then the third. When the fourth button was freed the dress slid down her shoulders to reveal her breasts. His hand molded one, then the other.

There were a thousand clichés he could have uttered, but he chose silence. He leaned closer to kiss her neck. Her head fell back, and she reveled in the feel of his hands and lips. When her dress finally fell to her hips, her arms were free. She stretched them toward him, pulling him closer. As her dress billowed to their feet, his lips found hers.

She undressed him as slowly as her failing self-control would allow. She bunched the fabric of his shirt in her hands, ignoring the hours of love that had gone into its creation. Palms pressed against his chest, she slid the shirt to his shoulders, then over his head. His flesh was warm against hers, hard where hers was yielding. She pressed herself against him as she found the waistband of his slacks, then the zipper.

"Are you sure you want to swim?" she whispered.

His answer was a kiss that went on and on. When it had ended, they were dressed in nothing except moonlight.

He led her to the edge of the pool. She couldn't look away. She had seen him in a swim suit, but now, completely naked, his masculine beauty took her breath away.

And he wanted her. His patience was nothing against the blatant evidence of his arousal. As the cool water closed over her, she was filled with anticipation. Any worries that Stefan's self-control was ruled by a lack of real desire had vanished. Their months together had been elaborate foreplay. He was a sensual man who genuinely savored each level of lovemaking as only the most sensitive of men could.

They were about to climb to the highest plateau together.

Pushing off from the side, she swam to the middle of the pool. When she surfaced, she couldn't see Stefan, but a gentle tug on her leg told her his location. She swam away from him, dolphin from shark, cutting sleekly through the water with her arms alone.

When she surfaced again she still couldn't see him, but another tug on her leg told her she hadn't escaped. She laughed and went after him. Under the water she could just detect a shape moving toward the shallow end of the pool. She followed. When he came up for a breath she was right behind him.

She circled his neck with her arms and kissed him. Then, before he could respond, she dove back into the water and started across the pool.

She was breathing hard when he finally trapped her in the shallow end once more. She laughed; then her laughter caught in her throat as he kissed her. She clung to him, her legs entwined with his. The water had done nothing to cool his response to her. He was warm and slippery, his skin like satin. She moved her hands over him, discovering each plane, each slope of his body.

Desire had tantalized; now it propelled. Effortlessly he lifted her, sipping the droplets of water from the hollow of her throat. Then his mouth slid lower. She gasped as his lips closed around the tip of one breast. She arched against him until her legs wrapped naturally around his waist. The water lapped at her thighs as his lips moved against her. She felt her body heat to fever pitch, and she was afraid she was going to dissolve against him.

"Stefan, stop. Not like this." She pushed against his shoulders.

Still holding her, he carried her to the wide, terraced corner leading out of the pool. He sank with her until they were lying against the top step with water lapping slowly around them. They had waited so long, been so cautious. Now they couldn't wait long enough to find a bed.

The tile was cool against her skin; the man was blazing hot. She embraced him as he entered her. He was fire, and she surrounded him like the water that cradled them both. She held him tightly, jealous of the moonlight between them.

He rose above her, his head thrown back in ecstasy. She knew she would always remember him this way, proudly beautiful, exultant and wholly immersed in their lovemaking. She raised her eyes to his and found them closed. She gripped him tighter, suddenly afraid and not certain why.

"Stefan?"

If he heard her, he didn't respond.

"Stefan!"

He opened his eyes and looked at her.

She wasn't sure what she saw there. In that moment, the most emotional of her life, he seemed completely remote. What she saw or didn't see might have been the moonlight reflecting off the water. It might have been simply the age-old fears of a woman who at last has given herself to a man.

"I'm here," she said.

"I know."

It was all she needed. She forgot her fears and demanded all of him. Without another word she asked him to give up everything to her, each thought, each part of himself he had never shared.

The asking took only moments. The answer would resound through her body and soul for years to come.

Chapter 10

That night in Key West was filled with lovemaking, with exploration and discovery, with whispered questions and ecstatic answers. Sometime just before dawn Lindsey finally fell asleep in Stefan's arms. Sleeping the whole night with a man was a new experience for her, but in the narrow bed in her room she cuddled against him as if they had slept together forever.

If Stefan still couldn't tell her what he felt, he'd had no trouble showing her how much pleasure she'd given him. She drifted into sleep as certain of her power over him as she was of her own needs.

She was less certain late that morning when she opened her eyes. Stefan was gone. She knew he must be somewhere in the house, but she wondered why he had gotten up. The bed was cramped, but she had loved the feeling of having him so close. Had he found it too confining or had the intimacy been too overwhelming? She didn't know how to make him tell her. He had shut his eyes, shut her out, at the height of intimacy last night. He was the most private man she had ever known.

She wondered if their lovemaking had ended the challenge for him. He was a man who needed challenges. Was he already forging ahead to whatever waited in the next moment, or the next?

She turned to stroke the pillow where his head had rested. He wasn't her first lover, but she wanted him to be her last. She hadn't been looking for commitment. She had planned on years of freedom, scores of adoring men and a life filled with color and music. She had not seen a medical student in her future; she had not seen herself as a doctor's wife.

And here she was.

A noise from downstairs interrupted her thoughts. A pan clanged against terrazzo, and something suspiciously like a curse followed it. She laughed, and her worries floated away. Her medical student was nothing if not practical. Perhaps all rational thought had disappeared last night, but this morning he was quintessential Stefan again.

Determined not to spoil his surprise, she lay back and waited.

The sun was higher in the sky when he finally appeared. He carried a tray that had last held her mother's silver tea service. There was a spray of gardenias beside white china plates and a teapot filled—judging from the smell—with coffee. On the plates were the most perfectly cooked omelets she had ever seen nestled against freshly steamed broccoli.

She sat up. "Broccoli?"

"Well, you refuse to eat bacon."

"Broccoli?" She held out her arms. He set the tray on the floor and took the kiss she offered. When he moved away she noted he was dressed while she was still gloriously naked. She felt not one bit of shyness, but she reached for her nightshirt just to even the score.

"There's a microwave downstairs," he said, tugging the nightshirt from her hand.

"Is there?"

"For heating omelets if they get cold."

She smiled. "And broccoli?"

"Particularly good for broccoli."

"I think we should give it a test."

"Later. Much later."

Despite his words, he didn't move closer. Florida sunshine flooded the room, and in the light of day she saw his doubts, his fears—or at least she imagined they were visible. When he couldn't seem to reach for her, she touched his arm. "I know, Stefan."

"You know what?"

"How unlikely we are together. It doesn't matter anymore."

"Doesn't it?"

"No. Does it matter to you?"

"Last night was..." He shook his head.

"Pick an adjective, any adjective."

"I don't know what I'd do if you left me now."

Her heart seemed to pause midbeat. She knew what that statement had cost him.

"There's some part of me that you touch," he said after a moment. "Only you. I don't ever want to lose you."

"I'll never leave." She embraced him, sure she could never let him go again.

It was much later when they ate. The broccoli was limp, and the cheese in the omelets had congealed. But the meal and the moment would never be forgotten by either of them. Nor would his words—even though she never heard them spoken again.

"You don't mind if I join you, do you?"

Lindsey opened her eyes to see Stefan in the doorway with a tray. She knew where she was. She knew what day it was. But for a moment she didn't want to believe that so much time had passed. Or that so much loneliness had filled those days. She managed a smile. "No. Have you eaten anything today?"

"Breakfast." He set the tray on the end of the bed as she wriggled into a sitting position. Before she could protest he reached for an extra pillow and tucked it behind her head. "You should take better care of yourself."

"Look who's talking."

He waited until she was settled to hand her the tray.

"I'm planning to take it easier," she said. "How about you?"

"According to my colleagues, that's all I've been doing lately."

She was filled with remorse. "I'm sorry. I really am. It does seem like you've done nothing but respond to crises this summer."

"Well, at least there's been a wide variety."

"The widest." She picked up her spoon. "This smells wonderful."

"That's a good sign. I could go for a steak, myself."

"There were eggs in the kitchen. You could have made an omelet."

"There's nothing interesting to eat with it."

Surprised, she looked up. She wondered if his thoughts had turned to one special morning, too. But if they had, he didn't show her. She, on the other hand, had been so immersed in memory that it was hard now to remember which Lindsey she was.

She watched him start on his soup. "You really didn't have to come. I'm feeling much better. I would have called you if I really needed help."

"Geoff was worried about you."

"He's not used to me being sick."

"After you eat, I'm going to do an exam."

"Are you? Without my permission?"

He flashed one of his rare smiles. "I'm going to get your permission."

"We'll see. You know Alden already checked me over."

"He thought I should take a look, too."

"Are the two of you conducting research?"

"The two of us are worried."

"That's silly."

"So tell me about the last week."

Lindsey found the intimacy of the situation bittersweet. They were a man and a woman eating a cozy meal together in bed. Teasing each other. Changing the subject to avoid arguments. Discussing their lives. A judge had ruled that they no longer deserved this pleasure. With a few mumbled sentences he had freed them both from caring and sharing. Yet here they were. Again. Still.

She took a few bites before she spoke. "You used to ask me about my week regularly. Even when we were married, we never seemed to have time to talk everyday. If we were lucky we'd only have to catch up on a week at a time."

"I don't remember that."

"I should have complained then, but I wanted to be an understanding wife."

"That sounds like you're admitting something."

"I never thought the divorce was entirely your fault."

"Didn't you?"

"Although, like I've told you, I did think your habit of answering me with questions had a lot to do with it." She smiled a little to take the sting out of her words.

"And you didn't think I could change that?" He caught himself and smiled, too.

"Anyway, you asked me about my week."

"That's right."

"Well, I kept busy. Too busy. I think I wanted to forget what nearly happened to Geoff. So we ran here and there, and I exhausted myself. That's why I'm sick."

"I kept busy, too." He told her about his week, about the old woman who had been misdiagnosed and sentenced to die mute and disoriented in a nursing home until a nurse he had once worked with called him to plead her case. "I evaluated last Tuesday and performed surgery on Wednesday,'' he said. ''By the beginning of this week she was calling the staff by their first names and asking them about their families. She'll go back to the nursing home to recover, then home to her own apartment.''

''That's wonderful.'' She touched his hand, genuinely proud of him.

''That's science.''

''No, that's a human being applying the principles of science.''

''It's the principles that cure.''

''It's the human presence that cures.''

''I'm sure your friend Alden would agree with you.''

''I'm sure he would.''

He reached for her cup to fill it with hot tea. ''How are you feeling?''

''Better by the moment. Your human presence is curing me.''

''Good nutrition.''

She laughed, sobering slowly when she realized they were staring at each other. The intimacy was becoming more sweet than bitter, and frighteningly addictive. She couldn't pretend otherwise any longer. ''When, exactly, did our differences become so fatal?''

''When we stopped trying to understand each other.''

''Maybe.'' She picked up her cup but didn't bring it to her lips. ''I wanted to understand. I even thought I did.''

He waited so long to answer that she thought he was going to change the subject. But he didn't. ''What did you understand?''

She thought she was absolving him. ''That you loved me as much as you could love anyone. That you never, never meant to hurt me. But that love would never have much of a place in your life. You'd never find the time for it.''

''Then you never understood at all.''

She met his gaze again, even though she knew its dangers. ''What didn't I understand?''

His voice was cold. ''This isn't the right time for this.''

"Maybe it's way past time."

"Maybe we should have had this conversation before you told me you wanted a divorce."

"Maybe I thought if you knew how desperate I was, we *would* have this conversation. But we didn't. You stared at me, and you said, 'All right. If that's what you want, I'll see my attorney.'"

"Did you ask me for a divorce just so we'd talk about the problems in our relationship? Was it a means to an end, a game with rules you didn't bother to explain?"

She set down her cup. "No! By then I was too hurt to live with you anymore. Besides, I knew you well enough to understand that nothing, not even the threat of a divorce, was going to make you talk about your feelings."

"And if I had?"

"I don't know. That was a year ago."

"If I had?"

"You didn't."

He finished his soup. She was too shaken to eat the rest of hers. A lump had formed in her throat. She wanted nothing more than silence and privacy to cry.

When he cleared away the tray she pulled the covers higher. She expected him to leave, but he sat down on the side of the bed again.

"I probably ought to get some more sleep," she said.

"I'd like to examine you first. Are you going to let me?"

There was nothing she wanted less, but she knew if they argued again she would cry. "If you think you have to."

"I want to."

"Go ahead, then."

"Rest for a few minutes. I'll be back."

She couldn't rest. Stefan's answers—and lack of them—kept ringing through her head. Something else bothered her, too. Her own answers. Had she been telling the truth? Had she ever? Without admitting it to herself, had she asked Stefan for a divorce as a last-ditch attempt to reconcile their differences? Had she tried and failed to make him see how much she really needed him?

At the time, she had convinced herself she truly wanted him to leave. Now she had to wonder if she had told herself lies. A year had passed and the divorce was a fact. But had any measure of peace come with that final decree? Almost more important, had she ever believed any would?

"Can you sit up?"

If he was bothered by what had occurred, it didn't show. He looked like any physician doing rounds in a hospital filled with strangers. With nothing left except to get this over with quickly, she propped herself against the pillows. "You're out of your element. This is like hiring Frank Lloyd Wright to nail shingles on a roof."

"I still remember my basic training."

"Just don't recommend brain surgery because you can't think of anything else to offer."

He touched her cheek. Her eyelids closed involuntarily. One touch, one casual touch, and she felt tears gathering under them.

He wrapped something around her arm, and she knew he was taking her blood pressure. She lay quietly and told herself not to cry. Things were already too complicated.

"Open your mouth."

She made the same gagging noise she had made for Alden. She was absolutely rigid while he looked in her ears. When she felt his hands at her neck, she opened her eyes. He was looking at her, not over her shoulder at the wall as her general practitioner would have done.

His hands felt wonderful. As tense as she was, as emotionally volatile, she could feel their healing magic. She wanted to beg him to stop, and she wanted to beg him not to. Instead, she tried to keep her voice light. "Do you know anything yet?"

"You're sick."

"Thanks. I'm glad I'm not paying you."

His fingertips massaged each inch of her neck, moving

slowly under her hair to the back of her head. "Does this hurt?"

She made a sound that could have been a yes or a no.

His thumbs caressed the soft skin under her chin. "Swallow." She did. "Did that hurt?"

She shook her head.

"I don't think it's a cold. You don't seem congested."

"Some other virus, then."

He continued to knead her neck. "You're very tense."

"You're very close."

"I'm not going to hurt you."

She knew that wasn't true. She looked away. His hands moved to her shoulders and continued the same slow massage. "How did you feel this morning before Alden treated you?"

"Dizzy. My head ached."

"Was today the first time that's happened?"

She hesitated too long to lie. "No. But today's the only time I haven't been able to ignore it."

"Lind...sey." He shook his head. "You promised me you'd tell me if you started having any unusual symptoms."

"Headaches come from tension, Stefan."

"Sometimes. Tell me about them."

She did, responding to all the questions he asked. "So what now? Do you pull out the chain saw and set to work?"

"No, I pull out my light." He didn't pull out anything. His hands continued their exquisite torture.

Her eyelids drifted shut once more. "You should go."

"I'm not done."

"That's what I'm afraid of."

"Are you?"

"This isn't like any examination I've ever had."

"Different from Alden's?"

"Yes."

"Good."

She felt his hands leave her shoulders; then she felt his

lips against her forehead. She opened her eyes, but he was already bending for his bag.

The light was bright, but not precisely like the one Alden had used. He took longer than she'd expected, but he had always been thorough. When he flicked it off and sat back, his expression gave nothing away.

"Well?"

"Layman's terms?"

"Please."

"I don't know what's wrong."

She laughed a little.

He smiled a little. "But I do want you to get some more tests. I'm not sure what I see. I need some more information."

"What are you worried about?"

"I'm not trying to put you off, but I can't really tell you. It's…" He shrugged, turning his hands up. "It's probably nothing. Your blood pressure's a little high. You may be anemic. Both could be due to a virus. But with the symptoms you've been having, we don't want to rule out possibilities."

"Possibilities?"

"That's the best I can do unless I get obnoxiously technical."

"Don't."

"Will you come in for a workup?"

"I had a workup."

"Not a complete one. Besides, some time's passed. If anything's happening, we'll have a baseline to compare it to."

"Will you be the one in charge?"

"That depends on you. If you'd like me to be in charge, I will."

"Of course. If I come in."

"I'm not finished yet."

"What else do you need to know?"

He put his light in his bag and got his stethoscope. "I'm

going to listen to your heart and lungs. Unzip your jump-suit.''

"I'm breathing fine."

"I'm sure you are. But let me see for myself, okay?"

She had never been shy with him, not even at the beginning of their relationship. She told herself she was being foolish and grasped the zipper, opening it six inches.

He opened it another six. She wondered if he had guessed that she wasn't wearing a bra.

He warmed the bell of the stethoscope against his hand. "Have you had any pain in your chest? Any coughing?"

She didn't meet his eyes. "No."

"Lindsey, I'm a doctor."

"You're my lover and husband." She realized what she'd said. "Were," she amended.

"Take a deep breath."

She found that part easy, but she jumped when he touched her. The stethoscope was cool, but his hand was warm. It brushed against her breast as he moved the stethoscope into position. "Let it out."

The sensation growing in the most intimate parts of her body had nothing to do with illness. She felt blood rising to her cheeks, and her breath caught as he moved the stethoscope again.

"Another breath."

"Haven't you heard enough?"

His eyes met hers. "Another breath."

She took a deep one and held it. His left hand kneaded her shoulder; his right moved again. "Good. Now let it out."

She knew her heart was speeding. It seemed unfair that all her responses were right there for him to read when his were so hidden. "Doesn't this bother you?" she demanded. "Or is it just me? After everything, how can you be so objective?"

"One more."

"One more what?"

"Breath."

She pulled enough oxygen into her lungs to last an hour.

"Good. Now turn around. We'll just slip your top down."

She turned her back to him. "Not we. You. I'm not helping. And there's no nurse in the room."

"Professional jargon."

"Professional hooey." She felt his hands against her skin. The jumpsuit slid slowly over her shoulders. Slowly enough to be suspicious. This time she didn't jump when the stethoscope touched her. She squeezed her eyelids shut and forced herself to be still.

"Take a deep breath."

"Stefan, get this over with quickly."

"One more."

She obliged him. Then she lifted her arms to pull the jumpsuit back on. Stefan gathered the fabric in his hands and slowly slid it up her spine. She shuddered when his hands stopped at her shoulders.

"I didn't protest when you asked me for a divorce," he said softly, "because I didn't know how. I didn't know how, Lindsey. I thought you didn't love me anymore. I thought everything must be over between us. I couldn't believe you'd want a divorce if you loved me at all."

So many mistakes. So many misunderstandings. A tear escaped and slid down her cheek. "It was for the best. It doesn't pay to look back and wish it had been different."

"No? Then I waste time everyday."

"How could anything be different when we're the same people we've always been?"

"I'd like to know."

"You don't want me. Not really. You look at our marriage and see a failure. You've never failed at anything in your life. You're confusing that with wanting me."

"I want you." He turned her slowly toward him. "I know the difference."

"You want sex. I want sex. We've both been alone too long."

"Because we chose to. Because neither of us wants anyone else."

She opened her eyes and saw the man she loved, the man she would always love, staring back at her. All she had to do was reach out and whatever he could share would be hers again. How many nights had she reached for him since he'd moved out of their house? How many nights had she reached out to find him gone?

She was too weak, too needy, to resist any longer. She made a noise of surrender low in her throat. Neither a yes nor a no, it left everything up to him. He framed her face with his hands, and she was surprised to find they were trembling. His lips were firm and unbelievably sweet against her own. She sighed against them and reached out to pull him closer.

"God, how I've missed you, how I've missed this." He whispered the words in her ear as if he couldn't say them out loud. His lips touched her earlobe; his breath caressed it. She shuddered, as responsive to his lovemaking as she had been on that Florida night.

"I've missed you, too," she said. "So much. So much."

He parted her jumpsuit and eased it back over her shoulders. There was nothing of the physician left in his touch, except that as he caressed her bare shoulders, she felt energy and strength flow into her. His energy. His strength. And something more, something as mysterious and healing as Alden's magical cure.

She fell back against the pillows and let his touch, his warmth and weight heal her. She could not absorb sensation quickly enough. She wanted to savor and she wanted to fly. Most of all, she wanted to forget the fears still hovering at the edge of consciousness, to forget so completely that there would be nothing left between them except clothes they could easily shed.

"Have you missed me?" he asked softly. "Why didn't I know? Why didn't you tell me?"

He kissed her neck, and her eyes fell shut. More tears

gathered under her lids, but they were tears of welcome. He felt so right against her; his hands felt so right on her shoulders, her arms. When he cupped one breast, that felt right, too, gloriously, perfectly right.

"What God has joined..." She hadn't meant to say the words out loud.

"Let no man put asunder," he finished.

Her tears began to flow. "No man did, Stefan. We did."

"But it doesn't have to be that way. Not anymore." His lips found hers again. She tasted regret and hope. She tasted a new beginning. Fear faded, tears dried. She had always believed in happy endings. She and Stefan could try again. They could bring a new maturity into their marriage. How could they not try when they shared this passion for each other?

When he unzipped her jumpsuit completely, she shrugged it off impatiently. The buttons of his shirt gave way easily under her experienced fingers. Hungrily she smoothed her palms over his chest. He was still so beautiful, had always been so beautiful. Touching him was both enticement and satisfaction.

He left her for a moment to finish undressing. Only a few seconds' absence, but she felt cheated, bereft. Even seconds were too long now, after all their months apart.

Under the sheet together, she explored him with her lips and hands. As if they had never been apart, she remembered exactly what he liked best, where he liked to be kissed and where he liked to be touched. He remembered the same so perfectly that he seemed to know her desires before they were clear to her. She pressed herself against him, wrapped her legs around his, circled him with her arms. She wanted to merge; she wanted to dissolve into him so completely that there would never again be a moment when they were separated.

"I love you, Stefan," she said fiercely. "I never stopped loving you. Never! I never can."

He silenced her words, absorbed them with his lips, but

he didn't speak his own. He turned her so she was on her back and slid into her so easily that it was as if they had never been apart.

She gasped, and she knew for the first time just how alone, how empty, she had been. She arched to meet him when he withdrew, seeking his warmth again, then again. She dug her fingers into his back, fighting release because it meant he would leave her. She never wanted to be separated from him again. They had lost a year together. She wanted all of him now and forever.

He rose above her, and she gazed at him, expecting, praying, to see a reflection of the same emotion she felt.

His eyes were shut.

A cold wave of fear washed over her. Now, even now on the brink of ecstasy, she didn't know what he was feeling. After everything, after a year of pain and loneliness, she still didn't know. She wanted to beg him to tell her, to show her, but her body betrayed her. Her eyes squeezed shut, too, and she felt herself falling through space.

And Stefan wasn't there to catch her.

He moved away from her almost immediately and lay beside her without touching. A long time passed before he spoke. "Are you all right?"

Her answer caught in her throat. "No."

"Did I hurt you?"

"More than I can say."

He turned toward her. Solicitous. Concerned. "What hurts? Where?"

"A place you can't see. A place you probably don't even believe in."

"What are you talking about?"

She touched her chest. "My heart. My soul."

He reached for her. "Lindsey...."

"Don't!" She sat up. "I love you, Stefan. I said it. I showed you in every way I knew how. I thought maybe something had changed and you could do the same. But nothing's different, is it?"

"Nothing needs to be different."

"Maybe not for you."

"What is it you want?"

"I want to know who you are. I want to feel it inside me when we make love. I want you to give yourself!"

"Just words, Lindsey? You want me to tell you I love you? I do. I've never loved another woman."

"Thank you for the impassioned speech." She swung her feet over the side of the bed. If there was a response to her sarcasm she couldn't see it. She cut him from her vision as surely as he had cut her from his heart.

"What you want isn't possible. You're demanding the impossible."

"I see couples, old couples, sometimes. Hand in hand. They walk slowly together, like each of them knows exactly where the other one will step. The woman stops to pick a flower, but before she does, the man slows for her. He knows what she's going to do even before she does. He's been there for her for so many years." Her words caught on a sob. She felt his arms circle her, but she pushed him away. "Maybe what I want *is* impossible. Maybe I'm crazy to think I deserve that kind of devotion."

"You're ill. You're vulnerable."

"And you're rationalizing. Don't you see? Nothing's changed! Why did we let ourselves in for this? I don't need this kind of pain, and neither do you."

"Then stop causing it."

"I'd like you to leave."

She felt his weight leave the bed. She didn't watch as he dressed. She pulled on her jumpsuit, carefully avoiding him.

"I'll leave," he said. "And we'll be right back where we were before I came here tonight."

"We're already there. We made a mistake. Just go."

"I'll go. You figure out how happy it makes you. But don't make the mistake of thinking it's what I want, too."

He stood in front of her, fully dressed. She could no

longer avoid looking at him. "If you know what you want," she said, "then you're the only one who does."

"I want you. I want our marriage."

"You want a wife to live with and a family to come home to on those rare occasions when you bother. You don't want me. You want somebody who can express all the feelings you don't have. You want somebody to be warm when you can't be."

His eyes were not shut now. They were filled with emotion. And she was no more sure of how to read it than she had ever been. "Tell me if I'm wrong," she begged. "Show me somehow!"

For a moment she thought he was going to reach out to her. She was ready, foolishly, to go back into his arms. Then he turned abruptly and left the room.

She reached the window more by feel than sight. Nearly blinded by tears, she stood there and listened as his car pulled away. As the sound of his engine faded, she knew what it felt like to die and still live.

She rested her cheek against the glass and clutched her chest. The house was so still. She couldn't bear the awful silence. She imagined she could hear her heartbeat, an erratic pounding that filled her head until she was afraid it would explode.

She had to leave. She stumbled to the dresser and pulled a comb through her hair. There was only one place to go, one person who might understand.

Outside, moonlight illuminated the lane between her house and Alden's. The evening was warm, but she shivered as a breeze played over her bare arms. Halfway there she wondered if she would make it. Her feet were leaden, and her head ached unbearably. She had no tears left, but the emptiness that had taken their place was worse.

When she had almost reached Alden's house she was suddenly unable to go on. She sank to a boulder beside the road and rested her head in her hands. She was growing increasingly dizzy, and she wondered if some passerby would find her in the morning, as she had been found in May. But there were no colored lights in the sky tonight, no feeling of well-being, no unearthly music or perfect communion with strangers from another world. There was only the absence of communion with the person she loved most and an emptiness that threatened to destroy her.

After a while she realized there were no night sounds, or at least she couldn't hear them over the roaring in her ears. There were no crickets, no calls of nocturnal birds. Even the forest was still, as if all the tiny animals who lived there were waiting for something, too.

She lifted her head, afraid to take another breath, afraid to disrupt the moment.

And then the music began. Clusters of notes, soft and inviting. Notes that could hardly be called notes. Music that deserved to be called by some word more magnificent. The roaring in her head disappeared, filled by the weaving of note with note, instrument with instrument. She stood, and the dizziness subsided. She started toward the music, following the path to Alden's house. At the edge of his yard she paused and listened, awestruck.

Music seemed to swell the walls of the little cottage. And light, light in radiant colors whose names she didn't know, shone through its windows. She gazed at the gate on the fence around Alden's garden, and the design was suddenly familiar. She had seen it before, on another night. Seen it in a more intricate form, a design on the body of a space-craft. She managed to raise her eyes to the night sky, but there were only stars above her.

Slowly she lowered her eyes to the sounds and sights of the cottage. Alden stood on the front porch bathed in colored light. She knew it was him, although she couldn't see his face. She could only see the outline of his form. She wasn't afraid. She was entranced.

"Lindsey."

She heard his voice over the music. Clearly. She lifted her foot, but she was already being drawn toward him. She felt no fear. She glided over the space between them until she was in his arms.

Chapter 11

There were lights on in his attorney's cottage when Stefan returned the Peugeot. Frank Barnes—twice divorced himself—was a hardheaded, workaholic success story. Christened Francis Barniak by immigrant parents who sold kielbasa and pierogies at a market in Chicago, Frank had long ago distanced himself from his ethnic heritage and the wide circle of relatives who wouldn't let him forget his roots. A judge had given him his new name, and the air force had given him an education. Out of the service and law school, he had risen quickly to the top of one of Cleveland's finest firms.

Stefan didn't really like Frank; there wasn't much about the man that was still there to like or dislike. He was all business; he rarely did anything that wasn't calculated to accelerate his climb up the social or professional ladder. When he had offered Stefan the use of his island cottage, Stefan had realized it was because Frank wanted Stefan to recommend him to other physicians at the hospital. Since Stefan had never had any qualms about recommending

Frank—there was no sharper attorney practicing law in the city—the arrangement suited them both.

Now Stefan considered parking the Peugeot and heading straight for the landing to catch the last ferry off the island. He didn't want to talk to Frank. Especially not now. He was raw from his encounter with Lindsey, raw, confused and angry. There was no reason to discuss her with Frank. He knew Frank's opinions of women. He was rarely called on to represent one. Most women seeking a divorce recognized something of the man they were leaving in Frank and sought counsel elsewhere.

Still, Stefan knew that Frank would have seen that the Peugeot was gone. No matter how he felt, he had to return the keys and pay his respects. Whatever Frank's motivation, volunteering his cottage for Stefan's use had been helpful.

Frank was in the kitchen when Stefan entered. He was a short man, barrel-chested and balding. His shirt and knee-length shorts were such resort wear perfection that Stefan expected to see price tags. Like Stefan, Frank had little use for leisure time.

"I see you're back." Frank held up a beer in invitation. "Caught up with Lindsey and the kids?"

Stefan didn't know how to answer that honestly. He doubted it would ever be possible to catch up with Lindsey. She was a shooting star, blazing through his life to leave sparks and memories of glory before she burned up in the earth's atmosphere. Blazing through his life to demand the impossible.

He reached for the beer reluctantly. "Lindsey's ill. I came to check on her."

"She doesn't have a doctor of her own?"

"She didn't call me. I heard from my son."

"She's not much trouble, is she? Seems like I hear from one ex or the other every week. They need this, they need that. Never seem to think I give them enough child support or alimony."

"Do you?"

Frank laughed. "Oh, I could live on what I give them. But if they worked, they'd have plenty more. Neither of them wants to lift a finger. I guess I just married the wrong women."

"What would the right one have been like?"

"Lindsey, maybe."

The thought of Lindsey with someone like Frank unnerved Stefan. "You hardly know her."

Frank lifted a half-full bottle of beer to his mouth. He finished it before he spoke. "I get the impression that you hardly know her, either."

"What does that mean?"

Frank shrugged and held up the empty bottle. "I've had too many of these tonight."

"And I probably haven't had enough."

"Since I've had so many, I'll tell you. Then we can both say it's just the alcohol talking."

Stefan prepared with a long swallow. "Go ahead."

"There was a girl I knew when I was growing up. Marinna. Her parents sold baked goods at the market where mine sold sausages. She was a pretty thing, blond, round and rosy, and eyes so blue...well. Her parents spoke Polish at home, and she spoke it when she was with them. Sometimes she wore clothes that her grandparents sent from the old country, you know, the kind with the embroidery here, and here." His hand swept from his neck to his knees. "She always smelled like cinnamon and vanilla, like something delicious right out of her father's display cases. She went to church for every feast day and twice on Sunday, and she knew how to dance all the old dances and sing the old songs."

Despite himself, Stefan was interested. "Go on."

"I loved her, but I was ashamed of her. She was perfectly, effortlessly happy. Do you know what I mean?"

Stefan shrugged, although he knew exactly what Frank meant.

"Living was what mattered to her. Taking bread out of the oven and cutting the first slice. Laughing. Praying. Eating. Kissing her was like kissing sunshine and fresh air, all the good things in life. But I wanted more than good things. I wanted everything.''

"What happened to her?''

"She married someone else after I broke her heart. A grocer. She has kids, a pack of them, of course. Once I went to the old church on Christmas Eve when I was back in Chicago and saw them with her. They were all blond, like her. On the way out the door I saw one of the boys take his father's hand.'' He paused. "My kids take money. That's as close as they want to get.''

"I gather you wish you'd married her.''

Frank turned his back to open the refrigerator for another beer. He seemed to search longer than necessary. "I would have dragged her with me, wherever I went. She would have gone, too. She wouldn't have been as smart as your Lindsey. She wouldn't have known when to let go. She would have kept trying and trying....''

"Trying?''

"To make me something I'm not. See, I wasn't ever the person she thought I was. I wasn't good or kind. I wanted to use that soft, plump body, and I didn't want the woman living inside.''

"Maybe you're kinder than you thought.'' Stefan remembered the night he and Lindsey had first made love. In the restaurant garden she had warned him about their differences, but he hadn't been as kind as Frank. He had taken what he wanted.

Frank shut the door and faced Stefan. "Marinna would talk to me, and it was like she was talking on another frequency, one my radio couldn't pick up. Your Lindsey talks on the same frequency.''

"My Lindsey.'' Stefan shook his head.

"But there's a difference between you and me. I couldn't tune in Marinna's station. You don't want to tune in Lindsey's.''

"Aren't you carrying the analogy a little far?''

"Sorry. Juries love that kind of thing."

"What makes you think I don't want to...tune in Lindsey's station?"

"I held your hand during the divorce. Remember? And I watched her try to talk to you. Over the years I've gotten good at listening to people talk. I can hear what they're really saying. I have to, or I'd lose every case I take on. You didn't want to listen to her. I don't know why, but you didn't."

"I listened."

"No. I don't buy that. If you'd listened, you wouldn't have gotten a divorce. You loved her. She loved you. Now you're both using this UFO thing as an excuse to be together."

"The UFO thing, as you put it, is more to Lindsey than an excuse to see me."

"I'm not saying she invented it for that purpose. But it has brought you back together. Maybe she was so lonely she transformed something with a perfectly rational explanation into a UFO sighting. Maybe she got something from that experience that she never got from you."

"Like?"

"Communication? Attention?"

"Now you're a psychologist?"

"Any attorney who wants to go places has to be."

"If there was an alien culture trying to make contact with us, they'd do it through somebody like Lindsey."

"Because she's a flake?"

"Because she's open to anything and everything. Because she listens more than she talks."

"Not like me, huh?"

Stefan had thought he didn't really like Frank. Now he realized he was changing his mind. "Not exactly." He finished his beer.

"Are you saying you think she really saw a UFO?"

He didn't think so. But he couldn't bring himself to say

Lindsey was a lunatic or a liar, not even to Frank, who dealt respectfully with both on a day to day basis. "Who better?"

"Sorry, but I think you're the alien in her life. The two of you are from different planets. And you don't speak the same language."

Stefan thought of the evening past, of perfect lovemaking that had ended in ashes. "I try."

Frank smiled. It was that special smile men saved for each other, a smile that said, "I've been there, too, buddy, and it ain't no fun."

"Go ahead and get whatever it is off your chest," Stefan said.

Frank shrugged. "Okay, I will, but you're not going to like it. I'm sorry, but I don't believe a word you've said. I can't shake the feeling that not only don't you speak Lindsey's language, you don't want to hear a translation."

The music was softer now, a melodious, bubbling waterfall of sound. The lights were dimmer, nothing more than a pastel haze of color illuminating Alden's living room. Alden lifted his hands and swept them gracefully from left to right. The music grew softer still.

"Who are you?" Lindsey asked. She had stood in his arms on the porch, and the interval had been timeless. She didn't know if it was now the same evening or a century hence. They hadn't spoken. She had been bathed in the light and music and in his total acceptance. Then he had brought her inside.

"You know who I am."

"I know you're not from this world."

"No."

"And you were on the ship that I saw, the spaceship."

"Do you remember?"

"I think so. But you weren't...you didn't..."

"Have a body?"

"No."

"I still don't. Not as you know it. Our race evolved beyond the need for solid form and oxygen a hundred millennia—by your measure of time—ago.''

"But I can feel you when you touch me."

"But I can't feel you, not exactly as you feel me. I can see you, because we still have that ability when we transform to this state.''

"You seem human."

"To you, perhaps. Not to your dog."

"Kong? That's why he's always so furious when he sees you?"

"He can't sense me or smell me. So when I pop into his line of vision, he's enraged. He knows he's been tricked. These animals you keep on this planet, they're much smarter than you humans give them credit for.''

"Can you taste?"

"Ah, you sensed that problem all along, didn't you?"

She smiled at him. She was sitting in a summer cottage with a being from another world, and she felt as if she had known him forever. "If you visit earth again, don't come as a chef.''

"Lindsey." He took her hand. His was as warm as any human's. The expression in his eyes was warmer. "How do you feel?''

"I don't know. Are you really a physician?''

"A physician in my world means something very different than in yours. We have no bodies to heal, but even in our usual form, we can be…ill?'' He shook his head. "I don't like that word. Off center? Outside the light? You have no expression that comes close enough. But yes, I am a physician. I heal in a way that doesn't compare to anything you know.''

"Why are you here? Why are you back on the island?" She searched her memory as he sat quietly beside her. The night in May was becoming clearer and clearer. "You weren't supposed to be here at all, were you? Landing here was an accident. There was some malfunction on your craft.…''

"Yes."

"And I wasn't supposed to witness the landing. No one was."

"Our tracking system malfunctioned, too. There was no reading of human life on this end of the island. We wouldn't have landed here if they'd functioned correctly."

"First you asked me to return with you. Then, when I refused, you asked my permission to help me forget everything I'd learned while I was with you."

"You were a wonderful surprise. We've encountered others who breathe, humans, as you call yourselves—sometimes on purpose, sometimes accidentally. They were not receptive. They were too frightened to see that we wouldn't harm them. Except the children. Children always understand."

"What happened to the others?"

"They forget. Willingly and totally. They wake up and think they've had a strange dream, then they go on with their lives. You were supposed to forget, too. And you tried. We know you did. But your consciousness is too developed to be overruled that way."

"Is that why you came back? Because I failed to forget?"

"Not exactly."

Somehow she knew he would reveal his purpose when she was ready to hear it. He seemed to be slowly leading her toward an answer. "Is your name really Alden?"

"No. Our study of English turned up thousands of useful names. Alden comes from your old language. It means wise protector."

"Protector?"

"The name I was given at formation was—" He uttered a string of sounds that she knew she could never hope to duplicate. "Of course, it sounds different when it's spoken without vocal cords, as it is at home. But you can see why I became Alden here."

"And Fitzpatrick?"

He smiled. "One of us saw it on a sign in front of a

house. That's a curious concept, isn't it? Selling a house. We own nothing, so we can't sell what we don't own. I had to study hard to understand how to rent this cottage."

"Why do your people come here at all?"

"We come periodically to see if you have need of us yet. We have much to offer, but only when you're ready to receive it.

"Are we ready now? Is that why you came back to the island?"

"Not nearly. First you have to learn to be at peace with each other. You have to take care of your children and your old people. You must stop destroying the earth."

"I'm afraid you missed your chance. You should have come in the sixties."

"We'll have a chance. But it seems that it's taking longer than it should."

"Many people would agree with that."

"You among them."

"Yes." She took a deep breath. She could almost feel the colors and the music in her lungs. Everything else was drifting away, the pain in her head, the agony in her heart. For the first time since she had awakened by the roadside and been taken to the hospital, she had not the tiniest doubt about her sanity. She only wished that she could share this with Stefan, that he could be here beside her listening to Alden.

"I should have recognized you," she said.

"In a way you did. You were suspicious immediately, although you didn't quite make the connection."

"Were you in our cottage before we got there? Mandy told me someone had been inside..."

"I had to learn everything I could about the way you lived. Objects communicate much to us. They've been handled, imbued with something of the persons touching them. And I had to be familiar with human things. I understood most of what I saw, but the toys confused me."

"Toys? Geoff's basketball? He said it had lost all its air."

"With a little help, I'm afraid."

"And it wasn't mice that attacked the stuffing in Mandy's bunny?"

"Attacked would not be my word choice."

"I thought it was Mandy's imagination."

"She's very observant, remarkably so. She would quickly learn everything we know if she was given the chance."

"And will she be?"

"I wish it could be so."

"But it can't?"

He shook his head. "She'd have to come with us. And it's against all the principles we live by to take someone from their home unless we must. Mandy will be needed here. This world needs her talents more than we do. She'll make great contributions, and so will Geoff."

"Geoff, too?"

"But you sensed that already."

"I've always suspected it." There seemed to be too much to comprehend all at once. Restlessly she walked to the edge of the room, toward the light. It seemed to come from nowhere. She couldn't detect its source. "Alden, if you're not here to take anyone back with you or to stay and help us, what does that leave?"

"Place yourself back in time. To the night we first met."

She let her mind drift. There had been a moment of fear when she'd seen the lights falling toward earth and heard the music. But the moment had quickly given way to excitement. By the time she'd been drawn toward the ship, she had been more than willing to go. She had known unequivocally that she wouldn't be hurt.

"I was welcomed," she said. "I felt as if I knew you, all of you. I was examined…" She paused and looked at him. "You examined me."

"That's right."

"In the UFO abduction stories I've read about since then, little rat-faced aliens probe and poke and terrify the people they've kidnapped."

He laughed. "Rat-faced? Different aliens, obviously."

"Are those stories true?"

"There's life throughout the universe. It's absolute arrogance to believe otherwise. And our race hasn't yet encountered all life forms."

"You examined me to...to see if I'd been hurt!" She looked at him. "I remember now. You were concerned. You hadn't expected to find life here. There were problems with your ship. Some type of shield, a screening device, wasn't fully operational. There was some fear that I might be affected, changed physically by our encounter."

Alden let the new memory ripen before he spoke. "And part of the reason you remember that now is because you *were* changed, Lindsey. Your own mind and your own powers are strong, too strong to be fooled by our suggestion that you forget what happened. But you also evolved that night, both from the things you witnessed and the physical realities of coming in contact with our ship when the screens weren't working properly."

"Evolved?"

"Your body suffered a severe shock."

"The headaches? Dizziness?"

He nodded. "We were afraid you might not recover, particularly when we saw that you remained unconscious for such a long time after we left you. You were supposed to wake up soon after we were no longer visible, but you didn't. So I was sent here to watch over you."

"Wise protector." Now she understood the meaning of his name.

"I hoped I could protect you."

"You protected Geoff. You saved him from drowning. Mandy said you flew through the water. Did you?"

"In a manner of speaking."

"And the way you twisted him to get him breathing again?"

"That comes from the medical history of your own race. I've read everything your people have set down on paper through the ages. Do you know how much knowledge has been lost on this planet simply because it's no longer fashionable? Every culture has pockets of great wisdom. Then, as people become more educated in traditional Western medical opinion, they throw away what they know.''

"Why have you studied so extensively? Do your people need help?"

"I've studied to help you."

She couldn't be afraid with the pastel light pulsating around her. But she was no less aware of frightening things, even if she didn't feel fear. "Do I need help?" she asked. "Are the headaches going to get worse?"

"That will be the least of it."

"And the most?"

"Death."

"Soon?"

"Much too soon." He moved to her side and took her hand.

She raised it to her cheek to comfort him. "It's not your fault, Alden."

"No one intentionally caused you harm."

"Have you learned anything in your study that will help me?"

"We can help."

Strangely, she hadn't been afraid or even sad when he'd talked about her death. But now she was filled with relief. She wouldn't be leaving the children to grow up without her. And she wouldn't be leaving Stefan.

She said his name out loud before she'd even planned to speak. Despite everything, she knew in that moment that she never wanted to leave Stefan. It was a revelation, a blinding flash of truth beyond wishing he were different, beyond hoping he would change. Beyond anger.

"He's a very good doctor," Alden said. "Already one of the best in this country. Someday, he'll be one of the best in the world."

"How do you know?"

"I can see what's in a mind."

"Can you? That's not an altogether comforting thought."

"But only if it's necessary. We believe strongly in privacy."

"How can you help me?"

"First, tell me why you don't want to leave the children and Stefan."

She found the question strange. "Don't you miss your loved ones when you're away from them?"

"But I never am. They are with me."

She could feel the truth in what he was saying, but the concept was beyond conscious human thought. "My family is with me, too, in a way. Memories, feelings. But that's not the same as having them where I can touch them and see them."

"I think perhaps we lost something important when we evolved beyond touch."

"I think perhaps you did."

"You won't be able to touch them if I help you."

She contemplated that. Now fear was beginning to seep through the light, the music and Alden's enveloping warmth. "What do you mean?"

"There is only so much I can understand from study. Much of what we once knew about humanoid form has been erased from our memories as useless. I've never had experience, none of us has, with healing a human body. If the things that are not right in your body were traditional human illnesses, we could cure you. We could find a record somewhere, a chapter, a sentence, that would help us understand. We could devise a treatment based on what we read."

"But what's happening isn't traditional?"

"There's a deterioration of cells, of nerve pathways, of your vascular system. It's like no recorded human disease. You see, it's the first step toward evolving beyond your body. But because you aren't ready, it will be deadly."

"Then how can you help?"

"We can make you ready for the evolution. We can take

you with us, teach you what you have to learn, expose you to things you have to see. Then you'll be ready, and the process won't be fatal. You'll become like one of us. You will *be* one of us. You'll live with us, work with us—''

"But you said it was against all your principles to take someone from their home!"

"We caused this problem. We are allowed, in this circumstance, to take the necessary measures to cure the problem we created."

"But my children, Stefan—"

"Can't come. Think a moment. How fair would it be to take them away from everything they know? How fair would it be to take them from a planet that needs them? They're already part of history. Stefan will—" He stopped.

"Will what?"

"Will help your race evolve."

"Stefan will change history somehow?"

He only smiled.

"You won't tell me more?"

He shook his head.

"But I can't go without them!"

"Of course, we would never insist."

An idea struck her. "Could I go, be cured and return? You have a body. Couldn't I transform again after I'm cured?"

"Earth as you know it would no longer exist," he said gently. "Your family would be long dead, Lindsey. Time would not stand still while you were away."

"Are you sure I'm going to die? You said yourself that you lack experience with humans. Are you sure?"

"As sure as I can be. If there was some way that I could absorb all the experience, the human intuition, I have no access to, maybe I could tell you absolutely. But I can't do that. I can only read and make a calculated guess. Your husband—"

"Stefan? Could he help if he understood?"

"Perhaps. But I'm not certain he could understand.

There's a strong flow of—'' He paused, then he uttered another of the words, like his name, made of sounds she didn't know how to form. "I'm sorry," he said in English. "There's just no translation. It's the principle that guides us, that teaches us, that acquaints us with all we can't see. Your husband possesses a large measure of it, but he is terrified to use it."

"Love," she said.

"As close as any word in your language."

Tears sprang to her eyes. "Frightened? Why?"

"I don't know why. Perhaps he's afraid of surprises or the unknown."

"But he wants to know everything."

"Everything he can see, and nothing he can't."

She stood and moved to the window. "I can't leave him. I can't leave my children."

"You will leave them when you die."

"You don't understand, do you? I don't want to live without them."

"I don't understand," he admitted.

"This principle that guides you, this—" She tried to utter the word as he had and failed.

"Thank you for trying," he said.

"Love! Haven't you ever loved anyone or anything so much that you couldn't bear to be separated from it? Wouldn't you give your life for someone or something?"

"Certainly I'd give my life. But only if there was a purpose. You will give yours without one."

"But I don't want to live without my family. If I really am going to die—and I'm not convinced I am—whatever days are left to me here can be spent with them."

"This is something I can't understand."

"I don't want to evolve to your level, then. I think in this we're the ones closer to—" This time she made the sounds more coherently.

"I think I'd like to feel as strongly about it as you do."

"No, you probably wouldn't."

She felt his hands on her arms. There wasn't anything provocative about his touch; there never had been. He seemed to melt into her in perfect accord with her thoughts and feelings. She was simultaneously warmed by his presence and frightened. This was what she would have if she chose to save her own life. And how different it was from what she had with Stefan. This was love, too, love as Alden understood it.

It was not the love she understood. Not the love she wanted. She wanted this perfect understanding with Stefan, not Alden, but she wanted it locked together with the passion, the intensity of emotion, she had always felt for him.

"I can't leave them," she choked out.

"You have time to decide."

"How long?"

"I don't know exactly. We'll be able to tell by your symptoms."

"Then you'll stay here with me? You'll wait?"

"I'll stay as long as I'm needed. I can make you more comfortable, as I did today."

She turned to him. He put his arms around her and held her close.

His comfort was infinite.

She wished, with all her heart, that it was Stefan holding her.

Chapter 12

Stefan had chosen his apartment because it was only five minutes from the hospital. It was one of four in a solid, unpretentious stone building owned by another physician. Someday Stefan planned to buy a house, but in the past year he hadn't even browsed through the classifieds. Home was still a Cape Cod style cottage with a plant-adorned front porch in Rocky River, and until that irrational feeling disappeared, there was no point in house hunting.

After the divorce, Carol, the nurse-practitioner who worked at his side, had chosen furniture at his request. He had drummed up some color preferences, and she had done the best she could. But neither of them had possessed much enthusiasm for the task. The only things of interest inside the apartment walls were framed samples of Mandy's and Geoff's art work that Lindsey had given him for Christmas.

On a Saturday morning two weeks after his last trip to Kelleys Island, Stefan stood sipping his coffee in front of a crayon portrait of a bear that Mandy had drawn when she was three. The apartment still smelled of last night's dinner.

He had made his chicken paprikash for a friend, the ex-wife of a colleague. Ellen had recently been cast aside for a younger, more adoring patient of her husband's, and she was still hurting. Stefan had run into her by accident at the grocery store, and they had gone for a drink together. The drink had turned into two, then dinner here.

And if either of them had wanted it to turn into more, neither of them had been able to make it happen.

He had thought he wanted Ellen. He had wanted someone to wipe away the feel of Lindsey's body, someone to drown the fragrance of her skin, cool the lingering warmth where she had lain against him. But Ellen, with her black curls and million-dollar smile, wasn't the woman, because no one could be. They had parted with unspoken regret, and he hadn't gotten her phone number.

He stared at Mandy's bear and imagined it speaking to him. Grow up, it insisted. Be a man if you can't be a bear. Put the past behind you and forge a future.

No advice on just how to do it was forthcoming.

In the operating room he was God. He didn't believe in his own omnipotence; that sort of arrogance could prove fatal to a surgeon's career. But when he performed surgery he held life and death in his hands, and no one asked him how he was feeling. What did feelings matter, after all, compared to the slip of a hand or a lapse in concentration? What mattered was what he did, not what he felt.

Now it seemed all he could do was feel, waves of anonymous emotion surging over the dikes that had always restrained them. Waves washing away logic and concentration and the little peace of mind he'd attained since the divorce. There had been no peace since Lindsey had sent him away once again, and no real hope of finding any.

He heard footsteps on the stairs and the laughter of children. He told himself that everything was going to be fine this morning. Lindsey probably didn't want to see him and wouldn't be accompanying Geoff and Mandy to the door. He had maintained a careful distance on the telephone when he called to tell her he wanted the children for the weekend. She had volunteered to bring them herself, assuring him that she had things to do in town anyway. But there had been nothing personal in their conversation. He imagined that she had wanted to get off the telephone as quickly as he did.

The front door buzzer sounded, and he abandoned Mandy's bear for the child herself. He lifted her and hugged her close, breathing in the smell of floral shampoo and little girl. With his free arm he reached out for Geoff and saw Geoff's mother.

"Hello, Stefan."

For a moment he didn't know what to say. He nodded and turned his attention to his son, but his throat was dry. He listened to the babble of both children, sorting, responding, praising. He couldn't seem to put Mandy down, and Geoff was hopelessly clamped to his side in an embrace that was making him squirm.

Only when the children demanded to go inside and see what was new did he detach himself. Lindsey stood four feet away, watching him.

"I didn't expect to see you," he said.

"Why? I told you I was bringing them."

"I know. But I expected you to drop them off."

"Did you?" She was wearing pink, a dusky, feminine hue that at one time might have highlighted the rose and cream of her complexion. But today she was pale. Much too pale.

He stepped aside. Politeness dictated his question. "Would you like to come in?"

"That would be nice."

He was as surprised as he had been when he saw her. "All right. I've made coffee. Would you like some?"

"Yes, thanks."

As he followed her to the kitchen, he watched the way she moved. She drifted instead of danced. There was something about the way she held her head that told him it ached.

In the kitchen she sat immediately, as if the short walk

had tired her. He poured her coffee and warned himself that he had no right to worry about her.

"Are you all right?" He sat across from her at the tiny wooden table. His warnings had been nothing more than an exercise. He leaned toward her. "Are you?"

"I don't think so, Stefan."

He heard the children whooping from their bedroom. He had bought them each presents, and he knew they had found them. In a moment they would be in the kitchen to show their mother.

He started to cover her hand, then thought better of it. "What is it?"

"I think you'd better have a look at me."

Two weeks had passed. Two, and his pride had stopped him from calling and checking to see if she was feeling any better. Now shame filled him. "Same symptoms?" he asked.

"Same, but worse."

"Have you seen a doctor?"

She smiled a little. "Alden. Have a good weekend with the children, Stefan. Don't worry about me. I'll come to your office on Monday. That will be soon enough. But Geoff and Mandy need this time with you. You've...you've got to get to know them."

His hand danced restlessly along the table edge. "Just what does Alden say?"

"He says that I should see a specialist. You, preferably."

He didn't have time to probe any deeper. Geoff came in to show his mother the wood carving tools Stefan had bought him. Mandy was right behind with a doctor's bag that made the instruments in Stefan's look antique.

Mandy demanded orange juice; Geoff demanded milk. Stefan was glad to have something to do while they showed their mother their treasures. He found glasses he had bought just for them, whimsical cartoon characters he had seen one lonely afternoon when there hadn't been enough work to keep him busy.

He turned away from the cabinet and saw Lindsey lift a scarf from the floor. It was silk, with black and hot pink geometric designs that had suited Ellen's vibrant coloring. He remembered her removing it with a laugh last night. The scarf was new. She hadn't wanted to risk spilling one drop of the paprikash on it.

He watched Lindsey examine the scarf, pull it idly through her fingers as if she were learning about its owner from the feel of the silk. She lifted it to her face as if to investigate the scent of Ellen's perfume.

Something surprisingly like shame filled him, although he had nothing to be ashamed of. He was divorced, and Lindsey had made it clear that she didn't want him back. Words leapt to his tongue to explain, but he suppressed them. An explanation would embarrass them both.

When he returned from the refrigerator, she had neatly folded the scarf and placed it on the table against the wall.

She was preparing to leave before they were alone again. He told himself he needed to know where she would be in case of an emergency. "Are you going back to the island?"

She shook her head. "I want to spend the weekend at the house. There's business I have to take care of, and I—"

"What?"

"I don't know. I just want to be there and make sure everything's all right."

Her explanation made him uneasy. "Isn't Mrs. Charles taking care of things while you're away?"

"It probably sounds silly, but I just want to go home. I want to sleep in my own bed again."

"Did anything happen on the island?"

"I saw lights in the sky and my life changed."

"You know I mean recently."

"If you can't believe that, what would you believe?" She smiled gently and touched his cheek.

He was surprised. Her fingers were electric. Anger—at himself, at her—followed swiftly. He stepped away, and her hand fell to her side.

"I'm sorry," she said.

"And I'm sorry you're ill. But don't use it as an excuse to change your mind about us again. Maybe you think I don't have any feelings, but I damned well do."

"You're angry."

"Did you expect something else?"

"It's a start, isn't it?"

"No. It's a finish."

"I didn't touch you to make you angry. I touched you because I needed to."

He felt her words inside him. Funny that words could feel like both a slap and a caress.

He pretended to ignore them. "Shall I drop Geoff and Mandy at the house on Sunday night?"

"Please. Shall I come to your office on Monday? Or shall I find another doctor?"

"Come. I'll set you up for a complete exam."

"There's so very little we know. We think we understand...everything. And we understand nothing." She turned away.

"Come early. Plan to spend the night in the hospital. I'll make the arrangements today. The children can stay with my mother."

She didn't argue. She just drifted toward the stairs and left him filled with emotions that were larger than he was.

The house in Rocky River was dust-free, and the plants freshly watered. Lindsey walked through it, smoothing her fingertips along mantels and walls. She held a pillow—Mandy's first needlepoint—against her cheek; she caressed the fading sea serpent that Geoff had fashioned of papier-mâché.

The house and all its memories were so dear. She gazed into corners and saw Mandy's first steps and Geoff's tears over a broken toy. She could smell the pine and peppermint fragrances of Christmas, the cardamon-flavored Easter bread that was Hilda's specialty, the first roses of summer. She could feel the warmth of childish arms around her neck and hear the melody of laughter.

And she could sense Stefan's presence. The year he had been away had done nothing to diminish his place here. The sofa, his special place on the left, still held the imprint of his body. She had resisted reupholstering it when she had redone the rest of the room; now she understood why.

There, beside the front door, was the table where he always threw his gloves and hat in the winter. And behind her were the stairs he had once carried her up in an uncharacteristic fit of Rhett Butler impatience.

Two weeks had passed since she'd been sentenced to death. Two weeks of the rest of whatever life was left to her. It had taken her those two weeks to come to terms with Alden's news. She had needed more time—anyone would have—but time spent adjusting was time she couldn't spend with the people she loved. That time was so short now that she couldn't let it be any shorter. How had she believed for all those years that her life would be unending? How could she have deluded herself into believing that she wanted to spend any of it away from the man she loved? Or let something as nebulous as pride and self-pity steal any of the days granted to them?

In the kitchen she picked up the shell Stefan had found for her that long-ago night in Key West. It had maintained a place of honor on the windowsill by the sink since the day they had moved into this house. After Stefan moved out she had not parted with any memories. She had consciously held on to pieces of him. Despite the lies she had told herself, she had hoped he would change.

But now she knew that changing Stefan was not only beyond her power, it was unthinkable to try. He was not a piece of clay to mold. He was nothing more nor less than the man she had married, a man with faults and a man with strengths. Why and when had the first become so important that she had failed to appreciate the last?

She held the shell to her chest. For a moment the light in

the room seemed to swirl in shades of purple. She swayed
and reached out to steady herself against the counter. The
shell fell and shattered at her feet.

"Stefan!"

He was no longer there to hear her cry. She had asked
him to leave their house and leave her life. But she had
never wanted him to go.

Who, of the two of them, had failed to reveal true feelings?

Lindsey had furnished Stefan's offices herself. They were
tucked inside the hospital building, at the end of a seemingly
endless corridor. But the view from his windows made up
for the inconvenient location. Instead of a parking lot, his
wing looked over the parklike grounds and a small pond
where young patients and their families sometimes fed the
ducks.

She had taken her color scheme from the newest residents
of the pond. The walls were a warm ivory, the curtains a
deeper yellow. Audubon prints decorated one wall, and on
the other, at a lower eye level, were framed illustrations of
the classic children's book, *Make Way for Ducklings*.

Today she found little comforting about the room. Even
the matched set of decoys perched on the reception counter
seemed merely lifeless. She wanted to be outside feeding
the real things, stroking their feathers. She did not want to
be here.

Carol had come to greet her, and Stefan's receptionist had
been more than cordial, but she still felt ill at ease. It wasn't
like Stefan to make anyone wait. No matter his own stature,
he treated others as if they were just as important. But she
was waiting. Her watch told her she'd only been there
twenty-five minutes, but she felt as if it had been hours.

For the first time since she'd left his apartment on Saturday she allowed herself to think about the scarf she had
found on the floor. Who was the woman it belonged to, and
what was she to Stefan? She knew it couldn't be a long-

term relationship; he had told her there had been no one since the divorce, and she had no reason not to believe him. But that was before she had thrust him out of her life and bed once more. Had he finally conquered the feeling that they were still married? Was another woman now the solution to the empty space in his life?

He deserved to have that space filled. Sometime in the near future there was going to be a permanent space that she herself could never fill again. She was going to die, and he was going to live. When she was gone he deserved more than lonely days of longing for the impossible. He deserved warmth and love. She wanted that for him.

But not while she was still alive to witness it.

The door opened, and Stefan entered from the hallway. No one had told her he hadn't been in the office. Relief was only one of the emotions that ran through her at the sight of him. His gaze swept the room until he found her. He smiled at the other patients and exchanged a few words with an old man in the corner; then he gestured for her to follow him.

He took her straight to his private office and closed the door. He had dropped the children at the house last night without getting out of the car; now she searched his face for some clue to his feelings.

"Carol's going to do a routine physical," he said. "If she finds anything worth noting immediately, she'll call me. Otherwise, she'll take you over to the hospital and help you settle in. You have a private room on the second floor. I've already given my mother your telephone number, so the children can call you when you're not having tests. I know you'll be worried about them."

She thought of all the years of their lives when the children wouldn't be able to call her. "I'm sure they'll be fine. They need to know their grandmother better."

"Do you have any questions?"

"Do you hate me?"

He stared at her. "How can you even ask?"

"I've been wrong about so many things."

"This isn't the time or place for confessions."

"There was never a time or a place like that, was there? There should have been."

"More criticism?"

"No." She leaned forward. For a moment shifting her balance made her dizzy. She hesitated, trying to regain her equilibrium.

Stefan sat back. "Look, Lindsey, all I want to think about now is finding out what your problem might be, if you have one. Let's not confuse that with anything else. Doctor to patient while you're here. This will be easier for both of us that way."

She couldn't fault his logic, but she didn't risk a nod. "I'm sorry."

Something passed over his face, something unfamiliar. "Don't apologize."

"That's not allowed either? This might take some getting used to."

"Why? You should be used to not communicating. That's why you said you left me."

She stared at him, effectively cut off from an answer. "Will you talk to me when we're done here?" she asked at last. "Please, Stefan? I need to talk to you."

His fingers danced along the desktop, but he controlled his expression. "Let's worry about later, later."

"Later..." The word had new meaning for her. "Later is a luxury." She stood slowly as Stefan reached toward his intercom.

"Carol will explain all the tests to you after your exam. Some of them might not seem necessary to you, but—"

"It's all right. I want a complete workup."

His hand paused over the buttons. "No arguments?"

"None."

"Well, good."

She steadied herself on the edge of his desk. "When will I see you?"

"This afternoon, probably. If not, this evening."

"For once I'm glad you work too hard."

He summoned Carol. She watched as they compared notes; then she followed the older woman out of his office. At the door she turned for one more look.

"I don't want you to worry," he said.

She smiled sadly. In the summer sunshine outside his window ducks swam on a sky blue pond. She memorized his casual elegance, the way the ducks glided effortlessly through the water, the excited shouts of a child.

"Thank you," she said. "I know I'm in good hands."

Chapter 13

A herd of residents on their daily rounds thundered by the nurses' station, white coats and pants, ID cards glistening in the artificial glare, stethoscopes dangling around necks thrust forward in anticipation. Stefan barely saw them pass.

"I defer to you, George. You've seen Lindsey's chart. Now you've seen all the test results. What have I missed? What the hell have I missed!"

"Let's find some other place to talk about this."

"Name it."

George LeGrande looked at his watch. "Coffee room."

Stefan followed him to the elevator. Those already on board stepped respectfully to one side as they entered. There was an unspoken hierarchy here, as there was at many hospitals, and Stefan and George were well at the top.

Both men wore light blue scrubs, but the resemblance stopped there. George was in his late fifties, an extroverted, attractive widower who wasn't a surgeon, although he often observed surgery when the patient was his own referral. He was the chief of neurology, and it was George himself who had flown to New York, where Stefan had done his residency, to convince him to join the staff at the Cleveland Neurological Hospital.

Outside the elevator, George stopped to give instructions to a passing nurse while Stefan went ahead. The coffee room was the size of a suburban basement and even less appealing. During the hospital's last cosmetic overhaul, the coffee room had been overlooked or abandoned as hopeless. Worn carpet, battered tables and a coffee machine that dispensed milk and sugar at random were the major attractions. One Christmas a wistful resident had installed a Norfolk Island Pine under the lone window, but no one had ever thought to remove it, even after its demise. Now, occasionally, someone decorated its needleless branches according to the holiday. At the moment it was still dressed in plastic Easter eggs.

Stefan took a table in the corner, sweeping disposable cups into the nearest trash can. He returned with coffee and gestured to George to join him when he arrived.

"First, you've got to calm down," George said. "Whatever we're missing, we're going to keep on missing it unless you get hold of yourself."

Stefan stared at his coffee. "I'm not missing anything because I'm upset."

"You, of all people, should know how little good it does to berate yourself."

"Me, of all people?"

"You're the soul of rational thinking."

Stefan laughed, and the sound was as bitter as the coffee. "All that rational thinking isn't getting me anywhere. I still don't have a clue what Lindsey's problem is."

"You're a step farther than you were a week ago. You're sure she has a problem."

"And if I take each step one week at a time and she continues to deteriorate at the same speed, she'll be dead before I've gotten halfway across the room."

"I can send copies of her records to a couple of people I respect out of state."

"I faxed two friends yesterday. Both called back with a list of disorders I'd already ruled out. I went back to the records. I ordered some more tests. Lindsey was reluctant to come back in, but I insisted. We did an MRI, another lumbar." He picked up his coffee.

"And nothing panned out."

"No."

"She's still here?"

"She's checking out again late this afternoon. I have to talk to her before she goes."

"You've looked at the possibility of parasites? Vitamin deficiencies? Toxic chemicals?"

"You know I have. Neither the X rays nor the blood work points toward any of them." Stefan looked up at George. "There's a doctor summering out on the island, a man named Alden Fitzpatrick. He was the first one to check her over. He called it a deterioration. I berated him. And you know what? We've got hundreds of scientific diagnoses, Latin names, syndromes named after researchers and physicians, and not one description comes as close as that."

"A very swift deterioration."

"Damn it, yes!"

George put his hand on Stefan's arm. "There's a possibility it's a rare type of multiple sclerosis or some kissing cousin, something we just haven't seen before. You could treat it accordingly. Steroids. Hyperbaric oxygen, if you're desperate enough. There's a physician over at the Clinic who's testing a new drug."

"I don't want to use Lindsey as a guinea pig."

"Has she had any more visions? Any additional hallucinations?"

"If she has, she refuses to discuss them."

"I'll confess that the story about the UFO baffles me more than anything else. Hallucinations and delusions don't fit with the rest of the profile. What we could be seeing is a coincidental onslaught of several different conditions.''

''I'd be happy just to isolate one. Just one for a start!''

George sat back. ''You need to take yourself off this case.''

Stefan drank half his coffee and didn't taste a swallow.

George continued when Stefan didn't answer. ''You have your pick of people to take over for you. She doesn't need a surgeon.''

''Are you saying I'm not doing enough? That I'm not good enough?''

''You know that's not my point. You're too close to this. You care too much.''

''No one else will care enough.''

''No one in practice here would do any less for her than you can. It's an insult to your colleagues to suggest otherwise.''

''I'll consult with anybody who has a suggestion to make. But I stay as the physician of record.''

''Why?''

Stefan took a breath and let it out slowly. As slowly and carefully as he might during the most crucial moments of an operation. ''Because someone else might go an extra mile, but I'll run to the ends of the universe to find an answer.''

''You may have to,'' George said. ''Because if there's an answer on God's green earth, at this point I, for one, don't know what it is.''

Lindsey dressed in her street clothes. Stefan had made sure she had a room overlooking the pond, and when she had finished pulling on her shoes she went to stand at the window. She didn't turn when the door opened. She knew who was there. One of the benefits of her illness was a remarkably heightened awareness of what went on around her. She supposed it was preparation for that glorious moment when her body disintegrated completely and left her formless. Only her misinformed body didn't realize that instead of emerging as pure consciousness, similar to Alden, she was simply going to die.

"Lindsey?"

"I'm watching the ducks, Stefan." She turned and smiled, motioning for him to join her.

"There're more than usual this year."

She was pleased he had noticed. "You'll have to bring Mandy and Geoff to feed them when..." She stopped. She hadn't discussed the future with him. Submitting to the endless, sometimes painful tests, had been her way of announcing her impending death in terms he would understand. He would never have believed her if she had just told him she was dying. He had always been a man who needed proof.

Of course, there had also been a fragment of hope that he could do what Alden could not and find a cure, even without an understanding of the origin of the disease. From the look on his face, she knew that had been foolish.

"When they visit me here?" he finished for her. "I'll be taking care of them more frequently while you're ill, to give you time to recover."

"No!" She turned back to the window. "Not that I don't want you to have them. Don't misunderstand. But..." She tried to think of an explanation that didn't have some form of the word death in it.

"But what?"

"I need them with me now."

"How can you care for them? You can hardly stand up on your own."

"I'll be better," she lied. "I'm just weak from all the tests."

"I'm sorry I've had to put you through so many."

"I'm glad you did. You'd hate yourself if you hadn't been thorough enough."

"I'm not planning to hate myself."

"I hope not."

"Why don't you sit down, and we'll talk for a minute."

She knew what he was going to say before he said it. She could hear tension in his voice, even though he was trying hard to sound casual. She wanted to spare him. "Stefan, I know already."

"Know what?"

She could feel him come to attention beside her. She faced him. "That I don't have long to live," she said, still avoiding the word death.

"What makes you say that?"

"A body that's giving up on me."

"Sit down, please."

"If it makes you more comfortable." She crossed the room and perched on the edge of the bed.

He sat beside her. "The tests are inconclusive."

"Which is just a way of saying that you don't know exactly what's wrong, but what you know doesn't please you."

"I'm not pleased," he admitted. "You're sick and getting sicker."

She took his hand, even though she had to lean forward to do so. "I know. It's all right."

"It's not all right." He jerked his hand from hers and stood.

She watched him pace the room, a lion caged and helpless. "I can cope," she said. "Can you?"

"Cope?" He paused, and his brows were a solid, angry line. "You damn well had better not cope. I won't have you coping. It's the same as giving up. You're going to fight. We're going to fight until we figure this out and come up with a treatment."

"You've lost patients, Stefan."

"So?"

"It's not going to be any different this time just because you love me. You can't stop the inevitable."

He stared at her.

"I know you love me," she said. "I was a fool not to believe it, a fool to need proof, or more proof than you wanted to give me. But I'm not a fool now. I don't have time to be foolish. I have to be practical. I'm not going to waste my time on denials or bargaining for time. I don't want you wasting time on them, either. You can't cure me, but you can make me very, very happy while I'm still alive.''

His voice got quieter. "I damn well will cure you."

"Did you hear me?" she asked gently. "There were more important things I said."

He stood perfectly still. "Why now, Lindsey? Why talk about this now? You're not dying. I'm not going to let you. So don't say things you'll regret when the headaches are gone and your blood work is back to normal."

"Should I regret the truth? Let me expand on it, then, so I'll have more to regret. You love me, and I love you. I never stopped, and I never will. You are my soul, the space between my heartbeats, the air I breathe. I can no more change that than I can change what's happening inside me. I tried, and I failed, and I'm glad I did, because loving you was the best thing I've ever done."

"Stop this."

"I don't mean to frighten you." She stood and started toward him. The room spun crazily. She stopped and tried to regain her balance, but he was beside her before she could.

He slipped his arms around her and pulled her against his chest.

"The space between my heartbeats," she whispered.

"Lind...sey."

She had never heard such agony in one word. She shut her eyes and willed herself not to cry.

She demanded to go back to the island. He demanded to go with her and refused to let the children return until the next day, after she'd had a chance to recover a little strength.

On the trip back they sat on an outside bench on the ferry. Lindsey let the wind whip her hair against her cheeks. In the early evening air, with the ferry rocking madly beneath her, she felt very much alive.

Stefan was finishing a story. She guessed he was afraid to let the silence build, afraid of his own thoughts.

"So Mother went into her bathroom last night and found Geoff carving soap with a nail file. She says the sculpture looks just like you."

"Me? How lovely."

"An Ivory soap rendition. She cleaned up all the scraps—"

Lindsey laughed. "And saved them, I'm sure, for her hand laundry." She ended the laugh on a shiver, and he put his arm around her to warm her.

"Are you all right?"

"I'm fine. It's just the wind." She snuggled closer.

"Well, the upshot of the story is that after she cleaned up and lectured him on his sloppiness, she gave in to temptation and tried it herself."

"Hilda? Our Hilda?"

"She says her version looked like meat loaf. I think she has a new respect for Geoff's talents."

"Does she mind taking care of them so much, do you think?"

"No. In fact, I think they give her a much-needed break. If she isn't with them, she's working. They remind her that there's more to living than her books."

"I never wanted to impose on her."

"You never did."

"They'll need her more and more."

His arm tightened around her. "There's no point in thinking what you're thinking. There is an entire array of illnesses with some of the same symptoms you have that just disappear one day and leave patients with nothing more than a little recovery time."

Lindsey pretended he hadn't spoken. "And the children will need you." She put her head on his shoulder and sighed as he gathered her closer. "I'm so glad you've made such a good start with them this summer. They talk about you all the time now, you know.''

"That's funny. When they're with me, they talk about you."

"The divorce was hard on them." She felt him tense.

"Had you expected otherwise?"

"I'm not sure I knew what to expect. I'm not sure anyone ever does."

"It wasn't a boxing match. In a divorce, nobody calls for a clean break, counts points and declares a winner."

"Nobody won. Least of all the children."

"Every morning after I moved out, I'd lie in bed and tell myself I wasn't awake yet, that I was imagining the whole thing. It didn't seem possible. One minute we were married..."

She closed her eyes. "You never told me that."

"Was I supposed to beg?"

"No."

"What did you want, then?"

"You were right the last time we talked about this. I wanted to know you loved me."

"And you thought I could open myself up to you that way, when you were telling me you didn't want me anymore?"

"It was a terrible mistake. A selfish mistake. A desperate mistake."

"Desperate?"

"I needed you. I didn't know what else to do."

He didn't answer, but he didn't move away. She kept her eyes closed; watching the water made her headache worse, and without sight, she could almost imagine herself as one with the man who held her.

When they reached the island she stood reluctantly. Holding tightly to Stefan's hand to steady herself, she navigated the steps to the lower deck where the van was parked and waited wordlessly while Stefan searched his pockets for the keys to her van.

At the cottage he busied himself opening windows. "Are you hungry?"

She hadn't been hungry in weeks. She supposed her body was no longer aware that it needed nourishment. "There's some more soup in the cupboard."

"You need more than canned soup." He went into the kitchen and examined the contents of the refrigerator and cupboards. She sat down at the table to watch. "Pasta and steamed vegetables in cheese sauce," he said when the tour was completed. "Whole wheat rolls and fresh sliced tomatoes."

"You'd do all that for me?"

"I'd do anything for you." He didn't turn from the cupboard when he said the words, and his voice didn't change.

"Then would you take me upstairs and make love to me first?"

He stood very still. Oddly, she thought she could see colors in the room. It was nearly sunset, and the room seemed to be filled with them. The space surrounding her was violet and rose, undulating waves almost like the light in Alden's house. The space around Stefan was darker, denser, a midnight blue, the gray of ashes.

She tasted ashes.

"I made love to you not too long ago," he said at last. "And you sent me away."

"I won't send you away again. Not ever. I couldn't."

"Because you think you're dying?"

"Because I'm alive. Because somehow in the last years I've let fear take the place of what I've always known." She stood, and the colors swirled. "I don't know when it started, and I don't know why, exactly. I stopped believing what my heart told me and started believing your silences and your absences. But I know now that I was wrong not to trust myself and not to trust you."

"No. I was the one who was wrong."

The colors swirled, lapping at edges, violet to midnight blue. "How were you wrong, too?" she asked.

He looked away from her. He could not bear to watch her face. "I should have found a way to tell you." He cleared his throat. "I should have known I had to."

"To tell me?"

"What you meant to me."

"Can you tell me now? I'd like to hear it."

"You mean too much." He faced her again. "You talk about fear. Do you know what it's like to need someone so much that the first thing you feel every morning is terror?"

"Stefan." She put her hand on the chair to steady herself. "Terror?"

"I ran from you because I was terrified! It wasn't rational, it wasn't logical, to need someone that way. I told myself that it was better to keep my distance."

She stared at him. "But why?"

"Because I was afraid what I felt would overpower you! I was afraid you'd overpower me." He clenched his fists. "I don't know how to explain it. I felt caught in something I couldn't control. My feelings were controlling me."

"And so you stayed away?"

"I love my career, too. You don't know what it's like, Lindsey, because I've never been able to tell you. But I can change people's lives. I can make their world a better place, give them a chance they'd never have without me. But I can't do it if I'm not fully there for them. And sometimes I wouldn't be. I'd be scrubbing for surgery, and I'd be reviewing the operation in my mind, and then you'd be there suddenly. I'd think of something you'd said, or something you'd worn. I'd feel your smile, and I'd forget where I was for a moment."

"Just like any other human being."

"I can't be like any other human being when people are depending on me. I can't be!"

"But you are." She stepped toward him, the colors pooling together until there was a rainbow. She held out her arms. "You don't have to be more than you are, my love. But you can't be less, either. Oh, Stefan, you can't be less!

All you have to be is a man, a man with feelings he doesn't have to fight.''

He reached for her, jerking her against him impatiently, and the colors surrounded them. He buried his face in her hair, and his fingers moved convulsively over her back. ''When you asked me to leave, I was destroyed, but at least I thought I'd finally be free of the terror. And then...'' His voice broke. ''Then I found out what terror really was.''

''We don't have to be afraid again. Neither of us. Not ever. Not ever.'' She held on to him so tightly she was afraid she was hurting him.

''Lind...sey.''

She heard his torment. Clearly. ''I love you!''

''I didn't know what to do when I thought you'd stopped loving me.''

''I never stopped. I never will. No matter what separates us.''

''Nothing's going to separate us again!''

''Love me now.''

He swung her into his arms. She was lighter than she had ever been. He felt as if he were holding air. He held her tighter, afraid she would slip away from him.

Upstairs, he couldn't seem to let her go. He sank to the bed still holding her tight. She kissed his cheeks, his forehead, his lips. Everything about him was so familiar, so unutterably precious. She wanted to drink in all of him, to absorb the essence of the man with all her senses. She touched his face, and his warmth radiated through her fingertips. She heard his soft moan somewhere in the region of her heart.

He lay back, and she stretched out over him. Tears glazed her vision. ''How could I ever have asked you to leave me?'' she whispered.

He tangled his fingers in her hair. ''It doesn't matter now.''

''Remember this, then. Not anything else. If I...have to leave you. Remember this.'' She kissed him again, smothering his protest, until he turned her to lie against the bed. He half covered her so she couldn't move away.

"You won't leave me," he promised. "I won't let you. Do you hear me? I'm not going to let you leave me!"

She pulled his face to hers and framed it with her hands. His eyes were wide open, and every feeling there was hers to name. She swallowed her own despair and opened herself to him. "I'll always be with you."

When he kissed her again there were no barriers between them. The colors of sunset flooded this room, too. As Stefan united them, Lindsey watched the dying day wrap them in its final light.

She was not alone, and she was not afraid. The tears she cried were tears of joy.

Chapter 14

Stefan watched the sunrise alone. He left Lindsey in bed sleeping, even though leaving her at all was difficult. But he was restless, and she needed whatever replenishment she could get. He didn't want to wake her with his tossing and turning. He didn't want his fears to enter her dreams.

He buttoned his shirt as he descended the stairs. Outside the morning was cool, still fogged with mist from the lake. Wet grass tickled his bare ankles as he crossed the field beside the shore. He remembered criticizing Lindsey's choice when she had shown him the cottage for the first time. He hadn't liked the idea of owning property on the island, but since Lindsey was determined to, he had wanted something directly on the waterfront, because the resale value would be higher.

She had insisted that good things were worth working for, that she didn't think she could bear the overpowering view of the lake every time she looked out the window. She wanted to anticipate the vast blue sweep, the colorful sails against the horizon. She wanted the discipline of leaving whatever it was she was doing and walking to the water for her own moments of meditation.

For the first time he understood what she had meant.

He crossed the silent road and stood at the water's edge. The sun would rise behind him, so the complete majesty of it belonged to the people on the east side of the island. But watching the sky lighten, watching the wave tips glisten with the sun's first rays, was a pleasure, too.

He stood with his hands in his pockets and drew in breath after breath of fresh air. He felt cleansed inside and out. He had been hollowed out and filled with something new and powerful, as if a sparkling, pure river ran through him now. But dancing along the riverbanks was a different terror, one he understood better than he ever understood his terrible fear of intimacy.

Lindsey was ill, so ill that she was convinced she wasn't going to survive. So ill that he wasn't convinced she was, either. She wasn't going to die immediately. She wasn't even sick enough to need hospitalization. Not today. Not tomorrow. But after that?

He shuddered, though the air was warming. Medicine was mathematics. This symptom combined with this symptom combined with this test result yielded this disease. This X ray combined with this examination yielded this growth, this condition. Lindsey's symptoms were numerous; Lindsey's test results were baffling; Lindsey's examination showed a body…deteriorating.

He hadn't told her that she would need to go back to the hospital on Monday. She was scheduled for more tests and for examinations by two more physicians in addition to George, who wanted a chance to look closely at her. They had to find an answer, and even if that wasn't possible, they had to begin treatment of her symptoms.

And while she lay in bed submitting to the personal invasion of more tests, more exams, he would be in the hospital library poring over volume after volume. He had two interns researching for him now. Somewhere, someone else had to have noted a case like Lindsey's. And he was going to find the answer.

"Stefan?"

He turned. He hadn't heard her footsteps. She walked on air. He held out his arms, and she went into them as naturally as she had in their first blindingly happy days together.

"You should be sleeping," he admonished her.

"Sleeping seems like a waste of time. I wanted to see the lake. I wanted to see you."

"Did the walk tire you."

She held him tighter. "It doesn't matter."

"It matters to me."

"I love you." She turned her face to his.

"I love you." He kissed her tenderly.

"Do you want to hear a silly idea?"

"Yes."

"Breakfast right here."

"That's not silly at all."

"We could spread a blanket. I'll make coffee. You found rolls in the freezer last night, didn't you? They'd only take a few minutes to defrost in the oven."

"I'll do it. You stay here."

She started to protest, then fell silent. The cottage suddenly seemed a hundred miles away. The trip to the lake had not been easy. Her legs no longer seemed inclined to do what her brain ordered. "Maybe that would be best."

"Sit on the breakwater. I'll be back."

She watched him cross the field. He walked with purpose, just as he did everything. His stride was long; his arms barely moved, as if he were conserving energy. Smiling, she watched him disappear into the cottage.

Then the smile died.

She was going to have to tell him the truth. How could she ever have thought he would throw up his hands in defeat and let her die peacefully with Alden in attendance? Stefan was not a graceful loser. He was not going to let her go gently into that good night. He was going to rage for both of them, rage and storm and fight the dying of the light, her light, with every particle of his being. He didn't know that what was happening to her was inevitable.

She wasn't going to spend her last days that way. She refused to die in a hospital bed, hooked up to machines and cut off from the people and place she loved best. Alden had promised her comfort; no one could grant her a cure. She wanted comfort; she wanted Stefan and the children with her. And in the last moments, she only wanted Stefan. Not nurses. Not doctors struggling futilely to cheat their worst enemy. Stefan.

But would Stefan believe the truth? Could she expect anyone to believe her? Or would he believe that this was another delusion, a symptom of her yet undiagnosed illness?

She sat in silence, watching the sky grow brighter. Each moment seemed precious. Each gull that skimmed the waves seemed an extension of herself. She wanted to fly with them; perhaps she would one day soon. Perhaps death was no worse than that.

Minutes later she heard Stefan coming toward her, well before she should have. She was glad her senses were only affected positively by her body's deterioration. She wanted to experience the world in all its potency. Especially the man she loved. She turned when he was just yards away and smiled at him.

He paused midstep and smiled back at her. No words were needed. She wondered why she had ever needed them.

She waited while he spread the blanket. Then she sat and patted the space beside her.

He took a thermos from the picnic hamper, along with the rolls and fresh oranges.

"A feast." She reached to pour the coffee, but the cup trembled in her hand.

"Let me." Gently he took it and carefully filled it half full.

"I'll feel better when I eat," she said.

"I fed you at midnight."

"The best meal of my life." She flirted a little, regarding him under her lashes. "The best night of my life."

"Every night should have been like that. Every night of our future will be."

"Maybe we had to learn what it was like to be apart before we could really know the joys of being together."

"I don't like that kind of lesson."

Her voice caught. "Neither do I."

"Do you want to take this slowly, Lindsey?"

She looked up, surprised by the intensity of his tone. "What do you mean?"

"I don't want to raise the children's hopes if there's no reason to."

She set down her coffee and breached the space between them with her hand. "I want to marry you again. Soon."

He stared at her.

For a moment she was afraid. She couldn't imagine that she had mistaken last night for anything other than what it had seemed to be. But she had hurt Stefan terribly. Perhaps she had hurt him too much to ask him to try marriage again. Or perhaps he believed they needed time.

She had no time.

"I know what that sounds like," she said softly. "I know you're afraid. But—"

"Afraid? No." He covered her hand. "Are you sure?"

"We've never been divorced, not really. You've said it yourself. No piece of paper makes or destroys a marriage. It's what two people feel about each other. But I want us to make our vows again. Maybe here by the lake this time. I want to...know you're totally mine."

"I am."

"Then you'll marry me again?"

"Yes."

"Just as soon as it can be arranged?"

"Just as soon as you're feeling better."

"No!" She drew a deep breath. "I...we don't know when that will be exactly. I don't want to wait."

He watched her closely. She was so fragile that it seemed as if the lake breeze might sweep her to the heavens. His hand tightened over hers. "Do you want this because you're afraid you're dying?"

"I want this because I love you."

"I've told you. You've got to trust me. I'm not going to let you die. We're going to have years and years together. We'll watch our grandchildren grow up, and their children, too."

"Then let's be sure we get married soon. Our grandchildren might not understand if we don't."

He leaned forward, touching her chin so she had to look at him, too. "There's nothing I want more. Nothing."

"Stefan." She went willingly into his arms.

"He's a very talented sculptor and wood-carver," Hilda said. "Why is it no one told me that my grandson likes to carve? No one thought I'd want to know?"

Lindsey sat still and let the others take care of her. Mandy brought her a crocheted afghan and tucked it around her; Geoff had already brought her a favorite pillow. And Hilda had pumped ice water and vitamins into her from the moment she had arrived at the cottage with the children.

"I guess I didn't think you'd be interested," Lindsey said.

"Not interested in my own grandson? Everything about him interests me. And Mandy, too. Did I move to Cleveland to write books? I can write books anywhere."

"You've always seemed interested in more academic pursuits," Lindsey said tactfully.

"I talk about what I know. I want to know about my grandchildren."

Lindsey swallowed her gratitude, curiously manifested as a lump of tears in her throat. Hilda loved Geoff, just as she loved her granddaughter. God willing, she would be there for the children as they grew, offering some of the devotion that Lindsey could not.

"My grandfather was a wood-carver," Hilda said.

"He carved clocks. Cuckoo clocks," Geoff explained. "Grandmother showed me some."

Lindsey was ashamed. "I knew that. I've seen them in your house, Hilda, but I'd forgotten."

"He would have been so proud of Geoff." Hilda beamed at her grandson, and Geoff beamed back. Lindsey realized how often she had stepped between these two, keeping them from truly getting acquainted. She had been so concerned for Geoff, and there had never been a need. Both Hilda and Stefan were willing to accept him for the person he was. They had only needed a chance to know him.

She felt hands on her shoulders. Stefan's hands. She reached up to cover them and keep them there. She was glad that Hilda had agreed to stay the night. She wanted Hilda to hear what she and Stefan were going to tell the children.

She saw that Geoff had noticed the intimacy. He looked away.

"Geoff, Mandy," she said. "Come here, please."

Mandy came over from the corner, where she had been attempting to teach Kong to sit. Geoff moved closer, but he didn't meet his mother's eyes.

"Your Daddy and I have something to tell all of you." She turned to look up at Stefan. She wanted him to do it, prayed that he would.

"Your Mommy and I are getting married again. We'll be living together, just like we used to." He looked at each of the children, then at his mother. "And we hope you'll be happy about it."

"Do you think I'm surprised?" Hilda asked. "No, the only surprise you've ever given me was not understanding your own hearts. I'm glad you finally do, though it took you too long."

"Married?" Mandy frowned. "With a wedding?"

"Yes. Next weekend," Lindsey said.

"Do I get to be there? I wasn't the last time."

"Absolutely."

Geoff stepped forward. He looked straight at his father.
"Will you still spend time with us?"

Stefan nodded gravely. "More than I ever have."

"You didn't before."

"There are a lot of reasons for that, and none of them
were your fault. But there aren't any reasons now. We'll
spend lots of time together. All of us."

"Can you get married if you're still sick, Mommy?"
Mandy asked. She crawled up on Lindsey's lap and expertly
felt her cheeks.

"We're getting married no matter what," Lindsey assured her. She kissed the palm of Mandy's hand.

"Did you start loving each other again?" Mandy asked.
"Is that what happened?"

The room was quiet for a moment. Then Stefan leaned
over so his eyes were level with his daughter's. "We never
stopped loving each other," he said. "Sometimes grown-
ups just make mistakes."

"That's a pretty big mistake," Mandy said. "I'd be in
such trouble if I made a mistake like that!"

Lindsey began to laugh. She clasped Mandy and then
Geoff, who crawled up on her lap to join his sister. Stefan
put his arms around them all, laughing, too. Across the
room, Hilda's eyes were wet.

From the cottage window and in the same dress she had
been married in once before, Lindsey watched Stefan saying
goodbye to the children and Hilda. It was early evening, and
most of the rest of the wedding guests had already gone.
There hadn't been many. She and Stefan hadn't wanted the
renewal of their vows to become a circus. They had only
invited a few close friends, Frank—who had admitted he
liked attending weddings better than divorces—and some of
Stefan's colleagues.

And Alden.

She turned to face Alden now. They were alone in the

cottage. "Stefan expects me to go back into the hospital on Monday. I put him off a week because of the wedding. But he won't be put off any longer."

"He sees what's happening."

"Which is?"

His eyes were depthless. She could see all the sadness in the universe in them. "Exactly what I was afraid of. Faster than I'd hoped."

She nodded. She had sensed the truth. "I wouldn't be on my feet if it weren't for your treatments, would I?"

"They only give you a little more strength. They do nothing to stop the inevitable."

"And soon they'll only stop the pain."

"You're fast reaching the point when it will be too late to come with us, Lindsey."

"I already told you my decision."

"You need another treatment now."

"So soon? I just had one before the ceremony."

"Even at that, it may not take you through the night."

She turned back to the window. "I can't go back into the hospital. I don't want to leave the island."

"I'll help you wherever you are."

"No. I've got to tell Stefan I'm not going. If I go into the hospital, I'll never leave again. I want to be here. With Stefan. With you. With Geoff and Mandy."

"What will you tell him?"

For a moment she was afraid. She knew Alden had powers beyond her imagination. If he didn't want her to tell Stefan the truth, he could easily stop her.

"Don't worry," he said, as if her thoughts had been spoken out loud. "Nothing you tell him could harm us. I'm not going to silence you."

"Then can you help? Can you make him believe what I tell him?"

"No."

She saw Stefan start toward the house. "He's come so far. But has he come that far?" She felt Alden take her arm, and she felt the faint, familiar prick that made it possible for her to go on from hour to hour. "What can I say to him to convince him?"

"Nothing more than the truth."

She turned to ask him for an explanation, but he was gone. She closed her eyes and thought about all that had been revealed to her. She would trade every bit of it for precious years with her family, even the serenity that came from knowing there were many more wonderful things in the universe than she had ever contemplated.

The door opened. "Lindsey?"

"I'm in here." She forced herself to smile when Stefan crossed the threshold. "Are they all gone?"

"What about Alden?"

"He left a few moments ago."

"I didn't see him."

"He left a different way."

"Then they're all gone." He came to her side. "You look a little flushed."

"It's not everyday I get married."

"There's going to be a wonderful sunset."

She couldn't face watching the sun disappear. Not tonight. "Let's go upstairs."

He frowned and put his hand on her forehead. "I think you're hot. Lindsey, damn it, I knew you should have gone into the hospital this week! This was too much excitement. We could have waited for the wedding."

"Please. No fights. Not tonight. I'll feel better in a little while."

"Upstairs is a good idea." He swept her off her feet, but there was concern in his eyes, not desire.

"I can still walk."

"Not if I have my way."

She rested against him, grateful for his strength.

Upstairs, he lowered her gently to their bed. Someone had already turned down the covers in invitation. She sighed with relief.

Stefan touched her cheek. "I'll help you out of your clothes."

"I think that's to be expected, isn't it?"

"You're too tired and sick to make love."

Tears sprang to her eyes. She tugged him down beside her. "No, I'm not." She didn't add that she soon would be. "Don't deprive me of my wedding night."

"You need to rest."

"And I will. Afterwards."

He surrounded her with his arms so that she lay against his chest. "Do you remember another wedding night?"

"I do."

"You were so beautiful. No more beautiful than you are now, of course. I felt like I was in a dream. There had been so many things I'd wanted all my life. Some of them had been easy to identify. And some of them weren't. I'd wanted you forever, but I'd never even known you existed. Then, suddenly, there you were. And I hardly knew what to do."

Stefan wondered if he was making sense. Sometimes, even now, his feelings were tangled inside him in knots he couldn't untie. He knew that he would never be able to express himself as easily as she did. He also knew that perfect clarity didn't matter. Now Lindsey understood the most important thing. He loved her. He had from the beginning.

"You and the children are more important to me than anything in my life," he said softly against her hair.

She didn't answer. He felt the soft whisper of her breath against his chest and realized she had fallen asleep. Fear pierced the tender moment. He was tempted to shake her, to prove to himself that she was only sleeping. Instead he settled her back against the pillows and felt for the pulse in her throat. Her heartbeat was too fast and not nearly as steady as he would have liked it to be.

"Damn you, Lindsey," he said softly, fiercely.

He hadn't even undressed her. He did it now, as gently as he could. He debated calling the hospital to alert them that he was bringing her in tonight, but decided it would be better to wait until the morning. She would resist with all her strength. Unless she took a turn for the worse, she would rest better here.

"Stefan? Come to bed."

Her voice sounded as if it were coming from miles away. He touched her forehead. "How do you feel?"

"I'm waiting for you to get undressed."

He did, slipping in beside her to hold her in his arms. "You fell asleep."

"On my wedding night? I did not."

"Then it was a good imitation."

"You're…just nervous about making love to your new bride."

She felt so perfect against him, like the half of himself that had been missing for too long. He kissed her forehead, the soft blond hair falling over her ear, the nape of her neck. She sighed with pleasure as his hands roamed over her. He memorized the feel of her with his fingers, his lips, and told himself there was no need. She was his again. She wasn't going to leave him.

"Why do you suppose that people ever do anything but make love?"

He laughed a little, and the laughter felt like pain. "Because we aren't nearly as smart as we think."

"We missed a year of this."

"It doesn't matter now."

"Make it up to me?"

"All tonight? That's a pretty tall order."

"You're the man to fill it."

He kissed her tenderly, then not so tenderly. He couldn't lose the feeling that she was slipping away from him. She was there and not there. He could touch her, feel her, yet something was different. Fear clutched him, but he pushed it away. He didn't want to be afraid now. Something told him not to let fear spoil this moment.

She was the one who joined them. She wrapped her legs

around him and made them one as easily as the court had divided them.

Afterward, drifting on satisfaction, he cuddled her against him. She had fallen asleep immediately.

He stroked her hair, and she turned her head. Her cheek was too warm against his chest. The fear he had tried to shove aside haunted him once more. He had pored over her medical records again and again. He and his interns had set up housekeeping in the hospital library. Nothing he'd found, nothing anyone had found, offered any clues. Tomorrow, with Lindsey safely in a hospital bed, he would work even harder to find an answer. She could not continue this way.

"What are you thinking?"

Her question took him by surprise. He hadn't expected her to wake up until morning. "Honestly? I was thinking you still seem feverish. I'll be glad to get you into the hospital tomorrow morning."

"I'm not going."

He stopped stroking. "Go back to sleep."

"I'm not going to the hospital, Stefan." She didn't move. She couldn't make herself look at him.

"You have to. You're sick. You can't deny it. I won't let you."

"I'm not sick. I'm dying. And nothing anyone at the hospital can do will change it. I want to stay here. I want to die h—"

"What are you talking about?"

"I know what's wrong with me."

He lifted her chin so that she was forced to meet his eyes. "Are you really awake?"

"I wish I weren't."

"Then tell me what you're talking about!"

"There are things in this world, in this universe, that we don't understand. One of them came to earth in May."

"Are you talking about the spaceship you thought you saw?"

She smiled and touched his cheek. "Have I ever, in all

the years you've known me, seen something that wasn't there?''

"Yes. I look at the lake and see blue water. You look at it and see colors and patterns and light and fish swimming beneath it and clouds reflected in it. And then you paint it that way, or—''

"Yes, but it's still only a lake, and I only see what's there or what I know is under the surface. I looked up at the sky one night and I saw more than stars.''

She touched his lips to silence his response. "I saw a ship land in that field, and I was drawn toward it. But there were problems. The ship only landed because it was in trouble. And that same trouble exposed me to forces beyond our understanding, forces the human body can't withstand. And I'm dying as a result.''

He stared at her. He wished he could see into her brain, beyond anything a CAT scan could detect. Into the very firing of neurons, into the places where imagination and its black-hearted partner, delusion, existed.

"I know what you're thinking," she said. "I'm really not crazy, dearest. I wish I were. We might be able to cure that.''

"And how do you know this? Did you suddenly remember? Did an alien come back to earth to warn you?''

"Open your mind. Listen with your heart.''

"How do you know?" he demanded, sharper this time.

"Because Alden told me.''

"Alden!" Fury blazed through him. "What the hell is he trying to do?''

"He's telling the truth.''

"He's trying to exploit you, Lindsey. I've always thought there was something odd about him. I warned you right at the beginning. Has he been treating you? My God, is that the missing link? Has he been giving you something—''

"He's not from this world.''

He shut his eyes. "I'll kill him.''

"Open your mind. Listen with your heart." She touched his eyelids. "Look at me."

He opened his eyes, and she saw rage. "If that bastard has hurt you, he's a dead man."

"He didn't hurt me. No one hurt me. It was an accident. I'm dying as a result. Alden came back to help me, but there's nothing he can do except make me more comfortable. I recognized him from the ship, Stefan, not at first, but later. I know how this sounds. I know! But I did see a UFO. And I did go on board. And Alden was there. In a different form. He seems human now, but he's not. His race can take on different forms if necessary. There's nothing evil about them. They are what we might become someday. Pure. Guileless. In harmony with something we can't even see."

He thrust her away, but she grasped his arm. "Stefan!"

"Don't try to stop me." He loosened her fingers.

"There's nothing you can do. There's nothing he can do."

"Oh, he can do something, all right. He can tell me why he's feeding this fantasy of yours! He can tell me what he's been giving you to make you sick!"

"He's only helped me. If it weren't for him, I might be dead already!"

"I'm going to find him."

"Don't leave me now. Stay with me."

"I'm going to stay with you forever! But first I'm going to find your so-called alien friend and find out what kind of game he's playing!"

She struggled to sit up, to go after him, but he was dressed and gone before she had even swung her feet over the bed. The room revolved around her until she felt as if she were in the center of a carousel. She grasped the bedpost and stood, and the room whirled faster. She couldn't take a step. In despair she fell back to the bed and wept.

Chapter 15

"I thought you would come." Alden turned away from his living room window overlooking the moonlit lake. He stood without moving as Stefan slammed the front door behind him.

"Did you?"

"Lindsey told you why I'm here."

"Lindsey told me why she thinks you're here. You've twisted her thinking until she actually believes your absurd story!" Stefan advanced on Alden. His hands were clenched at his sides.

"And you don't believe her." Alden shook his head. "I hoped you would."

"Then you hoped I was a fool."

"I hoped you were the man we'd sought."

Stefan paused, poised like a lion about to spring. "We?"

"My people."

"Your people."

"Everything she's told you is true."

"What can you possibly gain by these lies?"

"Not a thing."

"You've been giving her something to confuse her."

"The truth can be confusing, yes. But she's not the one who's confused. She has a rare ability, one that for the most part your race has lost. She can sense truth. She sensed immediately that we wouldn't hurt her when she saw us land our ship. Later she sensed that I wasn't exactly who I led her to believe I was. You who breathe pride yourselves on logic, but you've forgotten the logic of intuition. Your animals still have it. Sometimes they're wiser than you."

"Enough!" Stefan stepped forward. "I want to know what you've done to her and why!"

Alden shook his head sadly. "I'm afraid we've hurt her terribly. We aren't infallible. We can still make mistakes."

"Your biggest mistake was staying here tonight!" Stefan sprang. His hands, a neurosurgeon's skilled hands, went right for Alden's throat.

Alden swept one hand in a graceful arc, and Stefan stumbled and fell at his feet.

"You have the ability to understand what I'm saying, too," Alden said.

"You bastard!" Stefan sprang to his feet and launched himself at Alden again. Alden halted him with the palm of one hand in front of Stefan's face. Stefan tried to move, but there was an inviolable space between them.

"Listen to what you know," Alden said. "Listen to what you know! You can't always touch the truth, Stefan. No more than you can touch me now."

"What are you doing to me? What are you doing to my wife!"

"Listen. Shut your eyes. Open your heart."

"This is insane!"

"Insanity is losing touch. Sanity is striving to touch everything you don't know. Do you know everything, Stefan? Can you be so arrogant that you think you understand the universe?"

Stefan stared at him. His mind refused to comprehend the

obvious. He was standing two feet from a man he wanted to kill. He was a healer, yet he wanted to wrap his fingers around Alden's throat and choke off his breath. And the only thing keeping him from his goal was two feet he couldn't breach.

"Close your eyes. Open your heart," Alden said.

Stefan stared at him. "Do whatever you want to me, but release whatever power you hold over my wife!"

Alden shook his head. "I only wish it were that simple. But everything she's told you is true. We don't have *enough* power. We harmed her unknowingly. Now we want to help. But we're limited by what we don't know. We aren't human. We can only understand so much about you." He waved his hand, and Stefan felt the invisible wall between them disappear.

He launched himself at Alden and shoved him against the window. For a moment his fiercest desire was realized. Alden was in his grasp, his flesh giving under the pressure of Stefan's fingers. Then he was gone.

Stefan fell forward, and his head bounced against the window pane. He turned, and Alden was standing behind him. Stefan grabbed for him again, and again Alden was in his grasp. Then he wasn't.

The third time was the same.

Stefan dropped to his knees and bent his head. The room spun around him. The world spun. Everything he had always known spun out of his grasp until he was empty. The river of feeling that had been released by understanding and expressing his love for Lindsey was now a raging torrent washing away everything he had ever believed.

And in the place of all he'd known and all he'd believed was nothing. Darkness!

"Did she tell you that I want her to come with me to my home?" Alden asked. "Did she tell you that if she does, I can save her life."

Stefan felt tears coursing down his cheeks. "No."

"It's the only way I can be certain to save her," Alden

said. "We've forgotten as much about the human body as we've remembered. Once we were much like you, much as you see me now. But we thought we had no use for what we knew, and so we discarded much of it. So much."

"What's happening to her? How can you save her?"

"Lindsey's body is preparing to transform, much as ours did thousands of years ago. But it can't happen here. She's not ready, and she can't be made ready here. So we must take her back to our home and help her make the transition."

"Then take her! Now. Don't let her die!"

"She refuses to go."

"She can't."

"But she does. She doesn't want to leave you or the children. She prefers to die here."

"Then I'll make her go!"

"You can't do that any more than she could make you believe in spaceships and extraterrestrial beings."

Stefan couldn't speak. The awful truth wrapped around his throat just as his fingers had wrapped around Alden's.

His love had doomed Lindsey. By loving her, by needing her and telling her so, he had sentenced her to death.

Lindsey fought her way toward the front door of the cottage. It had taken her precious minutes and energy to dress and make her way downstairs. She was in no pain. Rather, she felt as if she were deep inside a dream, struggling to put one foot in front of the other.

She had to reach Stefan.

She raised her hand toward the doorknob. Higher, higher. She could see her hand clearly, just in front of her, but she couldn't force it to move faster. Her reflexes weren't gone, they were just vastly slowed. Every movement required intense concentration. When she touched the knob at last, her hand slid over it once, then again. She demanded that her fingers close around it, screamed silently at them until they did. The door refused to give, but she leaned away from it, using every ounce of her weight to make it obey. She slid to the floor when the door opened at last and she crawled outside to the porch.

The evening air revived her a little. She swung her legs over the porch edge and stood when her feet contacted the ground. The path to Alden's house seemed a thousand miles long. For a moment she was sure she couldn't make it. What little strength she had left was quickly fading. Soon, perhaps sometime in the next minutes, it would fade completely.

"A journey of a thousand miles…" she whispered. She took a step before completing the rest of the saying. "Begins with a single step." Her journey had begun on a night much like this one. She had stumbled onto something so unbelievable, so impossible, that Stefan could not be expected to understand and accept what she had told him.

Where was he now? She had never sensed, never, that he was capable of the rage she had seen in his eyes. He had wanted to kill Alden. Perhaps by now he had tried. Tears welled at the thought. She had brought him to this. She should have gone with Alden, gone and left Stefan and the children to a life without her. What new pain had she brought them by staying?

She took a deep breath and released it. How many more breaths would she be granted? And Stefan? Would he die now, too? Would he die trying to save her? There was so little she knew about Alden and his race. What would Alden do when confronted with Stefan's fury?

One step became two, then a dozen. She was moving faster than she had expected. Here in the open her dizziness wasn't as bad. She could maintain her balance if she held her arms slightly away from her body. She fixed her vision on a spot in the distance, a tree that stood at the edge of Alden's yard, and forced herself to concentrate on reaching it.

Fireflies brightened the darkness with tiny flashes of light, and the moon sent its subtle rays to illuminate her path. Once she tripped, but she caught herself before falling. Almost to her goal, she tripped again and sprawled helplessly on the ground, striking her head against a root. She felt along it, inching herself across the ground until she could touch the trunk. Using it to steady herself, she managed to stand.

The landscape whirled around her, and she held on to the tree for stability. "Stefan." But her voice was no more than a whisper. She concentrated on breathing. In and out. In and out until the whirling receded and her vision was no longer blurred.

Across the yard Alden's cottage glowed with pastel light, and she heard the melodies she had heard there before. Carefully she leaned all her weight against the tree and released her hold on it.

She could make it. She could and would, no matter what the consequences. She took one step, then another, until the tree was no longer within reach. She stumbled again, but she didn't fall.

"Stefan."

Silhouetted in the window of the cottage was a man's form. And the man was not her husband. Frantically she lifted one foot, then the other. One step. The journey of a thousand miles.

One step.

"She's coming," Alden said.

Stefan knew what Alden meant, had known Lindsey was near before Alden had even spoken. "How long does she have to live?"

"I don't know."

"How could your people have doomed her to this?"

Alden turned to him. "The fault was my own."

Stefan stared at him and saw the anguish on Alden's face. "Yours?"

"I was the ship's first officer that night. It was my duty to monitor the screen that should have prevented her from being harmed. In my haste I neglected one part of the safety inventory. I sensed something was wrong, but there was no time to investigate. Ordinarily our intelligence systems would have alerted me to my mistake, but they were affected by the same atmospheric forces that damaged the ship.''

''That's why you're here!''

''No. I would be here anyway. I am also the ship's healer. It's my sacred trust to heal when I can.''

''But you feel particularly dedicated this time.''

''You understand.''

Stefan tried to rise. He wanted to find Lindsey, but he was bound to the floor as surely as if he had been tied there.

''We must finish this now,'' Alden said. ''Together.''

The door opened, and Lindsey stood on the threshold. She stared at Alden, then at Stefan. With a faint cry she stumbled across the floor to Stefan's side.

''Are you all right?''

He grasped her and pulled her to him. His tears fell on her hair. ''Lind…sey!''

''It's all right. It's all right.'' She circled him with her arms and rocked him as if he were a child. ''Nothing you could have done would have changed anything.''

''You have to go with them!''

''Never.''

He tried to push her away, but she wouldn't allow it. ''Go!'' he said. ''Don't you know I'd rather you were alive somewhere?''

''And don't you know I don't want to be? How could I live knowing I'd never see you again? How could I survive so far away?''

''And how can I live knowing my love killed you?''

She brushed his hair from his forehead and kissed him. ''Even if that were true, there are some things worth dying for.''

Alden crossed the room. He bent and touched Lindsey's face. She shook off his hand and laid her cheek against Stefan's.

"You must come with us tonight." Alden stepped back. "The time has run out on your decision."

"I've made my decision."

"Please, go!" Stefan tried again to push her away.

"Can't either of you understand?" she asked. "I can't go. I'm not strong enough. I can't live away from the people I love. Death will be kinder than that! How can I live separated from everything and everyone I hold dear? I don't want to be transformed. I want whatever days are left to me in this body, in this place, with you, Stefan, and with the children. Could you go, if it were you?"

He held her against him, and knew she had won. He looked at Alden and saw that he knew it, too.

"It's always been your decision," Alden told her. "Always."

"Stefan?" She framed his face in her hands. "Tell me you understand."

He couldn't say it, but she saw it in his eyes. She collapsed against him, exhausted. He held her as if he could stave off the inevitable.

"What can I do?" he whispered. "There has to be something I can do." He lifted his eyes to Alden's. "Help me. Help us!"

Alden gazed at him, but he didn't answer.

"There is something, isn't there?"

"Close your eyes. Open your heart. Listen."

Stefan gripped Lindsey tighter. He squeezed his eyelids shut and tried to still the chorus of voices inside him. Fear smothered everything else.

"Don't push away the fear," Alden said. "Open your heart. Follow the voices until they die away."

Stefan felt Lindsey against him. He saw her body in their bed at the cottage, naked and flushed from their lovemaking. Sorrow pierced him at what could never be again. Tears slid down his cheeks, and he gripped her tighter still.

In his vision Lindsey rose from beside him and moved to

the window. Sunlight streamed around her. She lifted her hand, and he followed. He bent his head to kiss her.

The vision disappeared, and he saw Geoff drowning. He floated in the air just above him, unable to reach for him, unable to move. Then, as he gasped and cried out in horror, he was no longer frozen. He dove cleanly into the water and fell to the bottom. His hand closed over his son's body, and they rose together.

The lake became an operating room at the hospital. A man lay on the table, and Stefan saw himself in sterile garb reaching to comfort him. His hand touched the man's head, and he knew, from touch alone, exactly how he could heal him. Power flowed through his fingers, power and magic and something else.

"Love." He opened his eyes.

"As good a word as any," Alden said.

"You love her, too, don't you?" Stefan whispered.

"Close your eyes, Stefan."

Stefan did. This time his vision was of Alden. He saw him reaching toward Lindsey. Reaching, stretching his hands in anguish. He saw tears in Alden's eyes; then he saw Alden transformed. He was no longer human, but something so glorious, so radiant, that Stefan wanted to shield his eyes. But he could not.

As he watched, the blaze of formless light stopped just inches from Lindsey. "Touch her," Stefan demanded. "Heal her!"

"I cannot."

Stefan opened his eyes again and saw the Alden of human form before him. "Why can't you?"

"I've told you why."

"Because you aren't human. And I am, but I can't heal her because I don't know enough! I don't understand enough!"

"Once I told you there was much we could teach each other."

"Teach me now! I'll learn whatever I have to. I'll do whatever I have to."

"Once, there might have been enough time," Alden said.

"There's not enough now?"

Alden shook his head.

"Why didn't you tell me then? Why did you hint at things couldn't understand?"

"Because you couldn't understand then. Now you can."

"No!" Stefan shut his eyes. "No!"

This time the vision was of a house. It took him precious seconds to recognize it. The house was theirs, but it was barren of all the warmth Lindsey had brought to it. He saw Geoff and Mandy, nearly grown. He saw himself reaching out to them, but even holding them in his arms, he felt empty. The house was empty. Their lives were empty. His heart...

He opened his eyes and knew that he could not survive more visions. "What must I do?" he asked.

"There's only one thing left," Alden said.

"Whatever it is, I'll do it."

"You may not survive."

Lindsey had been silent in Stefan's arms. She had been silenced, bound by the same force that had shaken his body again and again. Now she no longer was. She pushed against him, trying to force him to release her. "Stefan, no!"

"What is it?" Stefan demanded of Alden. "What can I do?"

"What can we do?" Alden knelt beside them, touching each of them on the shoulder. Lindsey stopped thrashing. Wide-eyed, she gazed at him.

"Don't hurt him," she begged. "Alden, no!"

"He must make this decision, just as you were allowed to make yours," Alden said.

"What decision?" Stefan demanded. "What? I'll do anything."

"What do you feel?" Alden asked.

Stefan concentrated. He could feel a tingling where Alden

touched his shoulder. But it was more than that. Alden's touch made everything seem clearer. "I...I don't know. I can't explain."

Alden moved away. "Stand up."

Stefan held Lindsey tighter for a moment. He kissed her hair. Then, firmly, he thrust her away. She tried to stand, too, but found she couldn't.

"Move away from her," Alden said.

Stefan looked down and saw she was sobbing. He hesitated.

"Now."

Stefan stepped away from Lindsey until there was a wide space between them. "Enough?"

"Yes."

Stefan watched Alden close the distance until they were separated only by inches. Alden turned to Lindsey. "There are emotions you breathers feel that we are no longer privy to. I think I understand the one you call envy now. This man is to be envied for having your love. God speed you on whatever journey you take."

She covered her face in her hands and wept harder.

He turned back to Stefan. "There is much we no longer know. I believe most of that knowledge belongs to you." He touched Stefan's forehead and smiled a little. "A very primitive storage area, don't you think?"

Stefan could hardly breathe. His hands were clenched at his sides. "Nothing I know is worth anything if it can't save Lindsey."

"And nothing I know is enough. But together?"

"You said there wasn't enough time to teach me what you know."

"Not to teach you, no. But I can give you my knowledge, just as you can give me yours."

"How?"

"By merging with me for a moment."

"Merging?"

"There is nothing equivalent in your history. There is no

way to explain. This is the way we exchange knowledge where I come from." He uttered a long, pleasing array of sounds. "My home."

Stefan spoke the word back to him. Perfectly.

"You are the one," Alden said. "I've thought as much all along."

"Then merge with me."

"It's never been tried before with someone of your race. We have no guarantee that you can survive it. We only know that most humans could not. I believe if anyone can, it will be you."

"Stefan, no!" Lindsey struggled to stand, but she was unable to move. "Don't do it!"

"And when we've merged, I'll be able to cure Lindsey?"

"That's what we hope."

"Hope?"

"Hope. Want. Pray."

"You said that we would teach each other."

"We were wrong to lose what we knew. If I survive with what you have to teach me, then you'll be helping us."

"If you survive?"

"There are no guarantees."

"And you would do this for Lindsey?"

"I would do anything I could."

"No!" Lindsey struggled uselessly. "Both of you. No! Please!"

"This race of yours. Are they all like you?" Stefan asked.

Alden smiled. "Are you ready to find out?"

Stefan gazed at Lindsey. He wanted to reach out to her, to reassure her. He held out his hand, as if to touch her, but he was too far away. She looked distraught. He turned away from her, his heart torn.

"Close your eyes," Alden said. "Clear your mind."

"Stefan, no!"

Stefan saw Alden pass his hand in Lindsey's direction. The room grew silent. He closed his eyes.

Lindsey battled to stand, but she couldn't move, just as

she couldn't speak. In horror, she saw Alden's hands hover in the air above Stefan's shoulders. Everything inside her screamed at them to stop, but she couldn't make a sound.

Sobbing, she watched Alden's hands descend. Slowly, so slowly. Then they settled, fingers pressing lightly against Stefan's neck.

The pastel light flared into a million shards of primary colors. She tried to cry out again, but she could not. Terrified, she fought to reach Stefan as the light grew more intense.

There was an explosion, light erupting, and a sound that almost deafened her. The two men seemed to become one. For an instant there was a single body so brilliant that her eyes closed and her mind refused to comprehend.

The room fell silent again. She tried to breathe, but couldn't, as if all the oxygen had been sucked away. Her last struggle was to open her eyes once more. She saw a man lying facedown on the floor. One man. Stefan.

Then there was darkness.

Daylight was streaming through the windows when Lindsey awoke. She didn't know where she was, and at first it didn't matter. She was filled with such a strong sense of peace and contentment that she lay still, staring at the ceiling, and let it fill her.

The song of a bird brought her back to awareness. At first it was only pleasant background noise as she drifted serenely. Then she began to concentrate on the melody. It reminded her of the music she had heard last night as she fought her way toward the cottage.

Peace disappeared as memory filled her, followed swiftly by terror.

"Stefan." Her lips barely formed the words. For a moment her head refused to turn. She remembered that the last thing she'd seen last night was Stefan, prostrate on the floor. She summoned all her strength and fought to turn her head once more. This time she was successful. Stefan lay only yards away.

"No!" She rolled to her side and stretched her hand toward him, but he was too far away to reach. She inched closer, drawing strength now from some new, mysterious reservoir inside of her. Closer, then closer still. Finally her fingertips rested against his hand.

His skin was warm. "Stefan!"

Just touching him energized her. She was filled with hope again and new strength. She inched closer until she could touch his arm, then his back. "Stefan, can you hear me?"

He made the sounds of a man just coming awake. She wondered if she could sit up. At first she was unsuccessful, but she managed after several attempts. Now she could clearly see the side of his face. She touched his cheek, and his eyes opened.

He lifted his head, then slowly turned to his side. He looked at her as if he didn't know who she was, as if he didn't know who he was. For long moments his eyes didn't seem to focus. Fear filled her again. He was alive, but what price had he paid to try to save her?

"Lindsey?"

She sobbed her relief. He pushed himself slowly upright and took her in his arms.

"I thought you were dead," she said. "Last night. Oh, Stefan, I was sure you hadn't survived!"

He held her without speaking, rocking her slowly back and forth.

"Say something. Please, just say something," she said.

"You don't have to be afraid. I'm all right. I'm here."

She held him tighter, filled with gratitude. "Alden's not."

"I know."

"Has he gone back to his ship?"

He was silent for a long time. "I don't think so," he said at last.

"Is he dead?"

"No. He's safe, wherever he is."

She was worried about Alden, but more worried about the man holding her. "Stefan, were you hurt last night?"

"No, I wasn't hurt." He kissed her forehead. "And you're no worse this morning, are you?"

She realized it was true. "No."

"Our exchange last night halted your body's transformation temporarily. Alden knew if you witnessed it, it would buy you some time."

"How do you know? Did he tell you?"

"In his own way." He turned her face to his. He looked at her and knew he had never seen the real woman. And he looked at her and knew he had never let her see the real man. Now he did both.

She made a sobbing noise low in her throat, but she didn't speak.

"Alden's gone, Lindsey. I don't know where, and I don't know if he'll ever be back. But he left what he knew with me. And he took my knowledge with him. Just as he promised."

She touched his cheek. She couldn't tear her gaze from his.

His gaze didn't falter. "What do you see?"

Relief filled her at last, as if a question had been asked and answered. "Stefan."

He nodded gravely. "But I'm changed, Lindsey. I'm still Stefan, but I'm not the same."

"I know."

"There was so much I never understood!"

"And now you do?"

"Not everything. Everything Alden and I knew was still only a small part of the universal puzzle. But I think I know enough now…"

"To cure me?"

"Yes."

"Do you really think so?"

"I can't make promises. But I understand so much more. There are so many ways in which doctors have been wrong, so many treatments and approaches that were nothing more than superstitions left over from another era. And now that I understand exactly what's happening to you, how your body is changing… I think…I know…''

He touched her forehead with his fingertips, resting his thumbs under her chin to steady her. He shut his eyes.

"What are you doing?"

"Shh…"

She closed her eyes, too. She could feel heat in his fingertips, and something more. Something both powerful and soothing. Something infinitely healing. Hope flared within her.

"Love," she said softly.

He opened his eyes, and they were bright with tears. "As close as any word in our language." He kissed her tenderly.

She held on to him and let the power of love infuse her and begin its healing magic.

Maybe Stefan couldn't make promises. But in that moment Lindsey knew she had the only promise she needed. They were together for whatever time was theirs to share.

And no one in the universe could ask for more.

* * * * *

When you're looking for a great miniseries,
look no further than

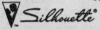

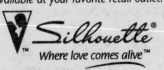

Silhouette®

SPECIAL EDITION™

Life, Love
& Family.

Silhouette®

Desire

Passionate,
Powerful and
Provocative.

Silhouette®

Where love comes alive™

Silhouette®

INTIMATE MOMENTS™

Romance, Adventure—
Excitement.

SILHOUETTE Romance®

From First Love
to Forever.

INTIMATE MOMENTS™

In February 2002

MERLINE LOVELACE

brings back
the men—and women—of

CODE NAME: DANGER

Beginning with
HOT AS ICE, IM #1129
He was frozen in time! And she was
just the woman to thaw him out....

Follow the adventures and loves of the
members of the Omega Agency.
Because love is a risky business.

Also look for
DANGEROUS TO HOLD in February 2002
DANGEROUS TO KNOW in July 2002

to see where **CODE NAME: DANGER** began

Available at your favorite retail outlet.

Where love comes alive™